# Poisson Da

GW00731352

Can Jake Poisson get his memory back in time to save the world?

# John I Carr

First edition

Published 2022

Copyright, 2022, by John I Carr

All rights reserved

All characters in this book are fictitious, and any resemblance to actual persons, living or dead, is purely coincidental.

# Preface

Who is Jake Poisson? Wiping his memory completely seemed the only way to avert a possible global catastrophe, but has his plan failed? As the possibility becomes a reality, Jake needs to regain all his skill, cunning, expertise and especially his training - to extricate himself from the extremely dangerous situation he is in. A situation which could threaten his very existence, a situation which could threaten the existence of his whole family (including the ones he didn't know existed), a situation which could even threaten the existence of everyone on the planet. Time is running out - perhaps it's too late, but one thing is certain – Jake won't give up without a fight!

# Chapter One

## Gordon Gekko's Moustache

The panoramic view of Brooklyn Bridge from the apartment window is striking, but the scene inside is much less impressive. Empty beer cans, wine and spirit bottles and various other unrecognizable items - some still dripping their sticky contents onto the Italian marble floor, lie strewn across every available surface. Food cartons containing leftover pizzas and curries appear to have been used as makeshift ashtrays. Crumpled items of clothing hang from lights and lamps, others leave a trail towards an open bedroom door. The stylus of the Technics SL 1200, which normally produces exquisitely clear sound, is locked in a cacophonic loop of static. As we move into the master bedroom, we see crumpled, stained satin sheets on a king size bed. A man's trousers hang from one bedpost - from the other, his jacket. On closer inspection, we see that the bed contains two disheveled occupants. One of them is Jake Poisson and he's not sure what has woken him from his fitful sleep, whether it's the excruciating pain or the strange squeaking noise emanating from the left-hand side of his king-sized bed. He opens his eyes, his mind slowly adjusting to the vaguely familiar surroundings. He closes them immediately, hoping he is having a nightmare - then slowly reopens them. It *is* a nightmare. It's his apartment, it must be, because he recognizes the limited edition print of Gordon Gekko on the facing wall – only he can't recall Gordon Gekko having a Zapata Moustache... The squeaking stops and out of the corner of his eye he catches sight of a tangled mass of hair popping out from under the quilt. As the events of the previous evening slowly, but surely, infiltrate his consciousness, he feels a bead of perspiration run down his flushed brow and into one eye.

'I'm sorry Georgia. I'm not normally the sort of person who would do it on a first date.'

'It's Georgette and you didn't.'

Jake feels slightly relieved. Carefully exploring the room with the one eye he can still see from, he returns his gaze to his guest's recumbent body. Her eyes are inches from his, her breathing is steady, her expression too enigmatic to read.

'Now would be a good time, Jake.'

'For what?' He notices a fleeting look of disappointment cross her face.

'Oh, nothing, Jake - I'm afraid I've got another appointment.'

Georgette hops out of bed, she's wearing only a pair of tiny, metallic gold panties. The squeaking noise returns. Jake is puzzled.

'Have you got a mouse down there?'

'A lot of men prefer the au naturel look, and from what I remember - you never complained last night.'

'I meant the sque...'

'Don't worry about it, Jake. I'll get over it. Just pay me the thousand bucks and I'll be on my way.'

'A THOUSAND BUCKS!' Jake turns to study Georgette - from a distance, she would probably look stunning, but close up – well, that's a whole different story.

'We had a contract.'

'I don't remember any con... '

Georgette jumps out of bed, she is almost naked, her golden tan matching her panties.

'Look at this!'

He tries not to, but his gaze is drawn to her tufts. 'Not that, this!'

She pulls down her briefs revealing part of her backside. 'This is your signature, isn't it?'

Jake glances at the signature and decides he can't bring himself to read any further.

'I don't keep that sort of cash around here. What if I just don't pay?'

'That did happen once. The agency didn't like it.' She makes the sign of a cross and shakes her head ominously. Then, jauntily, she takes a credit card reader from her bag.

'I take all forms of payment and I offer discount for Amex.' Jake looks around, sees his jacket hanging from the bedpost and reluctantly reaches into a pocket. Immediately he withdraws his sticky, gooey hand in disgust. Drying his fingers on the bedclothes, he makes another attempt. This time he is successful and manages to withdraw his card wallet. He would like the discount, but on this occasion, he decides discretion is the better part of valor and hands Georgette the first card that sticks to his fingers.

'Ooh - A Gold Card, someone's doing very well!' Jake remembers why he had been celebrating the previous night and he cheers up a little.

'Did I disclose anything personal last night?'

'Nothing important, it was only small talk. Oh, but you did mutter something about being offered millions of dollars for your business.'

Jake curses himself. 'That's top secret, I don't want you...'

'Don't worry about me, darling. I am always the soul of discretion.'

During their conversation Georgette has been busy running Jake's card through the machine. Now, handing him a receipt and slipping, or rather, sliding into her gold, sequined dress and matching gold, unfeasibly high, stiletto shoes, she adeptly finalizes the transaction.

'Well, it's been fun. I've left my business card on your bedside table – it's covering that deep scratch. Anyway, must dash. Next time don't leave it so long, my darling - MWAH!' As she sashays out of the room, Jake watches her through what appears to be a roughly sawn peephole in the door. He looks forlornly at her card. It reads:

Georgette

Model

Dan Corleone Agency

Reaching the bedroom door, Georgette glances back. 'When was the last time you saw your aunt, Jake?'

'I don't have an Aunt Jake.'

Taking another swift glance at him, Georgette notices his dejected expression and quickly changes the topic of conversation. 'Cheer up, Jake, darling, I know a divine cleaner – and he only charges an extra twenty-five percent to do it in the nude.'

'I'm not ga...' Jake looks around the room for support, but there's no one in the near vicinity.

'Of course, you're not, but you haven't seen him yet. I have, and so has my boyfriend, and I can tell you, he almost turned him! – Yep, and he's a man who has more testosterone than a sack of potatoes – oh, by the way, you can keep the diaper, free of charge.'

'What di...' Jake realizes he is talking to himself - all that's left of Georgette is a lingering whiff of tequila and cigars.

Gingerly lifting up the bedclothes, Jake sees he is wearing a cotton baby's diaper. He hurriedly tries to jump out of bed, but his first attempt leaves him flat on his face. Looking down he realizes what the squeaking was - his legs are enclosed in rusty shackles. He winces, then hobbles painfully to the bathroom where he carefully removes the slightly damp diaper. He half-jumps, half-hops into the shower, where the warmth of the water refreshes him, but as the water hits his buttocks, he has to stifle his impulse to scream. Jake turns his head to ascertain the source of the excruciating pain and notices both his cheeks are a crisscross of bright red weals. Five minutes later, Jake is standing in front of his self-defrosting, fully integrated Sub-Zero fridge freezer. He cautiously opens its fingerprint-covered, burnished steel door and frantically sticks his ass into it to try to numb the burning sensation shooting up his anus. He does feel some relief, but his eye catches something dripping onto the floor and he turns to examine the interior of his beautiful, but wildly extravagant purchase. The scene is one of utter carnage. Every shelf apart from one, is covered in a mixture of dripping cans and bottles or half-empty packs of food. On the one shelf which at first appears to be completely empty, closer inspection reveals that hidden in the far reaches of the back, there is, in fact, a large pink blancmange. A blancmange which, by the look of it, has had someone's fingers, or more worryingly, some other extremity, exploring it. As Jake stands there silently cursing his luck, the blancmange starts vibrating. He reluctantly plunges his hand into it and retrieves his cell phone.

'Jake, it's Lars, where the hell are you? - The Blowman Corporation are due here at ten thirty. I've been trying to get in touch with you for... '

'Lars, - that appointment is for Tuesday...'

'Yes, today - what day did you think it was?'

Jake looks at the Omega wall clock, its face is covered in graffiti, with the words

"Time to embrace your pain".

Making it almost impossible to read.

It's Tuesday, of course, Lars - I knew that.' Jake lies. 'It's all in hand. I'm just leaving home now.' Jake looks down at the shackles on his ankles. He dials a number into his cell phone. He hears laughter and the concierge's voice on the other end of the phone.

*'You were playing poker for tropical fish, man? Hey, that's one of the funniest things I've ever heard. Ha-ha, yes, that's the door to the car park – yes, just there, on the right, bye Georgette, careful with those fish. Oh, and don't worry about me telling anyone he's coming into millions. I'm always the soul of discretion."*

As Georgette disappears into an elevator carrying a container of tropical fish, the concierge's voice changes to one of excessive obsequiousness.

*'Good morning, Highclere Apartments. Sorry to keep you waiting, how may I help you?'*

Jake turns his head in the direction of his large, expensive, tropical fish tank. It's empty apart from one ugly-looking fish

with a moth-eaten fin. He looks down at his feet.
'Is Stavros there, please?'
The voice changes again to one of extreme superciliousness.

*'Oh, I didn't realize it was you Mr. Pisson.'*

Jake considers correcting the concierge on the pronunciation
of his name, but reckons that after a year and a half it's
probably time to give up on that one. The way he is feeling at
the moment, all he can muster is a short, ineffective retort.
'Obviously not.'
The concierge seems oblivious to Jake's annoyance.
*'Which Stavros do you mean, sir?'*
'How many Stavros's do we have working here?'
*'Well, there's Stavros the Chef, Stavros the Night
Watchman, Stavros the Porter, Stavros the Undertaker...'*
'We have an undertaker working here?
*'We have an aging clientele, Mr. Pisson – I think I've
mentioned all of them now, sir'*
'You've forgotten Stavros the Janitor.'
*'He's left.'*
'Oh, who's the new janitor?'
*'Crocodile.'*
'The janitor's called Crocodile?'
*'His mother's Australian and his father's Scottish – they
named him after her favorite movie star and the town in
Scotland where he was born - Crocodile Dunbar. His full
name is Crocodile Dunbar McTavish.'*
Jake wonders how in the world he has got into this
conversation and, more importantly, wonders how the hell
he is going to get out of it. He decides on the direct approach.
'Can you ask the janitor to come to my room without delay,

please?'

*'The janitor is on his break, Mr. Pisson. Do you need his services?*

Jake takes another look at his ankles. 'Yes, it's quite urgent, could you ask him to bring some bolt cutters?

*'Well, he's just started his half-hour coffee break. Do you really want me to disturb him?*

'As I've said, it is quite urgent and it does say twenty-four-hour service in the maintenance contract.'

*'Agreed, Mr. Pisson and at a charge of only seven thousand four hundred and sixty dollars per annum, I'm sure you will agree, that's excellent value.'*

Jake is starting to wonder whether the concierge secretly owns the building.

'No one could query such excellent value, particularly as I get my door handle polished once a month whether it needs it or not. I'm just wondering why it doesn't say twenty-three-and-a-half-hour service?'

*'If you look at the contract carefully, Mr. Pisson, you will find that on page one hundred and sixty-one, section thirty-two, subsection nine, paragraph sixteen, line four, it clearly states there is a surcharge of two hundred and twenty-six dollars, plus taxes, payable for urgent callouts. Do you wish me to categorize this as urgent, Mr. Pisson?'*

'That would nice, if it's not too much trouble.'

Unable to contain his frustration, Jake hurls his phone at the wall and watches in horror as it ricochets off his Timothy Oulton mirror and through the screen of his brand-new Bang and Olufsen television. *'At least the mirror didn't break.'* Jake thinks to himself. *'I won't be having seven years bad luck.'* The creak, inaudible at first, gradually increases in volume as the mirror loosens itself from its mountings. Jake watches helplessly as the movement of the mirror increases from adagio to allegro, he sighs, as it drops onto the marbled floor breaking into hundreds of tiny pieces and damaging at least a dozen floor tiles in the process. Taking slow, deep breaths, he promises himself that the first thing he will do with his money will be to attend an anger management course, the second thing involves the concierge's undergarments, a barrel of apple juice and a wasp's nest.

Twenty-four minutes later the janitor wanders into Jake's room and casually surveys the scene. 'I pulled out all the stops and I'm here early.'
He glances around the room. 'I don't do cleaning, Mr. Parson, but I do know someone who does. The bad news is - he's not cheap, but I'm sure that with all those millions coming your way, you'll easily be able to afford him. The good news is he only charges an extra fifty percent to do it in the nude.'
'I'd rather you didn't...'
'Your secret's safe with me, Mr. Parson, I'm the soul of discretion. Will you be wanting the extra services, sir?'
'I'll see to the cleaning myself. I just want you to deal with this.' Jake points to the chain around his ankles.
The janitor snips it with his bolt cutters, leaving the two ends snaking out from under his dressing gown.
'There you go, sir. If you change your mind about the cleaner just let me know, I don't think you'll be disappointed.'
Whistling happily, the janitor saunters out of Jake's apartment.

Ten minutes later and Jake is dressed, it would have been five, but he had a little trouble fastening the heavy chain to his legs. Frantically looking for his car keys, he ignores the noise of the now loose chain on his marbled floor. Eventually admitting defeat, he opens a wardrobe door and lifts the lid of a jar with spare car key written on it. He grabs the key from the pot and heads for the foyer. The elevator door opens into the lobby of the apartment block. The concierge glances up disdainfully and pointedly ignores the strange looking character heading for the elevator on the right. Even the clanking of the chain being dragged noisily across the polished, two-inch thick, Bocote wood floor of the foyer, fails to distract him from his critical morning duty of completing the crossword, although, to be fair, it *is* quite a hard clue.

*Seven across:  Have a boat, we hear (nine letters)*

Three floors later, Jake exits the elevator, urgently pressing his key fob, he rounds the corner of the car park, and waits for his lights to flash – they don't. Looking up from the key fob he realizes why - there's an empty space where his car should be. Jake sighs as he watches the tail lights of his car disappearing down the nearest ramp.

Three minutes later, a panting, perspiring, Jake appears at the door of the stairs in the foyer. The concierge has a pen in his hand, he puts it down, picks up the phone and waits expectantly. 'Shall I call you a cab, Mr. Pisson?' Begrudgingly, Jake accepts the offer. He glances down at the half-completed crossword - it offers a distraction from his pain. Addressing no one in particular, he effortlessly begins reeling off the answers.

*'Seven across - Ownership.'*

*'Nine down, apply some simple mentoring, nine letters –
Implement.'*

*'Seven down, Does Freddy cry wolf? No, he wisely loses his
head – Owl.'*

Jake takes less than a minute to complete the rest of the
clues before the phone rings. Richard, the concierge, answers
it.

'Your transport is here, Mr. Pisson.'

As Jake heads for his cab, Richard takes a cellphone out of
his breast pocket and presses 1 on his speed dial. 'Code red,
repeat, code R.E.D. R for Romeo, E for Echo, D for ...' 'Duck.'
'No, I don't think that's...'

The blow comes before Richard can turn to see his assailant.
As he slumps onto his desk, a gloved hand removes the cell
phone from his grip and bundles the unconscious body
under the reception desk. Later that day, a long-standing
resident enters the foyer and asks innocently.

'Where's Richard, isn't he normally on duty at this time?'

The new concierge's fixed smile belies his terse reply.

'Richard has been transferred to Miami.'

# Chapter Two

# Deal or No Deal

*Ten forty-five a.m.*

Jake enters his office and is met by his secretary, Sally.
'Where have you been Jake? They've been in there over
fifteen minutes!' As she gestures towards the meeting room
door, she suddenly becomes aware of Jake's disheveled
appearance - the tousled hair, the toilet paper-covered
shaving cuts and, finally, the chain snaking from the bottom
of one of his trouser legs. Jake notices her shocked
expression and offers what he hopes is a plausible
explanation.
'Car trouble, looks like I'll be carless for a while – man, those
cab drivers sure are crazy!' Judging by Sally's expression, he
realizes plausible might be too optimistic a description.
Rushing into the meeting room he sees three sharp-suited
young men sitting at the far end of his oak conference table.
He notices that their Blowman Corporation lapel badges are
each positioned at exactly the same spot on their jackets. To
Jake's right is Lars Arsen, his accountant. Lars jumps up
when Jake enters, the others stay seated. Lars ushers Jake
into the room as if he were royalty.
'See, I told you he wouldn't be long.'
Jake shuffles to the table, sitting down gingerly, he tries to
smile through the pain – he fails miserably
'Phew, made it. The traffic on the bridge was horrendous!
Still, I'm here now and that's the main thing.'
The nearest Blowman employee looks up.

'Brooklyn Bridge? We came over that, the traffic seemed normal then.'

'No, not Brooklyn Bridge.'

The next Blowman employee interjects. 'Which one?'

'Er, the other one.' The intercom buzzes, it's Sally's voice. 'Mr. Poisson, the cab driver says it's fifty dollars across Brooklyn Bridge to here and you only gave him twenty.' Jake shrugs his shoulders, shakes his head and makes an attempt to put on his best, innocently bemused, expression.

'Just pay him out of the petty cash Sally, please. Taxi drivers! - I was one once, so I know how easy it is to get confused. As I was saying, I've moved heaven and earth to get here. Shall we carry on with business?'

Unnoticed by Jake, the Blowman clones exchange knowing glances. The third Blowman clone's manner seems to make him the most senior, although physically, it would be difficult to tell them apart. The fact that he breaks the silence seems to confirm Jake's suspicions.

'Well, now that you're finally here Mr. Person, I'll get straight to the point.'

'It's Poisson.'

'Pardon?'

'French for fish.'

'As I said, I'll get straight to the point.'

'Yes, good. I like that.'

Clone three continues. 'As you know Mr. Fish, the Blowman Corporation has been considering purchasing a major share in Poisson Dating for the sum of three point five million dollars.' Jake tries to appear casual and realizes it will be better achieved by sitting on his hands. The pain renders him speechless. Blowman employee number one takes over.

'As my colleague has said, we'll get straight to the point.

Unfortunately, our accountants have found a number of anomalies in your figures - the deal is off.'

Jake is stunned. 'No, surely you can't do that.'

'Oh yes we can, no contracts have been signed.'

As Jake pulls a handkerchief from his breast pocket, Georgette's card falls out. An image of his signature on Georgette's butt fills his mind. He considers examining his own backside - he isn't optimistic, but asks hopefully. 'Are you sure there's no contract?'

'Oh yes, we are certain, so without any further...'

'Wait...WAIT! This business has high profit margins and very low overheads. Apart from myself, the only staff are my accountant Lars, here - one of the most respected financial experts in his field, our programmer Sven, Sally my secretary and our data input clerk, Candice.'

During this time, Lars has been busy using his laptop. At the mention of his name, he looks up, lowers the cover and looks smugly towards the visitors. As Jake appeals to them, the speaker on Lars' laptop blares out.

*"You have a message from Stewpothead."*

*"Hey Lardass, you won that one you lucky bastard, how about best of a hundred and..."*

Lars calmly closes the cover and stares nonchalantly at the visitors, his face expressionless. Clone Three rises to his feet addressing no one in particular, his words strike like arrows fired straight into Jake's heart. 'I'm sure I speak for all of us when I say that we are no longer interested in anything you have to offer.' The other two clones nod in agreement as Clone Two draws the meeting to a close.

'Goodbye gentlemen, we'll see ourselves out.'
Once outside, Clone Three takes out his cell phone and punches 1 on his speed dial. 'Can I help you, Number Seven?'
'I want Poisson's file on my desk by the time I return. It that clear?'
'Certainly, Sir.'
He turns to the other two clones. 'He obviously doesn't know about Candice. His guard is down.'

Inside his office, Jake isn't very happy, he heads for his room, passing a concerned Sally on the way. 'No calls from anyone, no, not one. None - not any.'
Jake enters his private office and sits in his chair. He looks at his office clock which shows 11.00am, lays his head on his desk and starts sobbing loudly. Later that day Jake wakes and wipes the saliva from his desk. Looking up at the clock he sees it's two thirteen p.m. He heads for his cloakroom and splashes his face with cold water. Above the sink is a motivational poster of The Terminator, it reads: FEEL BAD? DON'T BE SAD GET MAD Jake wonders when The Terminator grew a Zapata moustache. At the very bottom there's a lipstick kiss and a scribbled

Georgette xx

Jake storms out of the cloakroom into Sally's office, his manner one of steely determination. 'How's Candice, the Ice Queen getting on with the data input?'
'You shouldn't call her that, Jake, she's a lovely person when you get to know her. Did you know she once stayed up all night nursing her hamster?'
'I didn't, maybe she has a side to her that I've never seen.'
'She fed it warm milk through an eye dropper.'

'Aww – how sweet, what a lucky hamster.'

'Not really, it died.'

'Wow, she must have been gutted.'

'She was, but she's over it now.'

'When did it happen?'

' Let me see, it's Tuesday today, so it must have happened the day before yesterday.'

'So, where is she now?'

'She left this morning - went to an agency, the Dan something or other agency.'

'No! What's her job?'

'Typist.'

Candice was useless at typing, she was too frightened of damaging her immaculate nails, but when he had interviewed her, she was wearing the shortest micro miniskirt he had ever seen and he was so preoccupied with trying to catch sight of her panties that he forgot to ask her typing speed. He consoled himself by thinking of her other qualities. She was always punctual and – well - she was always punctual – she left the office on the dot of five. The main reason he was sad to see her leave, however, was that it meant he would have to give up his quest. Every day she would wear one of her miniscular miniskirts, every day he would try to get even the briefest glimpse of her elusive panties, and every day he would fail - but that only made him more determined. Jake can't hide his disappointment at the news.

'Who have we got to enter the new clients?'

'Nobody.'

'Could you do it, Sally?'

'Who would make your coffee, Mr. Poisson?'

Jake considers the question, then he remembers Sally's

dyslexia. He wonders whether Taf Watt is still on their books.

'True - I'll do it – what's the password?'

'Candice left it. Here it is.'

She hands him the slip of paper. On it is written THEFINGER all uppercase.

'What's wrong with that woman? I told her, always include a number. - Oh, look, it's folded. There's something written on the back.'

Jake turns it over and reads it. "2U" 'Well, at least she took some notice...'

Jake returns to his office, sits in his Nappa leather swivel chair and jabs at the intercom button. 'Can you send in Lars, please?'

'He had an urgent engagement.'

'Sven?'

'He had an urgent engagement too.'

Jake punches in the password with a vengeance. The maintenance screen appears with the header:

*POISSON DATING You Wish, We Fish*

Jake starts talking to himself 'It's been a while...'

The screen shows two options:

Monthly free trials:  6

Fully paid:      14

He chooses the Monthly free trials option. 'Hmm, might as well get rid of these first.'

The first applicant appears on the screen.

*Name: Georgette Occupation: Model Height: 5'5" Hair: Blonde Description: A gentle nature lover, I can promise you a nice, relaxing evening by the fireside.*

'And I'll throw in a sound thrashing for free.' Jake thinks to himself. Jake clicks on the photo icon. A beautiful portrait of Georgette fills the screen.
'She's very photogenic, I'll say that for her, maybe I just caught her on a bad day...'
Jake continues clicking

*Generate Matches*

The screen fills with thumbnails of handsome men.

*Select All.*

'All's fair in love and business.' He chooses the next applicant.

*Name: Lysette Occupation: Masseuse Height: 5'5"  Hair: Brunette Description: I'm an outdoor girl who likes physical activities, particularly horse riding.*

A photo of Georgette, different wig, different colored lipstick, fills the screen. Jakes feels a sharp twinge at the realization of why he keeps getting flashbacks of a riding crop. Noticing a poster on the opposite wall, he moves over to it and studies it.

*HONESTY IS THE BEST POLICY*

He turns it to face the wall. He reads the next name: Annette, looks at her photo and chooses

*Generate Matches, Select All*

and then clicks onto the next application. *Claudette*... Jake doesn't even bother looking at her photo. He furtively closes the blinds and continues.

*Generate Matches, Select All*

The next name to appear is *Collette,* Jake punches the intercom button. 'Any chance of a cup of coffee Sally?'
'Of course.'
Sally heads out of the office and, a few minutes later, returns with a cup of Starbuck's coffee - she pours it into a mug decorated with Jake's photo and the inscription I ♥ My Boss. She hands it to Jake who takes a sip from it.
'Wow, I don't know how you do it Sally – this coffee is delicious. Whenever I taste it, I'm reminded of why I employed you.'
'Was that the only reason, Mr. Poisson?'
Jake thinks long and hard about it and is about to be honest, but when he sees the innocent, expectant look on Sally's face, he relents. 'Of course not, Sally.'
Jake has another gulp of his coffee and leans back on his chair, relaxed and confident, congratulating himself on the way he has dealt with what could have been an awkward situation - his satisfaction doesn't last long.
'When you employed me, what other qualities did you think I possessed, Mr. Poisson?'
Jake nearly sprays coffee over his computer. Nothing immediately springs to mind, but then he notices a glass paperweight in the shape of a cherub.
'Too many to mention, my angel.'
'I love it when you call me your angel, Mr. Poisson. Do you remember that time at the Christmas party when you...?'
Jake could vaguely remember having to get the photocopier

fixed and disinfected, but he would be the first to admit that he'd had problems with his memory and these days it seemed to be getting worse.

'I thought we'd agreed not to mix business with pleasure, Sally.'

'Oh, I know Mr. Poisson, but just because you're my boss doesn't mean we can't be nice to each other, does it?'

'Of course not, Sally.'

'So just tell me my *three* best qualities.'

This time Jake can't avoid spraying the computer with coffee. 'Three!'

'Yes, Mr. Poisson, only three. My best three, in any order, if that makes it easier.'

The soreness in Jake's ass is beginning to spread though his body and, in addition, his head is throbbing. He grabs a couple of painkillers from his desk drawer and gulps them down, followed by some coffee. Unfortunately, there isn't enough coffee left and the tablets lodge themselves in his throat. Unable to speak he looks imploringly at Sally.

'I know, Mr. Poisson. You think you'll embarrass me, so I'll tell you what I think you'll say. 'Intelligence, ability and efficiency. Oh and, of course, my looks.'

She giggles. 'But you're not really supposed to say that!'

Jake is frantically nodding his head trying to dislodge the tablets. He manages to cough them up and they land on the screen of his monitor, covering the eyes of the photograph of Collette. Sally sees it and laughs. She's an attractive woman, Mr. Poisson. Do you know her?'

'I've never seen her before in my life.' Jake lies. Sally leans over his desk provocatively, showing her ample cleavage. This disconcerts Jake somewhat, as he finds he's enjoying the view more than he should.

'Well, I would love to sit here chatting to you, Sally, but as you know, we are a little short-staffed at present, so...'

'I know, Mr. Poisson. It's like the good old days this afternoon, isn't it? - Just you and me.'

Jake has a flashback. The pair of them sitting closely together in a dank, drab, tiny office. Sally breaks wind and turns to Jake. 'Sorry Mr. Poisson - must have been that curry last night.' As Sally reluctantly returns to her office, Jake sniffs the air.

'Have you been eating curry again, Sally?'

Sally turns round and gives Jake a sheepish smile.

'Oh, by the way, Mr. Poisson, your sister phoned. She said to remind you it's Tuesday, so you're due at your mom's for dinner.'

'I've got no car, so I won't be able to make it.'

'I told her - she says it's all sorted.'

'What the hell does that...?' His question is cut short as Sally closes the door behind her. Jake absently stares at his coffee cup.

'There must be someone else who can make coffee like this.' Jake leans back in his chair and, with a flourish, he expertly manipulates the keyboard. He clicks on Fully paid and turns up the sound on his speakers. With the sounds of *Dire Straits, Money For Nothing* filling the air, he begins to enter the details of his first fully paid client.


*Name: Elsa Eggblom Occupation: Film producer Height: 5'4" Hair: Blonde*
*Likes: Food, especially pizza, films, computers, nature.*


'Hmm... That name sounds vaguely familiar.' He selects

Photograph and slaps himself across the face. 'And that looks very familiar - could it be? – Perhaps it's a coincidence, someone who looks extremely like her, with a similar name...'

Jake has another flashback, this time to his days before college. He is delivering pizzas - dismounting from his moped he knocks on an apartment door. A young blonde opens the door wearing only a towel. As she reaches into her purse, the towel drops to the floor revealing that she is naked. Jake looks at the delivery note. 'Olga Oggblom?' Slowly and deliberately, the girl rummages through her purse 'Ya, eet is I. I only haf a hundred-dollar beal. You haf change ya?' Jake tries desperately to get his hand into his jeans pocket but there appears to be something hard stopping him. After a few minutes fumbling, he gives up.
'It's only twelve dollars. I could pick it up tomorrow if that's alright with you?'
'Ya zat iz gurd.'
'What time do you have your bath, er, get back from work?'
'I'll be in for sex.'
'Sex?'
'Ya, or sex turdy.'
'I'll be here at seven then - that should give you time to get unready.'
Jake watches through the letterbox as Olga crosses the room and switches her computer off. 'Not only beautiful, but also computer literate, that's my kind of woman...'

Jake's mind is troubled. The flashback seemed so real, but why has he not remembered it before? He tries, unsuccessfully, to put it out of his mind.

# Chapter Three

## Meatloaf

Back in the present, Jake is staring at his computer screen, eventually he scrolls down the options and clicks on

*Select None.*

The clock shows 5.30 - his intercom buzzes.
 'Your sister is here.'
 'Show her i...' Jake looks up and sees that his sister is already sitting opposite him.
 'Jake, you've been staring at that screen for ten minutes, lost in your own little world! - Come on, you know Mom doesn't like us being late.'
 'Liz – I wasn't expecting you - did Sally not tell you, I'm kind of in between cars?'
 'Worry not, big brother, it's all taken care of - follow me.'
Jake is on the pavement, standing alongside Liz, gazing fondly at a big, shiny, black Mercedes. Liz also seems to be looking at it.
 'What do you think, big brother?'
 'Nice, my favorite color too.'
 Liz throws him the keys and walks off in the opposite direction. As he turns, he sees her at the door of a nineteen-seventies, fluorescent orange and rust-colored Cadillac station wagon. The inside is covered in faded gold velvet and the trunk and back seat are full of boxes. The word pimpmobile has lodged itself in Jake's mind.
 'Come on, Jake, what are you waiting for? Mom will be

wondering where we are – by the way, this beauty is yours for as long as you want it.'

Five minutes later Jake is reluctantly driving the car. Liz is in the front passenger seat. 'It drives well, doesn't it Jake?' Jake somehow remains straight-faced.

'I'd almost forgotten I wasn't in my Porsche. Where did you get it?'

'Ernest got it from a friend of his, he won't be needing it for a while.'

'How long?'

'Ten to fifteen.'

'Days?'

'Years.'

After a pause, Jake resumes the conversation.

'Liz, I've been meaning to talk to you about Ernest. I mean, you're a reasonable looking woman with your own house and a good job with prospects. He's an out of work down and out with the sanitary habits of a circus monkey - I just think you could do a lot better.'

Getting no response from Liz, Jake continues. 'Where is he, by the way?'

'He's in the back.'

Ernest pops his head out from behind the boxes. 'Hi, Jake.'

'Hi, Ernest.'

'Hey, Jake, press that red button.'

Jake does as requested. The Cadillac starts jumping up and down like a bronco on its way to be gelded - Jake now knows what a piece of ribeye steak feels like while it's being seared on a griddle.

'Holy shit!'

'Good, eh? – Would you believe that upgrade only cost two grand.' There is a tinny, rattling noise as something metallic drops off the back of the Caddy. Jake drives on in silence. Ten minutes later, he turns to his sister. 'Liz, do you remember Olga Oggblom?'

'Umm.... Olga, yes, vaguely, I think – why?'

'Apparently, she's been trying to contact me on social media.'

Liz desperately tries to hide her surprise by looking out of the window, she needn't have worried, Jake is too caught up in his own thoughts to notice, but, just in case, she changes the subject. 'They're getting on well with that new restaurant over there - I hope it's a vegan one.'

'What's it called?'

'Everything But the Hooves.'

Jake pulls up outside his mom's house and rushes into the garage, loosening the tie holding part of the chain to his leg, he places his foot in a vice. He's gingerly using a hacksaw on the shackle when Ernest comes in carrying an armful of boxes and carefully places them on the floor.

'Jake, I'm getting married and I'd like you to be my best man.'

Jake, still sawing at the shackle, slices his leg open with the shock. His face contorts in agony.

'It would be an honor.'

Without commenting, Ernest takes the hacksaw from Jake's hand and starts sawing furiously at the manacle. Jake breathes a sigh of relief as, eventually, the chain drops noisily to the floor. He cautiously places his foot on the floor and looks down at his shredded, bloodstained trouser leg. Ernest holds up what's left of the manacle.

'I've had one of these, they're not real. You press this button to open them.' Ernest presses the button and part of the manacle falls onto Jake's bloodied foot. Jake winces in pain.

Ernest nonchalantly carries on with his conversation. 'Liz will be made up - you being best man and all.'

'What's Liz got to do with it?'

'Ha, Jake, you are so funny, it's Liz I'm getting married to.' Jake considers picking up the hacksaw. Reluctantly he decides against it. 'Does she know?'

'Ho, I can't wait for your speech, Jake. You'll crease everyone up!'

As Ernest turns to go into the house, Jake quickly bends down and presses the button on the other manacle, it opens easily. He sighs and throws it into the trash can. As he does so, he notices Chinese lettering on the boxes. 'Ernest, what's in these?'

'It's my new job. I'm a distributor. Hey, you'll love them.' Ernest opens one of the boxes and carefully takes out a small package. He shows it to Jake. 'It's new, talk into it.'

'I'd rather not.'

'Go on, it's fun.'

'I will if you will.'

Ernest delightedly plays it back to Jake.

'So, it's a message recorder.'

'But listen to this.' He plays a message to Jake. 'I'm stuck on the tube, I'll be late.' The voice sounds like Jake's and it has the sound effects of a tube train in the background. Jake is interested.

'It learns from your voice. It has over a hundred built-in messages and you can download more.'

'That's not bad, how much?'

'Normal retail, ninety-nine dollars. I can do one for you at cost, seventy-nine dollars, or forty down and ten dollars a month for six months.'

Jake reaches into his pocket and takes out a wad of money.

He counts out eighty dollars and hands it to Ernest. 'I'll take one.'

'Thanks man, they're selling really well.'

'That's good, how many have you sold up to now?'

'One.'

'So, this makes two?' Ernest stares at Jake. 'One? Well, I suppose you have to start somewhere.' Ernest wanders off into the house, Jake hears his mother calling to him through the open kitchen window.

'Jake, your dinner's ready.'

'What is it?'

'Meatloaf.'

'Just when I thought things couldn't get any worse.'

Jake, Ernest, Liz and Gloria (Jake and Liz's mother) are sitting round the dining table. Charles (Gloria's recent boyfriend) has left the table and is making coffee in the kitchen. Jake turns to his mother. 'That Charles guy seems to be making himself at home.'

'Don't be like that, Jake. You'll like him once you get to know him.'

'How well do you know him, Mom? – It's only been a few weeks and he seems to go away a lot. He acts like he's living here now.'

Gloria colors and hurriedly hands out the plates. Ernest is oblivious to the awkward silence. 'This is lovely, Mrs. Poisson, what is it?'

Jake can't stop himself. 'It's meatloaf Ernest, we've been coming here every week for the last year and every week we have meatloaf.'

'It's a new recipe.'

Jake tries it and is pleasantly surprised, it tastes a lot better than normal. 'What's in it?'

'I put some of those herbs I found in your bedroom drawer.'
Jake almost chokes on his food.' 'Mom, I wish you wouldn't
go into my room.'

'You moved out years ago Jake – besides I never look under
your bed.'

Ernest looks quizzically at Liz - she just shakes her head.
Ernest makes a rude gesture with his hand and she nods.
Jake tries to ignore the innuendo.

'I still use that room occasionally, Mom. I just think you
could be a little more thoughtful that's all.'

'Jake's always been very secretive, hasn't he Liz? Do you
remember that time when your father had to call the fire
brigade out to...?'

'Mom, Ernest doesn't want to hear about our boring old
family anecdotes.'

Charles has returned and is silently tucking into his food. At
the mention of Jake's misadventures, he suddenly becomes
interested.

'Oh, I do. I find the stories of Gloria's life before me very
illuminating.'

Jake's not happy, he swiftly changes the subject. 'We haven't
seen or heard from Pops for a long time now and there's
nothing much to say about him.' He glares at his mother,
unable to hide his annoyance. Gloria turns to Charles.

'That coffee should be ready by now, Charlie - would you?'
Jake immediately regrets his sharpness. As Charles heads for
the kitchen, he smiles at his mom. 'Mom, do you remember
Olga Oggblom?' Gloria looks surprised.

'Olga? No, I don't think so.' Liz is watching her mother's
reaction very closely.

'You do, Mom - she was the only girl Jake ever brought
home from college. She was Swedish.'

29

'She was Norwegian.'

'Are you sure she wasn't Russian, Jake?'

'No, Mom - she was definitely Norwegian.'

Gloria regains her composure a little, but stares fixedly at her plate, ignoring the intent gazes of her offspring. At that moment Charles returns with the coffees, he plonks the tray on the table.

Charles looks questioningly at Gloria. 'So, who is this Olga, then? But Jake makes it clear that he is putting an end to that particular topic of conversation.

'Oh, she was just a friend, nothing to concern yourself about.' Gloria tries to smooth things over

'I've made Jake's favorite for dessert - cherry pie, made to Grannie's recipe!'

'Charles, would you?'

Charles looks put out, but dutifully heads back to the kitchen. Gloria pats the back of Jake's hand as if he were about thirteen, which, in her mind, he still is. She senses how hurt Jake is - noticing that Liz and Ernest are deeply engrossed in each other, she whispers to him. 'Your father hasn't forgotten you, Jake. He'll be there when you need him'.

Rapidly composing herself, she turns to the others.

'It's nice to see my children getting along so well. What have you both been getting up to?' Liz manages to draw herself away from Ernest's scintillating conversation.

'Nothing much, Mom.'

Jake just wants to forget about the day he has had and this seems like as good a time as any to lighten up the conversation.

'Hey, Liz, Ernest sold me one of those recording machine things.'

'Oh yeah, they're great value for twenty dollars, aren't they?'
Jake looks at Ernest, or rather at the seat where Ernest was
sitting. A voice comes from the passageway to the kitchen.
'Mrs. Poisson, I'm just going to help Charles with that pie.
Does it have any of those herbs in it?'
'Oh yes, Ernest, I've been putting them in everything. While
you're in the kitchen you'd better check on Charles, he seems
to be taking a long time.'
As the two men return to the table, Jake notices them
exchanging glances, but he makes no comment. The meal
finished, as they head for the door Gloria takes Jake to one
side and gives him a hug. 'Fox would be proud of you, Son.'
'Do you think so, Mom?'
Jake feels an arm tightly gripping his shoulders, turning
slightly, he finds himself face to face with Charles.
'I'm sure he would.'
Jake shrugs off the grip as politely as he can. Unnoticed by
the others, Charles furtively slides a small package into
Jake's jacket pocket. Jake notices, but has no time to react
because, seconds later, he, Liz and Ernest are outside the
house with Charles and Gloria waving them off from the
porch. As Jake opens his car door, he turns to Sally and
Ernest.
'You sure you guys don't want a lift, it's only a few miles out
of my way.'
All three, but particularly Ernest, seem very vague after the
meatloaf and pie. 'Hey, far out man, but we are cool, we're
following that cloud.'
Jake and Liz instinctively look up at the clear, dark-blue sky.
'Well, that star. There - the one's that's moving.'
'Cool, I see it. Enjoy your trip, man.'
Ernest and Liz wander off arm in arm, with Ernest muttering

about how cool Jake is. Jake gets into the pimpmobile, waves to everyone and roars off up the drive. Charles and Gloria head back into the house. Charles is relaxing in his favorite chair; Gloria is scrolling down the screen of her cell phone.

'I think that was the best meatloaf I've ever tasted.'

'Thank you, Honey, it did seem to go down well. There's still quite a bit left though.' She moves over to him and attempts to sit on his knee, Charles tries to ignore the pain.

'I was thinking, Honey, do you think I should give Wes...?

'A call - yeah, why not? Just remind me - who is Wes?'

'He was a very close friend of ours when I was married to Fox, we lost touch. I bet he would enjoy a bit.'

Gloria picks up the phone. 'Hi Wes, it's me Gloria. Long time, no see. How are you getting on?'

On the other end of the phone is Wes, he is wearing only a towel and a cowboy hat.

'Hey Gloria, it's been a while - I'm great, how are you and...'

'It's Charles now. He's fine - we were just talking about you and we wondered if you might like to call round sometime. I've got a great new recipe for meatloaf.'

'Anytime, Gloria – just say when.'

'Actually, there's a piece in the fridge right now. I thought you might fancy a bit.'

'I'll be round in an hour...'

# Chapter Four

## Police, Guns and Bruises

Jake has been stopped by traffic police. One officer is at the window of Jake's car, another officer is radioing in to headquarters, both have their guns drawn and aimed at Jake.

'Can I see your driver's license sir?'

'Of course, officer.'

As Jake reaches into his pocket for his license, the officer using the radio makes a gesture to his colleague.

'Get out of the car, sir.'

Jake fumbles for his license, inadvertently triggering the recorder he had bought from Ernest earlier that evening. He listens powerlessly as his voice rings out.

'I'd rather not.'

Without realizing how it happened, Jake finds himself face down on the road with his hands cuffed behind his back. The two officers haul Jake over the bonnet of his pimpmobile.

The second cop kicks at Jake's legs 'Spread 'em.'

'I will if you will.'

Jake is horrified at how camp his voice sounds. The officers look knowingly at each other. One of them returns his gun to his holster and slowly pulls out his baton.

'Ooh, that's a big one.'

By now, the voice has turned soprano.

'That can't be right, it's broken.'

The officer looks lovingly at his baton. 'Not yet smartass, but it sure as hell will be soon.'

*Two hours later*

Gloria's phone is ringing. Charles drowsily gets out of bed to answer it. 'Yes, it is - where? Certainly sir, of course, sir - right away, sir.'

He puts the phone down with a crash.

'Who was it, Honey?'

'Jake has been arrested - he's down at the station.'

Wes pops his head out from under the bedclothes. 'Any of that meatloaf left?'

'Good idea. He'll be there a while, anyway.' Charles jumps out of bed and heads for the kitchen.

*Three days later*

Sally opens the door to Jake's office.

'Ooh, Mr. Poisson you scared the life out of me. That *is*, you, isn't it?'

'Of course, who else would it be?'

'You've been off for three days - I couldn't get in touch with you. Where did you get that black eye – and those bandages, and your poor hands – and those crutches?'

'Just a slight accident that's all. I'll be fine in a couple of weeks.'

Jake stands up and immediately falls over.

'Or so...'

Sally helps him back into his seat. 'But, why are you at work so early?'

'I came in early to catch up on my work. These are desperate times, Sally, they call for desperate measures. I want everyone in the conference room now – everyone!'

Jake struggles to his feet and, with the aid of his crutches, hobbles towards the conference room. Over his shoulder, he calls to his secretary. 'Could you bring me a coffee please, Sally? - The way only you make it.'

Ten minutes later, Sally brings him his coffee in his favorite I ♥ My Boss mug. She takes out her notebook.

'Sally, I need to tell all the staff about the recent developments.'

'Go ahead, Mr. Poisson.'

'I'd prefer to tell all the staff, rather than have to repeat myself.'

'Go ahead, Mr. Poisson.'

Jake puts his head in his hands and winces with pain.'

'All...the...staff..., Sally!'

'Go ahead, Mr. Poisson.'

Jake looks around the room and under the table. He stares at Sally with a puzzled expression.

'We are all here, is your coffee okay?'

'My cof...?' Jake takes a sip. 'Umm, yes, as usual - a lovely cup of coffee, I don't know how you do it.' Jake smiles to himself.

'Where are Lars and Sven hiding, those two crease me up – and what about Candice?'

'I told you before - Candice has gone to another agency.'

'Oh yes, I forgot – Lars?'

'I'm sorry to say he won't be coming back.'

'Lars has left? What happened?'

'He's gone to another company, Dan something or other.'

'Did he not say anything before he left?'

'He sent me an email, here it is.'

*"Please tell Jake I won't be back, it's been a blast, but it couldn't last."*

'There's one of those things on the bottom of it. It looks like a champagne cork popping off a bottle.

'GIF.'

'I always thought he was quite nice.'

'Me too, obviously he's never heard of the word loyalty though.'

'Do you want me to put that in the minutes. Mr. Poisson?'

'Er, no need for that - Sven?'

'I'm sorry to say he won't be coming back.'

'Sven has left - what happened?'

'He's gone to another company, Dan something or other, here it is – The Dan Corleone Agency.'

'Did he not say anything before he left?'

'He sent me an email, I'll read it to you.'

*"Please tell Jake I won't be back, it's been a blast, but it couldn't last."*

'There's one of those things on the bottom of it.'

'A bottle of champagne?'

'That would be very nice, Mr. Poisson.'

'No, no – I meant is it a champagne bottle on the bottom?'

'No, it looks like balloons floating up into the air, there's a blue one and a pink one and a...'

'That's fine, Sally, thanks, so there's only me and you?'

'Yes.'

'Fu...'

'Do you want me to...'

'No, no – you don't need to put that in the minutes, Sally.'

Sally closes her notebook and waits expectingly.

'So that leaves you and me, Sally, what's our plan of action?'

Sally re-opens her notebook and sits, pen in hand, ready for action. Jake stares at Sally, she returns his stare, Jake blinks first.

'Okay, Sally, let's brainstorm.'

Sally clicks her pen to the on position, Jake closes his eyes, his face a picture of concentration.

Ten minutes later Jake opens his eyes. 'I've got it, we'll go right back to the very start.'

'Where would you like me to sit, Mr. Poisson?'

'What do you mean?'

'When we first started, I used to sit on your kn...'

'Sally that was a long time ago.'

*'Long before the #metoo movement, and long before you started stuffing your face with curries.'* Jake thinks.

'Besides, at that time we didn't have enough chairs.'

'I had my own seat and desk.'

'Yes well, er, I knew we were in it for the long haul. I was trying to keep your work area tidy, remember?'

'Is that why you made me wear stockings?'

'That was for medical reasons, Sally. I showed you that article in Cosmopolitan.'

Jake takes a quick gulp of coffee.

'My, you've certainly proved you have a good memory, that's why I chose you out of all those applicants. That, and your fabulous coffee, Sally – any chance of another?'

'Of course, Mr. Poisson, you just sit there. I'll have one for you in ten minutes.'

Sally takes the empty mug and, ten minutes later, returns with it full.

'I never really thanked you for appointing me over all those other applicants, Mr. Poisson, how many were there?'

Jake casts his mind back. He remembers a twenty-one stone, semi-retired wrestler, after that his mind goes blank.

'Too numerous to mention, Sally - too numerous to mention! Anyway, the point I'm getting at, is that we were successful then, so if we follow the same steps, we'll be successful again.'

'That is a great idea, Mr. Poisson.'

'Jake please, Sally.'

'I called you Mr. Poisson then, Mr. Poisson.'

'Okay.'

'And you called me, Miss Jones. You always used to say "Take a letter Miss Jones." - didn't you?'

'Yes, good, good, it's coming back to me now.'

'And you would say, "Come and sit on my kn..." '

'You've already mentioned that, Sall..., er, Miss Jones.'

'I'm sor...'

'Oh no, Miss Jones, don't be sorry. This is good, but think back - tell me, what did we do? What ideas did we come up with?'

Sally looks blankly at Jake – he closes his eyes again - fifteen minutes later he reopens them.

'I've got it! We'll look at the files on the computer, the minutes, letters, flyers. Everything we've got on there. Show me the files, Sally.'

Sally heads to her office, sits at her desk and switches on her computer. Five minutes later, she returns. 'My computer has loaded up.'

Jake hobbles over to the screen. 'That's only the last two weeks, Sally - where's the rest?'

'I've deleted them.'

'Why on earth would you...?'

'You told me that storage costs money.'

'That was then, but now it's cheaper than a full body massage.'

'How much does that cost, Mr. Poisson?'

'Well, my last one was - never mind - you don't need to know

about that, Sally. Besides, the extras brought the cost up.'
'Miss Jones...'
'No, it was Miss Vixenne.'
'No, I'm Miss Jones, silly!'
'Sorry Sa... Miss Jones. That's a bit of a bummer, I'm just glad I told you to always print off hard copies. Where are they?'
Sally goes to a cupboard and returns with a box file. Jake frantically looks through it. 'I can only see the last two weeks documents here, where's the rest?'
'You told me that printing costs money.'
Jake sees a large box and rummages through it. He pulls out a mug and reads it, then another, and another. They all have I ♥ My Boss written on them, Sally looks on proudly.
'It's cheaper to buy in bulk.'
Jake puts his head in his hands.
'Do your eyes hurt, Mr. Poisson? They seem to be watering.'
Jake sobs silently. 'I need to think about this, Miss Jones. Can I call you Sally, please?'
'I prefer Miss Jones.'
'Okay, Miss Jones, any chance of another cup of coffee?'
'I'll need more petty cash.'
Jake rubs his eyes, forgetting that one of them is black and blue. He looks at his secretary with a puzzled expression.
'Starbucks have put their prices up.'
Jake takes a twenty-dollar bill out of his wallet - it's his last one. He passes it to Sally, his expression even more puzzled. As Sally reaches the door, she turns to him.
'Oh, by the way, Mr. Poisson. You never told me how you got those bruises.'
'It's a long story, Sally.'
'Miss Jones!' Sally giggles at her own joke.

By the time she returns with the coffee, Jake is in his office, waiting for his computer to load up.

'Here's your coffee, Mr. Poisson, I brought it to you in your favorite mug.'

'Thank you, but we'll do it differently this time, just call me Jake.'

'Certainly, Mr. Poisson.' With that, she leaves Jake to begin his search.

# Chapter Five

## Let's Go Round Again

Two nervous-looking, young officers are sitting in an interview room. A large, burly, brusque man walks in and sits down at his desk. He opens a folder, grimaces at the images it contains and looks quizzically at each of the officers in turn. They both automatically sit bolt upright. The folder contains photographs of a man, he's virtually unrecognizable, but there's something vaguely familiar about him. He studies each photograph carefully, then, wearily closing the dossier, he addresses each officer in turn.

'Well, well, well, who have we got here?' He points to an unfit-looking one. 'Tubbs?'

Then the one with long hair.

'And Crockett?'

The unfit-looking one replies. 'No chief - he's Crockett - I'm Columbo.'

'Columbo and Crockett? Somehow that just doesn't sound right.'

'It's right, Chief.'

'Let me see.'

He reopens the large, thick file.'

'Patrol officers, Christopher Columbo and David Crockett.'

'That's right, Chief, but most people call me Chris and they call him...'

'Don't tell me – Davy.'

'No, Chief - Geordie.'

'Why's that?'

'You'll find out, Chief.'

41

'I'm not sure I want to know - anyway, what's with this Chief crap? It's lieutenant, do I look like I've got a totem pole stuck up my ass?'

Both officers study the lieutenant carefully, Crockett nods his head, but fortunately for him, says nothing. Columbo is a little more tactful.

'Well, er, no. Not really, not very much, Che... - Lieutenant.'

'Which idiot put you two together as partners?'

'Ah can tell yer that, ah have it here.'

Crockett pulls out a stained, crumpled scrap of paper from his back pocket. 'It woz a leftenant Pussy.'

'What the hell was I thinking? I'm Lieutenant Harry Pusey.'

'Ah, so yor the pussy that every one's on aboot, the big boss, the head honcho, the numero...'

Crockett jumps up, stands to attention and salutes the lieutenant.

'There's no need for that Officer Crockett. Where are you from, by the way?'

'Ah'm from Newcassle, man. In the North East of Angleterre.'

'Okay, Crockett. This is a very serious matter - I think it will be better if Patrol Officer Columbo does the talking.'

'Alreet, marra.'

'Good - let's continue.'

Lieutenant Pusey picks up one of the photographs and grimaces again. 'He's claiming police brutality. That black eye doesn't look good – and the rest of his face looks worse...'

'Why man, that's obviously self-inflicted, he's a reet pussy, nee offence intended, Che...'

Pusey sighs. 'None taken, I don't think, Crockett.' Lieutenant Pusey looks questioningly at Officer Columbo.

Columbo shrugs and shakes his head.

'I've only been working with him for four months, sir - I'm not fluent yet.'

'That reminds me, how long have you men been on the force?'

'Fower months for me, Guv.'

Columbo feels the need to interpret. 'Four months for Detective Crockett and six months for me, sir.'

'Granted that's not long, but you should both know the department's policy by now - no visible marks.'

'That was my fault, sir. I was aiming for his nuts.'

'You were aiming for his nuts and you hit his head? Did you not learn anything in baton practice?'

'That was Crockett's fault, sir. He tasered him, just as I was taking aim.'

'It was a new taser, man, ah was jus' tryin' it oot.'

'Well, it obviously works.'

'I don't think we need to worry, sir. He hasn't got a leg to stand on.'

'You made sure of that - he's on crutches!'

'To be fair, sir. The curb was high.'

'He was in the middle of a three-lane highway!'

The two detectives stare innocently at the lieutenant.

'I've got to tell you, I'm in two minds about this.' He picks up the file and hovers between the Proceed and Drop trays. 'Who's the judge.'

'Hannan.'

'Hannan the Hangman?'

He reluctantly drops the file into the Proceed tray. 'Oh well, we'll all be retired by the time he gets out – so someone else can sort out this mess.'

As Columbo and Crockett high five each other on the way out, Lieutenant Pusey picks up the phone.

'Human Resources please, Betty,'
'Sure thing, sir.'
'Oh, hello, it's Lieutenant Pusey here. Are we still running those foreign language courses?'

*Jake's office - the same day.*

Jake is having no luck searching through the database. He limps into Sally's office.
'Sally, I saw a client's application yesterday and it's gone now.'
'It must have been deleted.'
'Where's the recycle bin on this system?'
'Ricicle – isn't that a breakfast cereal in the UK?'
'Not ricicle...'
'I'm sure it is, they "Snap, Crackle and Pop"!'
'No, I said...'
'I think you'll find I'm right. I had a pen pal in England and we used to laugh about it because I called them Frosted Rice Krispies. If there's one thing I know about, it's breakfast cereals. You can get organic Cornflakes now - and organic Weetabix...'
'I'm sure you f...'
'Mr. Poisson! - Were you going to swear there?'
Jake counts to ten, then another ten, and finally, another ten for good measure. 'Thank you for that, Sally, if I ever need any information about breakfast cereals I'll know where to come in future.'
'I'm also a bit of an expert on bagels too, did you know there are...'
'Perhaps some other time, Sally.'
'Oh.'
'It's not that I'm not interested, Sally. It's just that I haven't

eaten today and all this talk of food is making me feel
hungry.'

'Oh, you poor, poor soul - and you with those injuries, as
well.'

'To tell you the truth, your conversation is so interesting I'd
almost forgotten about them, but now that you mention it, I
suppose I should have a sit down. Before I do though, can I
just ask where the R E C Y C L E bin is on this system?'

'I've never seen one of those. The bin's in the corner there,
but I don't really have any use for it. There's a man comes
round once a week to collect any old printouts and bills and
so on.'

'After you've shredded them?'

'We don't have a shredder, you said...'

'Shredders cost money?'

'That's right.'

'I don't suppose you know who this man works for?'

'I do recall, he works for the something or other
corporation.'

'I think I'll have to sit down right now - I can feel the pain
coming back.'

'Would you like a cup of coffee, Mr. Poisson?'

'Yes please.'

'And a bagel? Did you know there are...?'

'Just the coffee, please.' Jake hobbles back to his office and
quickly closes the door. Clicking on the space bar to wake the
screen up, he is surprised to see: -

*Two new applications -*

'This is more like it.'
 He chooses the first one.

*Name: Christopher Columbo Occupation: Police Officer Height: 5'9" Hair: Darkish. Likes: Old cars, cigars, scratching his head, films, dirty macs, exploring.*

He chooses Generate Matches and selects *Evette.*

 'That'll teach you, you can explore the latest operatic blockbuster.'
He moves on to the second application.

*Name: David (Geordie) Crockett Occupation: Police Officer Height: 5'11" Hair: Blondish Likes: Fast cars, sunglasses, rolling up the sleeves of his jacket, massages, fast women, any women.*

He chooses Generate Matches and selects *Lysette.*

 'That'll teach you too, she can massage your thick head with that baton of yours.'
Feeling a little better, Jake lounges back on his chair, chanting an old Buddhist mantra in an effort to the relieve his pain. Five minutes later, Sally knocks on his door.
 'Here's your favorite coffee, Mr. Poisson.'
 'In my favorite mug, I see.'
 'Yes, and I took the liberty of getting you a Belgian bagel, you really shouldn't go without food, Mr. Poisson. Not in your state.' Jake feels a genuine twinge of affection towards her.
 'That's very kind of you, Sally.'

46

'*Sometimes I think I don't appreciate that girl enough.*' He thinks to himself. As she heads back to her office, Jake does a Google search *for   Do chubby women make better lovers?*

## Two weeks later

Jake is sitting at his desk, feeling quite pleased with himself. The last couple of weeks have gone well for him, his wounds are almost fully healed and he has attracted a number of new clients. He's had no luck yet finding out the whereabouts of Elsa Eggblom A.K.A. Olga Oggblom, but he has set the wheels in motion in his quest to discover the identity of whoever is sabotaging his business. His initial reaction was to wait for the bin emptying guy to turn up and then hit him over the head with a blunt instrument, but with his court case looming, he decides that discretion is called for. After watching his favorite film, *The Game*, an idea comes to him - misinformation.

'If he wants to play a game, then I'll play a game, we'll see who's the best game player.'

Jake's initial attempts at game playing are not particularly encouraging. He has a vague recollection of what to do, but his mind is in a fog. He puts it down to his recent encounters and perseveres. His initial chess games against the computer at level one are unsuccessful, although he does get one stalemate when cleaning his keyboard. Encouraged by this fluke, he decides to continue. Two days and *A Dummy's Guide to Chess* later, Jake has an idea. He is walking past an Indy bookshop and there it is, in the window - a used copy of *To Catch a Thief*. Jake hurries into the shop and picks up the well-thumbed paperback.

'That's what I need - whoever he is, he's stealing my staff and trying to steal my clients. I need a plan to catch him.'

'Well, you've picked the right book there, sir. I can highly recommend it.'

Jake looks up, realizing that he has been thinking aloud. He sees a very presentable young man, dressed in the store's uniform. Jake flicks through the book.

'Wow, nearly two hundred and fifty pages! Is there an abridged version or maybe... a comic?'

'There is a movie, starring Cary Grant and Grace Kelly, perhaps you've seen it?'

'I don't recall, what's it about?'

'Carry Grant is a jewel thief.'

'Is he? I thought he was an actor.'

'No, no – in the film he is a jewel thief.'

'Oh, I see – and he's working with Ned Kelly?'

'In the film he's working with Grace Kelly, she's an actress.'

'Of course, sorry, I misheard. It's coming back to me - she was the one who married that Prince of Morocco...'

'Monaco.'

'Yep, and she was killed on her motorbike.'

'James Dean.'

'Pleased to meet you, James, I'm Jake.'

'No, I'm not James Dean, he was the actor who was killed on his motorbike. Grace Kelly died following a car accident.'

'These are sad times, James.'

The shop assistant smiles indulgently at Jake.

'Indeed sir, I hope things go well for you and you catch the scoundrel who is stealing your clients.'

Jake is taken aback. It occurs to him that for the last few weeks he has only ever been exposed to people who have either wittingly, or unwittingly, caused him grief. This young man, a stranger until today, has restored his faith in human nature. He feels compelled to offer something in exchange.

'Thank you for that, and thank you for your help. Do you have a partner?'

'I'm not gay, sir.' The young man turns on his heels.

'Oh wait, I didn't mean... I run a dating agency – Poisson Dating Agency, *you wish, we fish*.'

You may have heard of us?'

Jake hands him one of his cards. 'I was just thinking you may want to take advantage of our new three-month free introductory offer.'

The shop assistant studies the card carefully. 'Poisson? Hmm... Don't you have an office near here?'

'Yes, just across the street.'

'A-ha, that's right, what a coincidence, I was in there just the other day. Now let me think... who did I speak to? Oh yes, A hot chick called... umm... Sally - yes, that was her name.'

Jake is incredulous. 'Sally – are you sure it was her?'

'Oh yes – what an ass she had – I'd love to fu...'

'Are you really sure it was Sally?'

'Oh yes! I could eat my dinner off that ass. I tell you, the fantasies I've had about that bootilicious woodteaser.'

'Er, well, she's not on our books at the moment.'

'I found that out, mate.'

Jake was amazed at how the thought of Sally had transformed this smart, intelligent, sensible and obsequiously polite young man into a wide-eyed, salivating, trainee sex fiend with the vocabulary of a Russian sailor. He could only assume that James had called in at a time when she hadn't been on the curries.

'But I'm sure we do have other women on our books who would meet your stringent requirements, are you sure you wouldn't like a three-month free trial. I could even extend it to six months.'

'It's nice of you to offer, but I couldn't.'

'Why not?'

'I'm married.'

'I suppose congratulations are in order.'

'Yep, three years next month, if you see that Sally, tell her that the wife's keen to meet her – and don't forget to mention that Max House has been asking after her.'

Jake decides that, in this case, discretion is the better part of valor and wishes the young man a nice day. As he steps out onto the sidewalk, he feels a gentle, warm breeze on his face and he smiles to himself, for the first time in ages he is feeling a little optimistic about the future. As he walks towards his office, he hears footsteps behind him.

'Excuse me, young man - I think you dropped this.'

As Jake turns around, an old woman hands him a flyer. Jake glances at it. 'I don't think...'

By the time he looks up, the woman has disappeared. Jake is deep in thought as he hurriedly heads back to his office.

'Mr. Poisson, I'm so pleased you're back. A man rang earlier, he said he would phone you back.'

'Did he leave a message?'

'No.'

'Did he give his name?'

'He said he was a dragon, you don't know any dragons, do you, Mr. Poisson?'

Jake looks around but can't see any untoward signs. He sniffs the air – nothing, not even the slightest hint of curry.

'Not to my knowledge, Sally.'

Shaking his head, he beats a hasty retreat for his office.

# Chapter Six

## Exit the Dragon, Enter Georgette

After drawing the blinds and settling into his comfortable leather chair, Jake begins to study the flyer, but his concentration is broken by his phone.

'Mr. Poisson, it's the dragon!'

'Poisson, is that you?'

'Jake Poisson here.'

'Ah, Poisson, thank God! I've spent half the morning speaking to some thick asshead, in an effort to contact you.'

'That would be Sally.'

Jake hears the click of the internal phone.

'And you are...?'

'I'm Antonio Dragoni, your attorney.'

'Ah, of course, Mr. A Dragoni how are you, sir? All prepared for my case tomorrow?'

'That's what I want to talk to you about Poisson, can I call you Jack?'

'Well, you can Mr. Dragoni, but my name's Jake.'

'Okay, Jack, goodbye and good luck.'

'What time will I see you there, Mr. Dragoni?'

'What? Oh, yes, nearly forgot. I won't be there – have to attend a charity golf tourney. Dam' boring if you ask me, but we can't let the senator down, can we?'

'Well...'

'Don't worry about it, Jacko, I've left you in the capable hands of one of our best trainees. A young chappie called, er...er... damn! – Got to go, being called to the bar.'

Jake hears the Honorable Antonio Dragoni shout, *"Make mine a large G and T"* and then the phone goes dead.

The flier, leaflet – he isn't sure what it is, lies on the desk where he threw it as he took the call. He picks it up and is about to read it, when his phone rings again.

'Mr. Poisson - I resign!'

'No, not now, any other time, but not now, Sally.'

'What do you mean, *any* other time, Mr. Poisson? Do you want me to resign, is that it? So, that *is* it, isn't it? Force me out so you don't have to pay me redundancy money. I know your game, so I'm not resigning.'

'Of course, you're not, I don't want you to, I just meant that at this particular point in...' Sally slams the phone down.

Jake picks up the flyer – a name jumps out at him.

'There's something strange about this booklet, it's too much of a coincidence, I can't quite...'

He picks up the phone again. 'Sally, could you do a search through our records, see if you can find anything out about a Doctor Florence?'

'No!'

'Why not?'

'Who do you think I am? - Your thick asshead?'

'Well, I thought you were my secretary and, if I may say so, probably the best secretary in the building.'

Since it was only a very small block, Jake thought there might be an ounce of credibility in his statement.

'That dragon called me an asshe...'

'No, no – you misheard him, he said classhead. He's from Rumenkia, or somewhere like that, it was just his foreign accent. It's a great compliment in that country, roughly translated it's like our class president.'

'Oh, I see, Mr. Poisson.'

'You can call me Jake, remember? Oh, and one last thing, Sally – is there any of your fabulous coffee on the go?'

'Coming right up, Mr. Poisson.'

As Sally places the tray on Jake's desk she glances at the leaflet - her surprise is obvious, but she says nothing. As he looks up, he notices that she's staring into his eyes - she starts to say something, then changes her mind, places her hand on his shoulder and smiles reassuringly at him.

'I'll be there to support you tomorrow, Jake.'

Sally's touching display of affection catches him off guard. He opens his mouth to say something in reply, but she is back in her office before he recovers his composure. Jake picks up the flyer, for some reason the same advert attracts his attention again:

*Dr Florence, Memory Specialist.*
*You won't forget the experience.*

He is about to peruse the rest of the booklet when he notices a Sprouted Grain bagel nestling behind his coffee. He takes a bite out of the bagel and phones Sally.

'Mmm..., Sally, thanks for the bagel. I'm going to be heading out shortly to prepare for my court case tomorrow, you can have the rest of the afternoon off. I'll lock up.'

'Ooh, thank you, Mr. Poisson, I can get my nails done – I don't want them to look chipped if I have to visit you in jail.'

'I can see how that would be a worry for you, Sally.'

As Jake puts the phone down, he feels a bead of sweat role down his brow. He waits for a few minutes, listening for the sounds of Sally leaving. He is about to throw the flyer into the bin, but then has second thoughts and places it in a secret compartment under the bottom drawer of his desk. Grabbing his jacket, he reaches out to open the door into

53

Sally's adjoining office when he hears someone trying the handle of the outer office door. After what sounds like a couple of hefty shoves and a kick, the would-be intruder seems to give up. Jake holds his breath, listening carefully for the slightest sound. Only when he is completely satisfied, does he open the inner door and rush to the outer door. He unlocks the outer door, opens it and surveys the scene. He catches a glimpse of a shadowy figure turning a corner at the end of the street and waits. Satisfied the coast is clear, he swiftly heads for his destination.

## *Later - Liz and Ernest's apartment*

'It's Jake's court case tomorrow, Ernest.'
'Oh yes, what was that for, again?'
'When he got arrested in that car we loaned him.'
'Surely not!'
'Do you not remember? I told you all about it, he was attacked by two policemen, on his way home from Mom's.'
'That's disgraceful. I can't understand the mentality of some people. Is the car alright?'
'The car's been fixed, all this happened weeks ago.'
'How come I'm always the last to know?'
Liz sighs. 'We need to go to the hearing to give moral support.'
'What time?'
'Ten A.M.'
'That's a bit early, but I suppose it *is* Jake, and he's kinda like a brother to me.'
'Yep, he'll be your brother-in-law soon.'
'Okay, I'll pop in and see him, but I've got an important

meeting in the afternoon. It won't take long to find him guilty, will it?'

'My brother isn't guilty, Ernest – he's never done anything illegal in his life!'

'There was that time when he...'

'Ernest, I don't want to hear unsubstantiated claims by unreliable witnesses, besides, that was years ago.'

'Point taken, but why was he actually arrested? Surely the police wouldn't arrest someone for noth...' He stops mid-sentence and looks over towards his wife-to-be. 'I suppose it *is* New York.'

'Exactly! I heard it had something to do with that voice recorder thing you sold him. He seemed to think it was faulty.'

'Impossible! They all go through two quality control checks before leaving the factory.'

'All I'm saying is what I heard, and I've got no reason to doubt Jake.'

'What about that time he said he'd...'

'Ernest, I don't want to hear about anything to do with something which may, or may not, have been of alien origin, besides, that was years ago.'

'Point taken, anyway, I have a plan, so there's no need to worry.'

'When you say you have a plan, Ernest - that's when I start to worry.'

The next day, at nine forty-five, Jake nervously enters the courtroom. A young man, who Jake takes to be a schoolboy, is seated in the foyer, reading a tome. He stands up and offers a hand to Jake. 'Good morning, Mr. Poison I presume.'

'Poisson.'

'Of course, I'm your attorney, Harrison Ward. No need to be nervous, sir. I'm nervous enough for both of us, ha-ha.'

He giggles at his own joke. 'I'm not nervous, Harrison. Mr. Dragoni's assistant told me you've never lost a case, how many have you won?'

Harrison looks as if he is carefully going over the cases in his mind. When a big, bear of a man slaps him on the back.

'What ho, young fella! Where's that old fart of an uncle of yours?'

'Uncle Antonio? He's got an important golf tournament to attend.'

'I suppose it's with that senator crony of his, eh?'

'I'm not sure, he didn't say.'

'No matter, Ward. No need to be nervous, lad. Your first case is always the hardest. Once you've lost this one, you'll feel better. You do know who the judge is, don't you?'

'No.'

'Hannan.'

'The Hanging Judge?'

'None other.'

'Shit - is that ugly, fat-assed, idiot still going?'

'Yes, he is.'

The bear of a man smiles pleasantly at an even bigger man who has impatiently been waiting to get past.

'Good morrow, Horatio.'

The man pushes Jake and Harrison out of the way, puts his arm around the bear's shoulder and walks off.

'Two o'clock okay for you, Perry? I've ordered us a nice plump pheasant, flown in specially from my grouse moor in Scotland.'

'Nice one, Horace.'

Harrison Ward looks on in awe as the two of them saunter off. Jake is confused.

'Who are they?'

'Well, the big, fat bastard is Sir Peregrine Featherstonehaugh, pronounced Fanshaw, he's the prosecuting attorney. The other one, with the scar on his face and the fatter ass, is the Honorable Judge Horatio Hannan aka The Hanging Judge.'

'He's the one who's trying me?'

'Apparently - now if you'll excuse me, there are a few pages of my book I need to read before we get called.'

Harrison sits down and reopens his copy of *Attornying for Dummies*. Jake is thinking things can't possibly get any worse.

'Hey, Jakey-Jake – we're here, worry no more.'

Obviously, he was wrong.

'It's us, your favorite future brother-in-law, and this is your sister, Elizabeth, but most people call her Liz.'

'Hello, Ernest, will you be staying for the hearing?'

'I'd love to, Jake. I've never seen anyone being sent down before, not even my mate, Rocky. He's the one whose car I loaned you. I was too busy - my horse was foaling. He went down for ten to fifteen for a piddly little motoring offence – he was only the driver for goodness' sake, it's not as if he blew the door off the vault - I blame the judge.'

'Who was it?'

'Some fat-assed, scar-faced bastard called Han something or other.'

Liz rushes to Jake. 'Are you alright, Jake. You look very pale?' Ernest rushes to support him from the other side.

'Chill, bro. It's all sorted.'

In the commotion Ernest slips something into Jake's jacket

pocket. 'Your sister, Liz, is staying for the sentencing. I have to go - I have an appointment with the vet about my...'
'Horse?'
'No, I've just got a bit of a sore throat I've had it for a couple of days.'
Jake watches Ernest as he swaggers out of the courtroom singing a Johnny Cash medley.


## Thirty minutes later


The court is packed. As Jake nervously looks around the room, he notices Sally, smiling reassuringly, she wiggles her fingernails at him and mouths. 'I put the answer machine on, what do you think?'
Jake is grateful for the distraction. He mouths *'nice'* back at her. Further back he sees his mother, Gloria, wedged in between a large, muscular guy and Charles. His mother has a glazed expression.
'Probably trying to hide her concern.' Jake thinks to himself. 'These courtrooms can play tricks with your mind, from where I'm sitting, it looks as if that big guy has his hand between my Mom's legs.'
Columbo and Crockett are situated to his left, injured looks on their faces. Columbo has a sling on one arm and Crockett has a bloodied bandage around his head.
Harrison Ward takes a nickel out of his pocket. 'Heads or tails?'
'Heads.' It lands on tails.
'I think we should plead guilty.'
'Whaa...'

### 'All rise for the Honorable Judge Horatio Hannan'

Everyone jumps to attention, apart from Jake, who has
caught his jacket pocket on his chair. A respectful silence
spreads quickly through the courtroom, punctuated only by
the banging of Jake's chair against the table, then a loud
ripppp... as his pocket comes away, then a jangly, metallic
clatter as something falls to the floor.

### 'Sit'

As everyone else sits, Jake manages to get to his feet.
 'Jake Poisson, you are here to be tried for the heinous crime
of assaulting not one, but two of this city's finest police
officers.'
Columbo and Crockett look searchingly around the
courtroom and then at each other, before shrugging their
shoulders.
 'A crime which, I may add, deserves the severest of
penalties, to serve as a warning to others who may be
tempted to follow in your villainous, unlawful footsteps.'
The judge surveys the hushed courtroom.
 'Does anyone else have anything to say before I deliver the
sentence?'
There is a gasp around the gallery, and a cross between a
groan and a moan from Gloria. The gasp is followed by a
hush as the judge picks up what appears to be a black cap.
The hush is then followed by a sigh of relief as he uses it to
blow his nose. Sir Peregrine Featherstonehaugh throws a
paperclip at Harrison Ward and indicates to him that he
should stand up - he does.
 'No, your honor.'
Sir Peregrine Featherstonehaugh stands up. 'Unusual as this

may be, since I am the Chief Prosecutor, I object, your honor. There has been no plea and no witnesses have been called.'

'Very well, could counsels approach the bench, please?' Judge Hannan whispers conspiratorially to Peregrine. 'I suppose you're right, Perry. Best call a couple of witnesses, before we find him guilty. We *should* follow the proper procedures.'

The judge nods in Harrison's direction. 'By the way, Perry, I like that young man's approach - brief and to the point. You should keep an eye on him – he'll go far.'

Ten minutes later, after Columbo and Crockett have given a completely new meaning to the phrase "lying through their teeth", the judge is issuing his verdict.

'Before I sentence this wretch, I will ask once again, does anyone have anything to say before I deliver sentence?'

An almighty crash reverberates throughout the room as the large wooden doors fly open.

'I do, your honor.'

The court is in uproar as a bride, complete with veil and long flowing train, strides majestically through the courtroom only pausing momentarily to pick up the object which had fallen out of Jake's pocket. As she reaches the bench the Judge tries to protest.

'I'm afraid I can't marry you, young lady. I'm too busy sending this recidivist to San Quentin.'

'I didn't mean "*I do*." As in *I do* give my hand in marriage, I meant I do have something to say.'

'This is highly irregular, young lady.'

The bride pulls her veil up with one hand and holds out her other hand revealing the small device.' 'And so is this!'

'Georgette!'

The two detectives catch a glimpse of her face.

'Lysette!'

'Evette!'

The judge puts his hand over the microphone. 'Georgette, what the hell's going on?'

'This is a recorder, Horace, it recorded everything that went on that night.'

'*That* night?'

'No, not *that* night – that video is tucked away safely in a bank vault.'

The judge breathes a sigh of relief.

'This recorder contains details of the night of the alleged assault.'

The judge lifts his hand from the microphone and bellows. 'Case adjourned, counsels to my chamber, now!'

He lowers his voice and whispers. 'And you too, of course, my beautiful, sweet temptress.'

*Thirty minutes later*

The courtroom erupts as Jake is declared innocent and awarded ten thousand dollars costs. His family and Sally crowd round, hugging and kissing him. He notices the big, muscular man who was sitting next to his mother.

'Jake, I'd like you to meet Wes, he was a friend of mine and your father's and now he's a friend of Charles and me.'

Wes takes Jake's hand and pumps his arm vigorously. 'Well done, young man - Gloria was ecstatic and so was I.'

Jake is unsure how to react, he considers punching him with his free hand, but something stops him. He can't quite put his finger on it, but there's something very familiar about this man.

Out of the corner of his eye he catches sight of Georgette sneaking out of the side exit. With great difficulty he manages to free his hand from Wes's vice-like grip and extricate himself from the proceedings. As he rushes from the courtroom he shouts over his shoulder - to no one in particular, 'I think I've left the gas on.'

# Chapter Seven

# Dr Florence and the Machine

Jake is hot on the trail of Georgette. He sprints to the exit of the courtroom and kicks open the door. As his eyes adjust to the bright sunshine, he feels a hood being put over his head and a little prick on his backside. Immediately he is plunged into complete darkness. When the hood is finally removed Jake finds himself in a large, dimly-lit, disused warehouse, naked and tied to a hard wooden chair. On a similar chair, sitting opposite him, is a pot-bellied, red-headed man. Thankfully, he isn't naked. Jake wishes he hadn't watched that James Bond film a couple of weeks ago - he really isn't in the mood for having his balls battered with a knotted rope. He knows he should be petrified, but, in some strange way, everything he has been through in the last few weeks has changed him. He feels braver, stronger – he feels as if he *is* Bond. Well, his younger, more handsome brother, perhaps. *'What is the worst this man can do, what would Bond do in a situation like this?'* Jake laughs.

'You are wasting your time, I'm like a Pacific geoduck, you'll get nothing out of me.'

'What's a Pacific geoduck?'

'It's a type of clam.'

'I could kill you now, what do you have to say about that?'

'You could, but then you wouldn't find out what I know about **Operation Slamdunk**.'

The pot-bellied, red-headed man looks stunned. 'You're bluffing, Poisson, you can't possibly know about...'

'Can you afford to take that chance?'

'My God, you're right, it's a risk I can't afford to take. Number One said you'd be a hard nut to crack. You've been trained, haven't you? CIA, FBI, KGB, SS?'

Jake has an itch on the back of his neck, he moves his head up and down in an effort to scratch it. His interrogator takes this as an affirmation.

'You seem to have me at an advantage, you know my name, but I don't know yours.'

'I'm hardly going to tell you that I'm Colonel Wilde, ex-Army Rangers, am I? – Oh jeez!, how did you do that – trained in interrogation, no doubt – am I right?'

'I can't remember...'

'Struggling with your memory, eh? Word is that you've been through MESH. Hell, there aren't many who come out of that in one piece. It requires a will of iron. I even heard a whisper that one man had put himself through MESH+. I didn't believe it, but by God man, – I'm beginning to realize now that I was wrong, I owe you an apology.'

'What's MESH+?'

MESH is short for memory wash, a procedure only ever reserved for the highest-ranking agents – if you went through MESH+, who the hell were you?'

'I don't know...'

'Well, I suppose that's my job – to find out, we need to know which side you're on – are there any questions you want to ask me?'

'Why am I naked?'

'That was Georgette's idea.'

'Georgette?'

'She was looking for bugs, she's very thorough. I'm pleased to tell you that she gave you a clean bill of health. Apparently, they can plant bugs in parts of your anatomy that I didn't even know existed. Any more questions?'

'Why did Georgette take my fish?'

'She has a theory that bugs can be implanted into fish, we had to examine them.'

'When will I get them back?'

'Don't worry about that, we'll get you replacements. It's not easy to examine a fish, you know, it wriggles around.'

'Replacements - did any of them make it?'

Colonel Wilde shakes his head.

'Not even Charlie, the big black and white one? He was my favorite.'

The colonel shakes his head again. 'But if it makes you feel any better, I can tell you he didn't suffer.'

'How was that?'

'We cut his head off, it was a quick death.'

'Who's the we?'

'Me and Georgette, all I did was hold him down, she did all the cutting.'

Jake fights back a tear. 'Why does my backside look like a red garden trellis?'

The pause is just long enough for Jake to realize that the colonel is secretly listening to instructions through a hidden earphone.

'Bugs - she has a theory that you can beat them out of a person.'

'Why did she take my Porsche?'

'Bugs.'

'When will I get it back?'

'We had to strip it down to the last nut.'

'When will I get it back?'

'We're waiting for a specialist mechanic. He's coming all the way from Switzerland.'

'I'm not getting it back, am I?'

'No.'

Jake jumps off his chair, triumphantly holding his arms in the air.

'The first rule of espionage, Colonel - read Escapology for Dummies.'

An incredibly strong, sharp shock on Jake's left buttock causes him to jump into the air and then collapse in a heap. As he loses consciousness, he hears a woman's voice.

'The second rule of espionage, always carry a super-strength cattle prod.'


*One hour later*


Jake wakes up, pleased to find he is no longer tied to the chair. He notices his clothes lying in a heap in one corner and within a minute he is dressed and surveying his surroundings. Apart from the two chairs, the room is completely empty. He calls out.

'Is there anyone here with a super-strength cattle prod – hello - anybody?' No response - Jake begins to relax.

*'Perhaps they're having an early lunch.'* He thinks.

He sprints to the door – it's locked! Within seconds he opens it with a collar stiffener. Darting through the door he finds himself in a small courtyard. He climbs onto a ledge, jumps over onto the opposite wall, shimmies up a drainpipe, swings on a vine through an open window and lands in a vault. He pours himself a whiskey, drains the glass in one go and uses the empty tumbler to unlock the safe. After checking the contents of the safe, he removes a gun, a wadge of banknotes and some loose change, for good measure. Jake turns, gun in hand and notices a figure lurking in the shadows. He drops his gun on the floor.

"*Clap, clap, clap.*"

'Seventy-nine seconds, very good Mr. Poisson – the previous record was three minutes forty-two seconds.'

'If I'd known I was being timed I'd have taken the less scenic route.'

'Why didn't you shoot me, Mr. Poisson?'

'A Ruger SP101, two and a quarter inch, thirty-eight-millimeter weighs at least seven hundred and twenty grams with one bullet in it, seven hundred and eight grams empty. I can tell by the feel of this one that it's empty - watch, I'll show you.' Jake bends down, picks up the gun and fires it into the air. A large lump of ceiling plaster falls on his head.

'Shit!'

'I had the stock lightened by twenty grams, Mr. Poisson.'

'Are there any more bullets in it?'

The man shakes his head, then flinches as Jake pulls the trigger again – click!

'Just checking.'

The man moves out of the corner allowing Jake to get a clearer view of him.

'Colonel Wilde, I assume you've finished your lunch.'

'Yes, thank you, I've had my main course, Mr. Poisson and for dessert I'm going to torture you.'

'Why don't I just give you a karate chop and walk out of here?'

'Because, Mr. Poisson, if you did, I would be unable to keep this button pressed down.'

'Is it a bomb?'

'Not quite, did you notice that band around your testicles?'

'No, I thought I'd just woken up with an early morning -

well, you know what I mean - we're all men here' , although after the cattle prod incident, Jake was starting to wonder. Now you mention it though, I can feel a little tingle down there.'

'If I loosen my grip – boom!'

'I was never thinking of giving you a karate chop anyway, it was only a hypothetical suggestion. If you'll excuse me, I'll just... '

'DO NOT MOVE, MR POISSON.'

'I wasn't going to move either. Well, only to re-adjust myself a bit, check that I was hanging properly. I've heard you can get headaches...'

'You would get more than a headache, Mr. Poisson. I can assure you of that. The only person who can remove it is my colleague, Miss Virtue, and I'm afraid she's...'

'You're not going to tell me she's on holiday, are you?'

'Nothing so dramatic, she chipped a nail placing that band around your cojones. She was really upset because it was gel nail varnish and it was only a couple of days since it was applied.'

'I must apologize to her the next time I see her, which will be - *when?*'

'She should be back from the nail clinic in half an hour or so.'

'Why don't you take a seat, take the weight off your thumb.' Colonel Wilde shakes his head. 'I'm alright where I am, Mr. Poisson. Do not try anything. This device has a delay - after two seconds you would be Miss Poisson.'

Jake shows no signs of fear. 'I think I should tell you, before I lost twice my present body weight, I used to be a Sumo wrestler.'

Jake's face turns purple as he grits his teeth and shakes his hips vigorously (retracting one's testicles is never painless, no matter what anyone says). Colonel Wilde watches helplessly as the untethered ball-band slides down Jake's trouser leg and is deftly dispatched towards the colonel's hand. The impact knocks the detonator out of the colonel's grasp into a waste bin and the explosive band into a sand bucket. After the dust storm settles the colonel opens his eyes - where Jake was standing there are only footprints. Wilde frantically searches through his pockets to call HQ for help, but there's no trace of his phone.

In less than a minute Jake is at the other end of the building, hooking Wilde's cell phone into the mainframe of the computer system. He takes out his own cell phone and at lightning speed swaps the sim cards back and forth. After a few swift adjustments and a comparison of both screens, he seems satisfied with his handiwork. Backtracking, he places the colonel's cell phone on the edge of the hole in the ceiling. Hiding in a storage cupboard, he leaves the door slightly ajar, holds down the number one on his phone and silently waits for a reaction.

'That's my phone, I'd recognize that ring anywhere -It's up there, it must have blown out of my hand with the explosion.' Miss Virtue has returned from the beauty salon, she takes a break from admiring her nails and places one of her extremely long, shapely, mini-skirted legs on the corner of the desk. With one swift, athletic move she hoists herself up and peers into the hole. Deftly retrieving the phone, she drops back onto the floor. Jake catches a brief glimpse of the outline of her head. Jake's mind is whirring.

'It can't be, can it?'

Even though the cupboard is cramped and he is still getting

the occasional twinge from the fading scars on his backside, Jake waits patiently, hoping to hear her voice.

The colonel answers his phone. 'I am unable to talk to you at the moment, please ring back later.'

Miss Virtue straightens what there is of her skirt and turns to the colonel. 'You idiot, if we don't get to him first, he could ruin the whole operation. Get back to headquarters and send out a KFC order'

Jake's blood runs cold. Firstly, he recognizes the voice, but secondly, and more importantly, he realizes he's not in line for a nice Chicken Dinner for One- in the recesses of his mind, he remembers coming into contact with men who

...........Kill For Cash............

*Sixteen hours later*

Jake stumbles into his office. 'Wow, Sally – I had a weird dream last night – any chance of a cup of that fabulous coffee of yours?'

'Of course, Mr. Poisson, you just make yourself comfortable in your office. I'll get – er, make you one.'

As Jake sits at his desk, he realizes his lace is loose, bending down to fasten it, he notices the secret compartment under his desk. He opens it and takes out the flyer. Hearing Sally opening the door to his office, he hurriedly stuffs it into his pocket. Sally places the tray containing a cup of coffee and a bagel in front of him. 'We didn't know where you'd gone after you won your court case, Mr. Poisson - were you alright?'

'What? – Oh yes – fine, I was just tired. I went home and slept most of the day.'

'Did you Mr. Poisson? Some people were trying to contact you, that's all. Nothing that won't wait, I'm sure. We thought you must have gone off to celebrate or something, your aunt was looking for you, but you were just at home, weren't you? When was the last time you saw your aunt? – Jake – Jake – do you remember?'

Jake feels himself drifting into a trance at the sound of Sally's hypnotic voice, but he snaps out of it as he feels his cell phone vibrate in his pocket.

'Whaa? - I... I... don't remember.'

Jake gulps his coffee down, grabs the bagel and heads for the door. He turns to his secretary.

'Sally, I need to go somewhere. If anyone calls, tell them I'm in a meeting.'

Five minutes later, flyer in hand, Jake is standing outside a bland office door in an unremarkable office block. He takes a quick look at the advert and then locates the nameplate.

*Dr Florence, Memory Specialist.*
*You won't forget the experience.*

'*Yes, this is the place.*' He knocks and after a short wait, the door opens.

'I've come about the ad...'

'Follow me.'

A rather rotund lady leads Jake into some sort of treatment room.

'Okay, if you'll just take your clothes off, I'll have a look at you.' Jake steps back in surprise.

'It's about the memory treatment, I'm starting to get flashbacks.'

'I'm sure, and I suppose that might be of interest to other medical charlatans, but I treat you holistically, so please get undressed.'

She surveys Jake from top to toe, front and back.

'I must say, you seem fine to me, those strange weals on your backside have almost gone. Half a stone perhaps, no more, that should stop you getting flashbacks to when you were slimmer, just take a sip of this, now pop this mask on and hop on this bed.'

Jake feels a chain being wrapped around the Gimp mask and then a padlock being locked.

'Now I just have to put these reinforced leather straps around your wrists - Health and Safety, you know.'

Jake can hear something being wound and the sound of sparks and crackles and...

'Hmm, - maybe a bit too much, but then again – nothing ventured, nothing gained. I need to ask you, just for the records, your name and occupation.'

'Jake Poisson, I run a dating agency.'

'Poisson Dating? Is that you?'

'Yes, would you like a three-month free trial?'

'I'm not sure my husband would like it. Not that I give a toss about him, did I tell you he ran off with all my money and left me in this shithole? Yep, left me penniless and destitute and only my body to provide me with an income. You know what my philosophy used to be with husbands? Trade in and trade up and it was working well, at least it *was*, until that last bastard, stitched me up like a kipper, left me in this shithole – penniless and destitute and only my body to provide me with an income.'

Jake is about to say something about her repeating herself, but is distracted by the sensation of having his balls shaved. He hopes the ointment being vigorously rubbed on them might soothe the nicks, but the jalapeno-scented cream disappoints. He tries to stifle a scream as she attaches the clamps.

'Silly me, I forgot the gag.'

The background humming sound increases and then, with the flick of a switch, his whole body is jerked a foot into the air.

'It works!'

She marvels at the effect of the machine on Jake.

'Oh yes - straight to the sweet spot!'

She gives a red dial a quick turn and gasps in surprise.

'Now that is a bonus!'

Jake can hear a rustling of clothes and then, as he recovers, he smells body odor, feels flabby flesh and hears what sounds like the howls of a Himalayan wolf. Fortunately, a combination of the drink, gag and mask have blinded him and obliterated his sense of taste. As his body reacts to the pulsating electrical charges, he drifts in and out of consciousness.

Hallucinating, he sees a strange-looking horse being ridden by a naked, frenetic jockey. On closer inspection, he realizes that he is the horse.

He has no idea how long he has been in this state, but suddenly, as quickly as it had begun, the sublime torture ends. Jake feels a tremendous weight being lifted off him then hears the sound of rustling clothes again.

'Half a pound in thirty minutes. I think I'm on to something here.'

Jake realizes that at some stage of his therapy the gag has been removed. 'Excuse me for asking, but what...?'

'It's my latest experiment, since my last husband stitched me up like a kipper and left me in this shithole – penniless and destitute and only my body to provide me with an income, I've had to try an' find something to get me a quick buck.'

'I'm sure an enterprising person like yourself could find an easier way...'

'Did you not enjoy it, Mr. Poisson? Maybe it needs a few tweaks, an oscillating frequency module or an anal stimulator, perhaps. Now let me see...'

She replaces the gag and opens the door of a cupboard. A loud knock at the main door spares Jake from his fate – three knocks, then a pause, then two knocks, followed by two knocks, then a pause, then one knock - finally, after another pause, another knock.

'Damn, my next client is early. I'll be right back in an hour or so. If you need anything - just wait. – Oh, by the way, if that three-months free trial is still going...'

She rushes out, leaving the door slightly ajar. As she escorts her new visitor down the corridor, Jake hears part of their conversation.

'Doctor Florence vacated these premises a couple of days ago. I'm using them now.'

# Chapter Eight

## Too Hard to Hide

Fifty miles away, in what looks like an underground car park, but isn't, two men are talking. 'If he's gone rogue, we are up shit creek.'

'A man like Jake Poisson would never go rogue, Boss. I'd stake my life on it.'

'You might have to, Pavlov – you may well have to. Maybe I shouldn't tell you this, but he volunteered for MESH+. He's the only guy on the whole of this bloody planet to have gone through that. God knows what that poor bastard has suffered for all of us, Jeez, what a guy!'

'He took a bullet for me in 'stan.'

'You know the guy personally?'

'He was the best platoon leader we ever had - and he was only fifteen.'

'Fifteen!'

'Joined at fourteen – lied about his age - rose rapidly through the ranks. Wasn't going by the name Jake Poisson back then, we knew him as E.T.'

'He had alien-like abilities?'

'No, he had sticky-out ears. It was before he had them done.'

'What name was he using?'

'Ed Travis.'

'Maybe that was...'

'He ate things that would make a billy goat puke.'

'What things?'

'Pot Noodles, and I'm not just talking about Chicken and Mushroom, I mean the really hot ones, the ones that make your breath honk like a sewer rat with a hangover.'

'Good God!'

'Strange thing was, even though every guy in the platoon wanted to be him, he never had much luck with the ladies...'

'You just never know with women, do you?'

'Affirmative, Boss - some say he was the reason our troops were withdrawn.'

'How so?'

'He held the pass for three days while the rest of the platoon finished their songs round the campfire and meandered back to base camp. Eventually he ran out of ammo and was overpowered in a hand to hand with thirty 'Ban.'

'Tragic - was he tortured?'

'I heard they fed him pot noodles in an effort to make him talk.'

'Did he talk?'

'Said his mother had taught him never to talk with his mouth full - they gave up on him eventually.'

'Did he escape?'

'In time, but not before they'd measured his testicles and found out his real age. They used him as a poster boy – to shame us – that's why they pinned his ears.'

'I don't understand.'

'They wanted a close up of his face in the video, but couldn't fit his ears on the screen.'

'Well, it was certainly an improvement. With his new appearance he must have been welcomed home as a hero.'

'Court martialed...'

'After what he'd gone through, surely not?'

'Top brass had him up for lying about his age.'

'How long did he get?'

'Got off with it. He'd put his age down as forty-one. His

lawyer said he had dyscalculia.'

'Sounds painful.'

'It's dyslexia with numbers.'

'Even so, I feel sorry for the poor kid.'

'I couldn't believe it when he turned up working for us. He made me swear an oath of secrecy, under pain of death. I swear, I've never told a soul.'

'Except me.'

'Except you. Oh, and a few of the lads at NBC.'

'At NBC? What the...'

'They were interviewing me about my *"take a child to work day"* and one thing led to another...'

'Well, all I can say is, I hope for your sake, Pavlov, that Poisson wasn't watching the news that night!'

'Well, boss, all I can say is, I'm not drinking vodka anymore while I'm at work.'


*Meanwhile...*


Jake flinches as he hears footsteps outside his room.

'Don't move, Mr. Poisson.'

'Saayeee!'

'Don't try to talk, Jake. I need to get you out of this place. What does this red knob do?'

'Arghieeee!' 'Wow, that's impressive.' Sally finds the effect fascinating. She turns the dial up and down, studying the results with interest.

'What would happen if I turned this up to maximum?'

As Sally carries Jake out of the treatment room, he notices a *"For Rent"* sign stuck onto the door with Scotch tape. He glances across the corridor and sees a polished brass nameplate - it reads *"Dr. Florence"*.

Three minutes later, Sally is helping Jake down the stairs.

'I'm sure the effect won't be permanent Mr. Poisson. It would be unnatural to have one that size all the time - and you'd have to get all your trousers altered.'

'Ahoeznot.'

'When we get back to the office, I think I'll be able to loosen that, Mr. Poisson, would you like me to call a locksmith?'

'Nnnnooooo!'

Thirty minutes later Jake and Sally are back in the office, Sally is tugging at Jake's trousers in an effort to free his jammed appendage, unfortunately she manages to catch it in his zip. With the gag still on, Jake cannot scream loud enough to do the pain justice, but the fact that he has ripped both arms off the chair, and the tears dripping from his shirt tails, would probably give an indication to any casual bystander.

'One good tug should do it, Mr. Poisson.'

One good tug does do it - for Jake. The pain is so exquisite he is unable to move even an eyelid – he wants to, so he doesn't have to watch the blood spurting all over his desk, but he is powerless to offer any sort of response, due to being caught in some kind of twilight world where every one of his senses registers only pain.

'I'll put a band aid on that, it'll be fine.' Sally takes one of his hands, prises his fingers off the chair arm and places them over the gash to stem the flow.

'We are going to need two fingers for this one.' She giggles. If you hold it tight it won't spurt so much, but don't do anything naughty.'

Sally heads for her office to find a band-aid. Jake desperately tries to remember the mantra a Buddhist monk gave him to use in times of extreme emergency. As Sally returns with a moth-eaten packet of band-aids, Jake is rocking on his chair chanting. 'Urmigurnu... urmigurnu... urmigurnu...' Sally picks up a nearby vase and throws the contents over Jake's head. The indentations of the plastic petals resemble a Māori tattoo.

'Oops, I always thought they were real! That seems to have stopped your fit though, Mr. Poisson.'

She carefully studies Jake's unfeasibly swollen member.

'I think you can loosen your grip now, Mr. Poisson – oh, maybe not, okay, hold it until I count to three – three!'

As Jake releases his grip, Sally sprays the gash with antiseptic and clumsily wraps three band-aids in the vicinity of the wound. Jake begins to realize there are various levels of pain and that, up until now, he had only experienced a small fraction of those levels. Sally stands back to admire her handiwork. In reality, there isn't much to admire, unless you're a fan of The Evil Dead. She smiles innocently at Jake.

'There we are, all done. Not a bad job, if I say so myself. Why don't you take the rest of the day off, Mr. Poisson, maybe play a round of golf?'

'Wurr abah eeez?'

Jake points to his mask and gag.

'Oh, I forgot about those. I'll go down to the mall. What do you think would be best - tin snips or a chainsaw?'

As Sally heads off to look for a hardware store, Jake frantically hobbles out of his office and onto the street. Wearing an old mac, a hat from the cloakroom and a broken pair of sunglasses he has fished out of the bin, he manages to limp two paces before he hears the police siren.

'And what do we have here, Geordie?'

'It looks some kinda pervy flasha tah me, man.'
'I agree Geordie, have a look to see what he's hiding under that coat.'
'Oh my God, that's hideous. The last time ah saw owt like that, it had crawled oota the sewer. Ah'm ganna hafta taser it.'

*Thirty minutes later*


Lieutenant Pusey's heart sinks as his two least favorite officers drag what looks like a bedraggled tramp into the station.
'I've told you two about bringing the homeless in here, take him to the shelter around the corner.'
'We've got a reet one here, Che... – Leftenant - Boss.'
'He just looks like another harmless vagrant to me, Crockett.'
'Aye, but take a look at this.'
Detective Crockett triumphantly pulls open Jake's mac. His delight is short-lived, the taser has staunched the blood flow and reduced the swelling in Jake's manhood. So much so, that the band aids have dropped off and the only evidence of his mishap seems to be a nasty gash, which the Lieutenant takes to be the result of the detective's over-zealous use of his favorite weapon.
'I've told you about that taser, Crockett – out, both of you. I'll deal with you both later!'
Lieutenant Pusey pulls out a seat and guides Jake towards it - as he does so, he notices the gag. 'My God, what have those two done to you?'
He takes a skeleton key from his desk drawer and undoes the padlock. 'There you are, sir. Sorry for the inconvenience.'

Jake takes off his hat and sunglasses and then breathes a sigh of relief as he removes the mask and gag, the Lieutenant jumps to attention and salutes him.

'At ease, Corporal.'

'I'll have those two down in the cells by tonight and I'll personally beat the sh...'

'No need, HP. They were just doing their job.'

'Whatever you say, Chief - God, it's good to see you! I cried buckets at your funeral, guess it was staged, huh?'

'I had to go out of circulation for a while. I'm still keeping a low profile, so...'

'You can rely on me, Chief, my lips are sealed but if there's anything I can do for you.'

'There is one thing, if you find out anything about an Elsa Eggblom, aka Olga Oggblom. Absolute hush hush – use the usual drop off point.'

'Sure thing, Chief, anything to repay that bullet you took for me in Bolivia.'

'Yeah, that was a close shave, HP. You'd have done the same thing for me, though. I still have that bullet on a chain around my neck. One millimeter to the left and it would have ruptured my anus.'

Jake takes the chain off his neck and offers it to the lieutenant.

'I want you to have it, I've left it exactly as it came out of my guts. I only take it off when I get washed.'

Lieutenant Pusey wipes tears from his eyes.

'I couldn't, Chief, really.'

'I insist, I'm only sorry I haven't been able to give it to you before now. It was touch and go for three months while I was on life support and then I went underground. Now turn round you big bobo, or you'll have me crying.'

'That'll be the day, when we see Chief Ironheart Custer crying!' Lieutenant Harry Pusey turns round and offers his neck to Jake.

'True HP, but I recently lost my favorite fish.'

'Not Charlie, the big black and white one...?'

Jake bites his lip, his voice quivers slightly. 'Yes.'

'Good grief, that's enough to make a billy goat cry!'

He turns round, but the man he knew as Chief Ironheart Custer has gone, The only evidence he'd been there is a scribbled note on the desk.

It reads:

*Next week you'll get a letter promoting you to Captain*

The Lieutenant picks up the phone. 'Get me those two assholes!'

'Crockett and Columbo?'

'Of course, how many assholes have we got in this precinct?'

'Well sir, there's...'

Lieutenant Pusey sighs heavily as he replaces the receiver.

*Five minutes later*

'Phoar! – What's that putrid smell?'

The lieutenant gingerly places the bullet under his shirt.

'Excuse me, sir. Have you been crying?'

'No way, Columbo. It's just a touch of hay fever.'

'The pollen count's canny low at the minute, Leftenant - it normally is in March.'

'Shut it, Crockett! When I want your opinion, I'll ask for it.'

'Or you could send me a text, boss.'

'Why the fu...?'

'That way, you would be sure I got it, Boss.'

The lieutenant counts to ten, he has a choice, count to ten again, or kick the waste bin. He decides on the latter and immediately regrets it.

'That looks nasty, sir. Would you like me to phone an ambulance or would you prefer me to text?'

'Who's the first-aider in here?'

'It's me, sir. Ah've got me scout's badge in forst aid.'

'It doesn't matter, Crockett. The bleeding will soon stop.'

'Ah knew a man who got a wound like that and he had to have his whole leg amp...'

'CROCKETT!'

'Yes, sir?'

'I've just remembered, the desk sergeant said they needed someone to restrain a wild, young, blonde who is running around naked at the front counter.'

'I'm on it, sir.'

Left alone with Columbo, Lieutenant Pusey feels he has a half-decent chance of a sensible conversation.

'Officer Columbo, I can't disclose that so-called tramp's identity otherwise I'm dead meat, but have you heard of the *"Bolivian Coffee Caper"*?'

'Everyone on the force has heard of that, sir. Some say that's how you made Lieutenant and that you wouldn't have stood a cat in hell's chance if it hadn't been for...'

'Okay, okay, Columbo – well, do you remember...?'

'The Chief of Police who took the bullet for you, as you were running away?'

'Not running away, Columbo, tactical evasion. Rule Number One in the Enemy Confrontation Manual.'

'You're not telling me that tramp was Chief Custer? I thought he was dead. He's my number one hero of all time. – He's the reason I joined the force.'

'Officially, he *is* dead. Anyway, he wants us to investigate a certain Elsa Eggblom aka Olga Oggblom.'

'Certainly sir, leave it to me. I can't believe it! That was Chief...?'

'How does Detective Columbo sound? Play this right and you could even make Lieutenant.'

'Lieutenant Columbo, I like the sound of that, sir. You can count on me.'

'But remember, this is strictly between you and me. You mustn't tell any other soul – not one person, no one.'

Lieutenant Pusey exaggeratedly zips his lips and then taps the side of his nose.

'You can count on me, sir, but if I were you, I'd take something for that hay fever.'

They are just finishing their conversation as Crockett bursts into Pusey's office.

'Ah've cracked it boss, she wasn't naked when ah got there, but I soon sorted that. Ah've left her in lockdown. Ah had to take her blanket in case she tried to harm hersel' with it.'

'This young woman, Crockett. Did she look anything like Commissioner Gordon?'

'Is she the one with the long blonde hair and the big bazoo...?'

'Yes.'

'Aye, come to think about it, she did bear an uncanny resemblance to her.'

'And, can I just ask - were there any men in lockdown?'

'Er, aye, quite a few.'

The lieutenant picks up the phone. 'Sergeant Dilko, could

you fill in a transfer request for Officer Crockett, please? Oh, and you'd better send someone down to lockdown to retrieve what's left of Commissioner Gordon.'

'That'll be all, you're both dismissed.'

'Thank you, sir.'

As they saunter out of the office, Officer Columbo turns to his colleague. 'Hey Geordie, you'll never guess who that tramp was.'

Pusey's phone rings.

'Lieutenant Pusey speaking.'

'It's the Duty Sergeant here, sir.'

'What is it, Dilko?'

'Commissioner Gordon says can she have just one more hour?'

# Chapter Nine

# Not Total Recall

*Four hours later*

Jake opens his front door to find a note has been left on his mat.

*You were out, so I left the package at the usual drop off point.*

He smiles to himself as he heads out of his apartment.
'I knew HP wouldn't let me down, it's nice to know he's just as quick as he ever was.'
At the drop off point, Jake is pleased to see that everything seems to be in order. The tree is still there, but as he approaches it, he realizes the bench that was beneath it has been removed. He upends a nearby trashcan and carefully steps on it to gauge its ability to withstand his weight. It seems okay. He gingerly reaches towards the hole and is about to feel inside, when...
'Are you alright there, young man?'
He turns to see an old lady walking her dog. 'Oh yes, I'm fine. There was a cat stuck up this tree, but I've managed to free it.'
'Are you sure it wasn't a squirrel?'
'Oh no, it was definitely a cat.'
Jake nonchalantly places his hand inside the hole.
'If you've freed it, why are you putting your hand in there?'
'I'm just checking to make sure there are no kittens in here, I

wouldn't want to make them orphans. No, nothing here –
have a nice day, lady.'
Jake is desperately trying to end the conversation - he turns
away from the woman and casually delves his fingers a little
deeper into the hole. As he regains consciousness, Jake sees
the old lady peering over him.
'See, I said it would be a squirrel!'

Realizing where the pain is coming from, He looks towards
his hand and sees a squirrel firmly attached to the end of his
finger. As he shakes it off, the dog chases after it, dragging
the old lady with it. Jake looks both ways to make sure no
one has witnessed the incident, jumps onto the trash can and
hurriedly retrieves the package. Stuffing it down the front of
his jacket, he nonchalantly saunters away from the
scene. When he feels he is far enough away, he reaches into
his jacket and opens the envelope.
'That's interesting!'
He sets fire to the envelope and note and lets them drop into
a nearby waste bin, as the fire in the bin takes hold, a
canister explodes deafeningly and shoots into the air. In a
flash, using his years of military training, he pulls down his
zip and extinguishes the raging flames. Turning, he sees the
old lady in the distance. By the look of her muddied coat and
torn stockings, the dog has obviously dragged her for some
considerable distance. She is too far away to be heard, but
Jake can lip read.
'Stay exactly where you are until I get a good look at you!'
Jake declines the offer and beats a hasty retreat.

The next day Jake meets Lieutenant Pusey at a secret
rendezvous inside Macy's.
'I'm pleased you could see me at such short notice HP.

Phoar! - what's that smell?'

'I can't smell anything, Chief.'

'Anyway - I needed to see you about that note.'

'Yes, Chief?'

'Are you sure that information is correct?'

'Yes, Chief – absolutely certain.'

'Two years ago, you say? Well, that alters things considerably.'

'Pleased to be of help, Chief – by the way, did you see anything suspicious at the park yesterday?'

'Nope, nothing at all, why?'

'Oh, it's nothing, I shouldn't really have mentioned it. It's just an old lady was walking her dog and she came across a flasher.'

'Did she give a description?'

'Yeah, about your height, your weight and hair color. She said he was very well-built, if you know what I mean?'

Jake smiles proudly. 'Did she really?'

'Yeah, but she said unfortunately he ran off before she was able to get a really good look. She has kindly consented to be a witness for a line-up if I can get enough men who fit the description.'

'I'd like to help HP, but I've an appointment at the doc's.'

'No matter, Chief, as I say, I really didn't want to bother you with it. I've got two of my be... - two of my fine... - er, two of my men on it right now. They'll catch him, don't worry about that.'

'Good luck with that – hey, I must go. Hope to see you soon, let's not leave it so long next time.'

'Sure thing, Chief.'

*Two days later*

Jake is back in his office, studying the leaflet. He hears the door being opened and hastily stuffs it in his pocket.

'I was worried about you, Mr. Poisson. When I got back here with the chainsaw, you'd gone. Where did you go?'

'There was no need to worry, Sally. I'd just popped out to see a friend, but it took longer than I thought.'

Considering what had actually happened, it wasn't a complete lie.

'A man or a woman?'

'A man or a woman, what?'

'Your friend?'

'He was male, actually - a former colleague of mine, why?'

'It was just, when I saw what that woman had done to you, I wondered...'

'If I'd gone to look for her? No, definitely not. I didn't know who she was. Do you know her name?'

'So, if you had known who she was, you'd have gone back to her?'

'No, that's not what I meant, I promised her three month's free membership, that's all.'

'Alright, if you're sure that's the only reason you're interested in her?'

'Oh, I'm dead sure of that.'

'Are you completely sure, Mr. Poisson. You know what your memory's like sometimes.'

'I think I would know if there was any other reason, Sally.'

Sally rummages through her handbag. 'She gave me her card - but I've lost it.'

Jake is curious as to why Sally appeared in that room at that particular time but before he has a chance to ask her, she moves around his desk and tries to unfasten his belt.

'Sally, what are you doing, for goodness' sake!'

'I'm just checking to see if your thingy is okay. It was very swollen and I fixed the bleeding for you, remember?'

'How could I forget?'

'Is it still bleeding?'

'No.'

'Is it still just as big?'

'No.'

'Aww - can I have a little look at it?'

'No.'

'I have some cream here - I could rub some on it. It's very good.'

'How do you know that?'

'I took that machine home.'

'What machine?'

'The machine that nasty woman used on you, I took it home. It came with instructions - it's designed to help women lose weight.'

Sally runs her hands down her backside, as she does a little pirouette. 'I've lost one pound already.'

'How the hell could you have used...?'

'The mailman. That's why I'm late and that's how I know the cream works.'

'Is he okay?'

'I think so, I told him to let himself out.'

'Well, I must admit. You do look good.'

Sally bends forward, her backside inches from Jake's face.

'Do you think it looks more toned?'

Jake has to admit, there is an improvement. She hitches up her skirt, revealing her stocking tops. 'It works well on the thighs, don't you think?'

As Jake considers his answer his office door bursts open.

'Sally, what the...!'

'Candice, what are you doing here?'

'By the look of it, I'm stopping you from doing something you will both regret.'

Jake has rapidly lost any interest he may have had in Sally's thighs, for some reason he blurts out the first thing that comes into his head. 'Beaver!'

'Okay.'

Sally hitches up her skirt a little more.

'Pull that skirt down now, Sally Chaste.'

Sally stares pointedly at Candice's micro-mini skirt before reluctantly obeying.

'And leave us, I need to talk to Mr. Poisson.'

Candice's tone leaves Sally no option, but as she reaches the door she turns to Jake with a hopeful expression.

'If you need me for anything, you know where I am – anything at all...'

Candice's tone is curt. 'Goodbye, Sally.'

Candice turns to Jake. 'How long has that been going on?'

'What?'

'You know! If I hadn't got here on time, you'd have been on her like a rat up a drainpipe.'

'There's nothing...'

'*I* know that, Donkey – I've been watching you long enough. Although I must say, I think you seemed to enjoy the other day's shenanigans a little too much for my liking.'

'Why are you calling me a donkey?'

'Ha, always the joker, Jake. Even when your life was in great danger you would always laugh about it. I'm not falling for that - I know you too well. Come here and kiss me. *I'll* rub your thingy better.'

Jake is puzzled, he can't remember the last time he'd had any success with the ladies. Now, within minutes of each other, two of them want to do unspeakable things to him.

He hears himself say. 'It's better' and now wishes he'd bitten his tongue. He regains his senses quickly. 'Not completely though, it still needs treatment.'

'Come here then, Donkey - Beaver will fix it for you.'

Jake is on his feet, hastily unzipping his trousers. 'I'm not saying I don't like it, but what's with the dirty talk, Candice?' Just as he is about to drop his boxers, Candice pushes him back.

'You don't remember, do you?'

'I remember some things, but other things I seem to do instinctively. This will be one of those things.'

'No way, Jake – not yet. I came here to debrief you. I've been waiting nearly two years to do it.'

'Please, let's not let a little thing like my memory get in the way of your plans.'

'I'm sorry, Jake, but I can't - not yet. I'll reveal all when the time is right.'

Jake takes a long look at Candice's micro-mini.

*'There's not much else to reveal'*, he thinks. *'But what there is, is the most lov...'*

'Ouch!'

The slap breaks his train of thought. 'Stop it, Jake!'

'Whaa...'

'I know what's going through your mind!'

Candice pulls Jake towards her and kisses him tenderly on the lips. 'It won't be long now, my darling.'

Jake rubs his face.

'Here use this.' She spits on her handkerchief and passes it to him. He closes his eyes and gently wipes his face with it. He opens his eyes, but Candice has gone. The smell of her hanky mixed with the saliva gives him a flashback. Candice is asking him a question.

'Now it's your turn – the first animal that comes into your mind?'

'Beaver!'

He sees himself turning to look at her, but at that point Sally enters the room breaking his recall.

'I'm here – and I have the machine with me.'

Jake rushes past Sally and out of the door. 'I'll have to take a rain check, Sally - maybe later.'

Sally stares at Jake's groin area. 'Well, don't wait too long, it might keep on shrinking.'


Before leaving the building, Jake looks carefully for any signs of unusual activity. Although everything looks fine, he senses that he is being watched.

'He's leaving the building now. No, he hasn't got it back completely yet, but it seems to be improving a little more every time his brain or body is stimulated. Oh wait, I think he's onto me.'

'Withdraw number nine, from what we've seen already, his instincts are also returning. That makes him extremely dangerous. We'll take it from here. You've done a great job, but remember, your safety is our number one priority. Don't do anything that might blow your cover.'


Downtown, five miles away, in an office above a Laundromat 'Did you get that, Pavlov?'

'Yes, Boss.'

'You need to get over there right away, take Elvis with you for backup.

'My smalls still have another ten minutes, Boss.'

'Your laundry? I'll get it. Time is of the essence, Pavlov.'

'Thanks, Boss, if you wouldn't mind checking them carefully. A couple of those boxers had some nasty stains on them.'

'Just get out, Pavlov – and don't forget to take Elvis with you.' As Pavlov leaves the room, he turns to the Boss.

'Just so you know, it's the green stripey ones and the...' Pavlov manages to duck in time to avoid the paperweight. He scurries off to meet up with his colleague, eventually joining him on the pavement outside the Laundromat.

'Ah, good, you've brought the car. The Boss is a bit grouchy today, don't ya think?'

'I think he's worried about Poisson.'

'I don't know why. We're on the case now. He's unlikely ever to see him again, isn't he Pav? - Pav?'

Elvis is staring at the spot where Pavlov should be, but there's no one there. He feels a tap on his shoulder and turns round to face his worst nightmare.

### Five minutes later

the Boss is shouting frantically into his long distance, encrypted, walkie-talkie. 'PAVLOV... ELVIS...come in please, where in the fu...?'

'Pavlov's sleeping like his dog and Elvis has left the building.'

'Poisson, is that you? What the hell have you done with my two best agents?'

'If these two are your best, then things have gone downhill since I...'

'Oh my God, you've got your memory back!'

'Not fully, but I remember that you owe me a hundred bucks.'

'It's yours, Jake – I haven't spent a dime of it. I have it here in my wallet. All you have to do is come and get it. In fact, you can have that thousand I was saving towards my wife's boob job. Just come in quietly, there's no one here but me.'

'I've got the lunch order for the guys, Boss. Seven Supermeals, five Big Whoppas, eight Chicken Gigantifries and a barrel of root beer. Would you like me to add you to the list, Boss?'

The Boss covers the microphone with his hand.

'Keep it down, Otto. Can't you see I'm talking to someone? - I'll have a Gigantifry and a massive full-sugar Coke, please.'

Jake is suspicious.

'Who was that?'

'Nobody, just a customer asking for directions to the bathroom.'

'Well, that's strange, because I can see the sign for the rest room from where I'm standing.'


The Boss rushes to the window and peers through the blinds. Beads of perspiration stream from his brow.

'Now Jake, don't do anything stupid. I know you can shoot the nob off a gnat from five hundred yards and I know you still have that second hand Remington 700 PCR I bought you for Christmas five years ago. Just remember, Jake, it was never anything personal. It was always business.'

'You talk too much, Adolf or are you going by Number Three now?'

'Shit!'

The line goes dead, the fat man peers out of the window, hands shaking, rivers of sweat pouring from his brow. He staggers back to his desk.

'I need to get back into training.'.

He nervously grabs his cell phone. 'Otto, make that a diet Coke.'

# Chapter Ten

# Sally's Aunt

*One day later*

Jake is sitting at his desk, staring vacantly at his computer screen as Sally casually opens the door to his office.

'My, you gave me a shock, Mr. Poisson. I didn't expect you to be in so early.'

'Obviously not, Sally, you're early too. Is there any particular reason for that?'

Sally looks flustered. 'Well, no...er...yes.'

'Which is it?'

Sally bursts into tears.

'Mr. Poisson, I've been so concerned about you!'

'There's no need to worry, Sally.'

'But, Mr. Poisson, I've seen strange people wandering around near this building. I was worried they might be looking for you.

'Why would they be looking for me, Sally?'

Jake is standing next to Sally now, his face inches from hers, his eyes looking closely for the merest hint of a reaction. Sally's expression gives nothing away. Jake is now gripping Sally's elbows. Wedged between Jake and the desk, she is unable to move. She stares expectantly into Jake's unblinking eyes. After an interminable wait, he loosens his grip and gently wipes the tears from her face with his thumbs.

'When was the last time you saw your aunt, Sally?'

Sally's mouth is dry, her body shaking.

'You mean the one in Denver?'

'No, the one in Milwaukee.'

'Thank goodness for that Jake.' She starts undressing. 'At last, I can get rid of this goddam' padding, it's been two uncomfortable, long and sweaty flippin' years.'

Sally is now naked, apart from her high heels. Her body padding thrown carelessly to one side. The door to Jake's office bursts open.

'I hope I haven't called at an inconvenient time, Mr. Poisson.'

'Not at all, Georgette. My secretary was just testing the new air conditioning unit, it seems to be working fine. That will be all, Miss Chaste.'

Sally gathers up her belongings and glowers at Georgette as she struts out of the room. Both Jake and Georgette stare open-mouthed, mesmerized by the jiggling of Sally's gorgeous, peach-shaped buttocks. As Sally slowly closes the door behind her, Georgette eyes Jake up and down and then back up a little.

'I see you've fully recovered from your injuries.'

Jake quickly slides behind his desk in an effort to hide his reaction. 'How can I help you, Georgette?'

'I have some urgent news I need to discuss with you urgently concerning...'

'Is it very urgent?'

'Yes, it's very urgent news that I need to discuss with you very urgently.' 1

Georgette looks carefully around the room then whispers conspiratorially to Jake. 'E or O.'

'ELO? You're not going to tell me they've disbanded? They're my favorite group, that *Showdown* is a classic.

Georgette allows Jake to finish before correcting him.

'Not ELO, E and O – ELSA aka OLGA!'

Jake puts his fingers to his lips. 'Woah, Georgette, walls have ears.'

'Okay, do you understand sign language?'

'Of course.'

'I'll use sign language then.'

'Have you never heard of hidden cameras?'

'Should I write it down?'

'They have ways of reading impregnations through five sheets of paper.'

'What do you suggest?'

'Charades.'

'Charades?'

'You know? Like...'

Jake starts waving his arms in the air.

'Is it a book, a film, a play? - That sort of thing.'

Georgette reluctantly agrees. She places two fingers on her arm.

'What does that mean?'

'It means two syllables.'

'Oh yes, I forgot - carry on.'

Georgette sighs and is about to continue, but she catches sight of Sally, whose tanned, glistening, naked torso is framed magnificently in the backlit doorway.

'I'm sorry to have to interrupt your games, but if you recall, Mr. Poisson, your specific orders were that I had to inform you immediately if there were any problems with the new air conditioning unit. As you can see, it's not working, so I'm afraid, madam, you will have to leave...NOW!'

Taken aback, Georgette picks up her Gucci handbag,

mumbles her apologies and storms out of the building. Jake scrutinizes Sally's body, noticing the rivulets of perspiration dripping from her face, arms and other parts.

'Is it that hot?'

'I've sprayed myself with water, I didn't know what else to do. I had to get rid of that woman.'

'Why, Sally? She said she had some important information for me.'

'I'm sure you'll find out soon enough.'

Jake is still distracted by Sally's transformation. His gaze has now reached her waist.

'Is that a spider behind you?'

Sally turns round sharply, in shock. Jake's eyes remain transfixed on her flawless, shimmering skin, he sighs contentedly as her bottom jiggles deliciously only inches away from his face.

'Jake, be serious. This is important! Have you come out of it? You gave me the code.'

'Well, if I'm honest, Sally, I've only regained ninety percent of my proficiency. I can sense danger and react instinctively. I've lost none of my cunning, but the other twenty percent hasn't come back yet.'

'What's that?'

'My reasoning and mathematical functioning.'

'Have you any idea when it will return?'

'At my current rate of improvement about fifty days, maybe a little longer – perhaps a month.'

'We haven't got that much time, Jake. We need to speed up your recovery.'

'I could maybe do it in a week, or ten days if I really worked at it. How's about we go somewhere nice and comeback when I'm fully better?'

'That's a great idea, Jake, my aunt has a place in the Rockies.'

'Your aunt in Denver?'

'No, the one in Milwaukee.'

'Let's go!'

'I'll just put something on.'

'Oh well, I suppose you'd better. There's something I need to do on the way there. How far away is your aunt's place, by the way.'

'It's over two thousand miles.'

'We'll be there before nightfall.'

'The sooner you get your mathematical faculties back, the better, Jake.'

'You're just going to have to trust me on this one, Sally. Oh, by the way, do you have your machine with you?'

'Yes.'

'Good, let's go.'

# Chapter Eleven

## Oh Yes - It's Major Tom

*Thirty-seven minutes later*

Sally is peering through the narrow slit of a two-inch thick solid iron cell door. The inside of the cell is sparsely furnished and on the floor two men sit back-to-back on the cold stone floor, handcuffed together by their wrists. Their cheeks are stained with tears.

'Oh, Jake – look at those two men, who are they? Have you come to rescue them?'

'Possibly, Sally – have you got your machine there?'

'Yes, I always carry it around in my handbag?'

'Just in case?'

Sally colors and smiles sheepishly at Jake. He returns her gaze, surprised by how much her big, blue eyes sparkle in the dim light.

'Sally, I...'

Sally waits expectantly for Jake to finish, but one of the men's wailing breaks the moment.

'Is there anyone there, please let me out, please, PLEASE!'

Jake tears himself away from Sally and opens the cell door.

'Wait here.' He strides into the cell.

'Thank God, Jake - you've come back – I can't take any more of this. I'll do anything you want. I can't take any more days and nights like this - I beg you.'

'It's been two hours thirty-eight minutes, Otto.'

'Oh, has it? It seems longer.'

'So, are you ready to cooperate then?'

'Sure Jake, anything.'

'What about you, Elvis?'

'I'm with Otto, just let me out of here!'

'I'm going to help you both to stand up, okay?'

Jake lifts the two of them onto their feet. He takes two hoods out of his pocket. 'I'm going to have to cover your heads.'

He places the hoods over their heads.

'Ooh, it's dark in here!'

'Don't worry, Elvis. This won't take long.'

Jake pulls down Otto's trousers and boxers and beckons to Sally to enter the cell.

He points to Otto's testicles.

'Do it.'

Despite being unable to see, Otto makes a valiant attempt at avoiding Sally's grasp, eventually, however, she manages to take a firm grip on his member and successfully attaches an electrode to each testicle. Jake energetically cranks the machine. A loud crackling noise reverberates around the cell, followed by a massive bang and a huge puff of smoke. Otto collapses onto the floor, taking Elvis with him. Sally tries to extinguish Otto's sizzling pubes with her perfume, but only succeeds in creating a two-foot-long plume of smoke and flames. Jake uses the slops bucket to good effect and once the fumes and screams have died down, he returns the bucket to its rightful place - the corner of the cell. He notices Elvis trying to escape by dragging the comatose Otto behind him and for a moment it looks as though he might succeed, but unfortunately for him, he walks straight into a wall. Jake mouths to Sally.

'What went wrong?'

Sally pulls a jar of Vaseline out of her bag and hands it to

Jake, he bends down to reassure Elvis, who is now lying prostrate across the unconscious Otto's body.

'Just a technical error, Elvis - teething problems that's all. Just lie back and think of England.'

Sally turns to Jake. 'I think he's settled down.'

'I think he's fainted, Sally.'

### One hour later

'Do you think we should have left them there, Jake? - In the park?'

'They'll be okay, Sally. That park is patrolled day and night by New York's finest, they'll be well looked after.'

Jake tries not to think of what's going to happen when Columbo and Crockett find them.

'How long will it take for you to pack a suitcase, Sally?'

'I don't need to, Jake. I have everything I need at my aunt's.'

'Great, I can pick something up on the way. We'll be there before nightfall if we go now.'

Sally smiles indulgently at Jake. He looks so pleased with himself - she doesn't have the heart to tell him it will take at least two days to get there.

### A little later

Sally has dozed off, but she wakes up in shock to see a soldier pointing a rifle directly at her head. As she looks around, she sees that they are surrounded by heavily armed troops.

Surprisingly, Jake appears completely unperturbed by it all. The officer nearest to them is speaking into his tactical radio, Sally can just about make out the crackly response.

'What the hell's going on soldier. You know better than to

disturb me when I'm having a top-level meeting.'

'Who is it, darling?'

'No one - aiyee! - just keep on doing what you're doing – aah, that's it -now, what is it, soldier? It sounds as if World War Three's going on out there!'

'There's an intruder at the main gate, General. Somehow, he managed to get through the first five levels of security. He's eluded all our attempts to stop him, sir.'

'Goddam it, soldier, put your bloody bodycam on him, and let me eyeball the bas...'

'That's him, General.'

The General's body reflexively jerks into a sitting position, almost choking his companion.

'Goddam it, man – stand down - that's Major Tom – yeeoww! – you've taken a chunk out of my...'

'I'm getting a lot of static, General – did you say Major Tom?'

'Goddam it, soldier – of course it is, do you not recognize him from the training manual? Open the gate immediately! – Would you get me a band-aid, please, Angel?'

'I'm sorry, General. He looks a little different without his moustache. I'm opening the gates now, sir.'

As the huge, thick iron gates creak slowly open, a whole platoon of men line up and salute Jake. Returning the salute, Jake drives through the gate - almost immediately his vehicle disappears from sight. The General's companion returns with the band-aid.

'Who's Major Tom, darling?'

'You've never heard of Major Thomas Tom – oww - careful, Applepieface.'

'The name sounds familiar, darling.'

'I should think so, Appie – if it wasn't for him, I wouldn't be here now.'

'Oh yes, he's the one who saved your life! If I remember correctly, it was in Area Fifty-One.'

'Damn right it was, Applepie – excuse my French. You've done a good job on that. It'll be as right as rain in a couple of weeks.'

'Would you mind telling me again, darling?'

'Of course, Appie. I never get sick of telling this tale. I was flying over Area Fifty-One on a clandestine reconnaissance mission when all of a sudden there was an almighty flash and I felt my joystick being pulled out of my hand. I swear to God it was some alien or supreme being doing it – although I never mentioned that to another living soul - they would have drummed me out of the force pronto, if I had.'

'Surely not, darling.'

'Don't you believe it, Pieface. In this business you're only as good as your last mission.'

'Go on, darling, this is exciting – what happened next?'

'Well, I was sent spiraling into a massive, irreversible tailspin. On the way down I made peace with my maker and, even though I'm not a very religious person, I said a little prayer. I even recorded my will - I leave everything to my Applepieface - that got me into big trouble with my wife. I can tell you.'

'Umm, but it was a nice thing to do, though.'

'So - there I was, seconds away from oblivion, when...'

'What saved you, darling?'

'Not what – who!'

'Major Tom?'

'None other! I felt a little nudge on my tail and, incredibly, I was airborne again. I looked around and out of the corner of my eye I saw Drum with that wry smile of his on his face, then off he went on his merry way. That was a few years ago and I've never seen him since. That accomplishment has gone down in the annals of flying history, though. We named a maneuver after him – The Hind-lick Maneuver.'

'Who's Drum?'

'That was Major Tom's nickname, I don't know why, but we all have nicknames in the military.'

'What's yours, darling?'

'I'd rather not say.'

'Oh, go on, please....'

'Do I have to?'

'I'll kiss it better.'

'Alright then, it's - Snake.'

'Why?'

'You've heard of Snake Plissken, haven't you?'

'No.'

'Well, I think it's got something to do with him.'


*Underground, inside the base*


'Why is it so dark, Jake.'

'Because we're three hundred feet underground. There's not much natural light around here.'

'I'm frightened, Jake.'

'Don't be scared, Sally – look!'

Jake opens the car door and a series of lights flicker on, lighting up a long corridor.

'Where is this place, Jake?'

'I suppose you could call it my garage, come on, Sally – follow me.'

Sally doesn't need any encouragement. She rushes out of the

car and races round to Jake's side, grabbing his arm tightly.
Jake pats her hand reassuringly and then gently loosens her
grip from his forearm.

'Don't worry, I'll explain everything once we're airborne.'

'Once we are what...?' She looks around, but Jake has
disappeared through an opening in the corridor, he is five
yards away, opening a locker. He turns and throws a flight
suit towards her.

'Put this on.'

Jake effortlessly steps into his suit and zips it up. He notices
that Sally is struggling with hers and he helps her with it.

'It's a perfect fit, you'd think it was made for me.'

'It was, I remember now.'

'Have you got your full memory back yet, Jake?'

'Almost, Sally – I'm ninety-five per cent there, just another
ten per cent to go.'

'And your sense of humor, too.' Sally looks happy and gives
him a playful punch, Jake just looks puzzled. The shrillness
of the siren startles Sally.

'That's the one-minute countdown - time for us to go.'


*Five minutes later*


'Jake, why are we flying so low?'

'To avoid detection, we can't be picked up by radar at this
height.'

'Why are we flying so fast?'

'Because we can, I'll slow down if you're frightened, but it
might take longer to get there.'

Sally wonders how Jake knows so much.

'No, I like it, it's exciting, but how do you know how to fly it after all this time?'

'As I told you, my instincts have returned fully. I'm able to do all the things I used to be able to do. In fact, I can do most things much better. I just need to ask, have you still got that machine?' Sally's face lights up.

'It's here in my bag, does that mean I'll be able to use it again?

'If you wouldn't mind trying it out on me again. I think that's what's enhancing my abilities.'

Sally's eyes are now closed, as she imagines the week ahead.

'Are you okay, Sally?'

'Umm, yes, I'm very okay.' Sally can't help giving a little sigh of contentment as she squeezes her legs together.

'Why is this engine so quiet, Jake?'

'It's a prototype, it uses reverse osmosis to regenerate sound as energy, that's why we can fly at five hundred miles an hour. Helicopters normally have a top speed of two hundred miles an hour.'

'That sounds very clever, Jake.'

'Not really, I designed it before I was thrown out of college.'

'You were thrown out of college, Jake – why?'

'Oh, it's boring really – I was researching the medicinal qualities of marijuana oil.'

'And they threw you out for that?'

'Well - that, and the fact I burnt the science lab down.'

'No!'

'I was a little unlucky – if it hadn't spread to the nuclear power station next door, I could probably have put the fire out myself...'

'That was bad luck, Jake.'

'Anyway, that's water under the bridge, a whole lake full, actually. To get back to your question - the mechanics behind this baby are quite simple really. The main benefit though, is that any excess fuel used comes out here as chilled, purified water.'

Jake removes a plastic beaker from a cup holder and fills it.

'Would you like a drink?'

Sally takes a sip.

'It tastes like gin and tonic.'

'That's an optional extra. I paid for that myself.'

'You haven't stolen this have you, Jake? – We'll have the whole of the United States Air Force after us!'

'Of course not, I was given it.'

'You were given it - why?'

'It's a long story, two reasons, really. When I left, they wanted to give me a present because I'd helped Snake out.'

'Who's Snake?'

'He was our Squadron Leader at the time – I think he got promotion and a desk job after our little exploit.'

'Why is he called Snake?'

'Rumor has it that one day his pet snake crawled up his trouser leg and bit him. He spent an hour running naked around the parade ground with the snake attached to his dongler. Eventually the surgeons had to cut it off.'

'His penis?'

'No, the snake, he was really upset - he loved that snake.'

'What a sad story, how did you help him?'

'It was nothing, really. He was in an irreversible tailspin and I just nudged his rear end with my undercarriage to take him out of it, it was a maneuver I'd always wanted to try out.'

'Wow, wasn't that dangerous?'

'There was a ninety-nine point seven percent chance we'd both be killed, but when a brother is in danger you don't think of the odds.'

'What was the other reason?'
'The other reason for what?'
'The other reason they gave you this helicopter?'
Jake is wrestling with the joystick.

'No one else could fly it!'

# Chapter Twelve

# The Yates Motel

*Two hours later*

Jake looks over at Sally, she's sleeping peacefully, a contented expression on her face. He is about to gently wake her from her slumbers when a crackly, car-splitting voice reverberates through his earphones.

*'Major Tom, Major Tom – Can you hear me Major Tom, can you hear me, Major Tom - can you hear... ? – Abort, Abort – Sabotaagh - no - not that!'*

As he glances across at his solitary passenger, she opens her eyes dreamily.
'Are we nearly there, Jake?'
'Just about, honey. I can see your aunt's lakeside home from here.'
Sally smiles to herself.
'I love it when you call me hon... What are you doing, Jake – is there something wrong?'
Jake is out of his seat and checking around the cockpit. He notices the parachute on his ejector seat has been tampered with and he double-checks Sally's 'chute.
'Nothing, honey – just last-minute landing checks.'
He hands Sally an attaché case.
'Whatever you do, hold on tight to this.'
'Jake, I'm worried.'
'It's nothing, Honeybunch. The landing gear's playing up,

that's all. I've taken the wind, temperature and atmospheric pressure into account, you should land on your auntie's porch – I'll meet you there – I lo... '

A whoosh of air drowns out the rest of Jake's sentence as Sally finds herself drifting towards the ground in her ejector seat. She catches a glimpse of Jake blowing her a kiss as the helicopter spirals towards the lake. Jake checks around the cabin and collects a few essentials. He bends down to pick up Sally's makeup bag.

'Mustn't forget this, she'd never forgive me.'

With seconds to spare he kicks open the door, throws out the bags and jumps out of the helicopter. With superhuman effort he dives towards the bottom of the lake. An almighty explosion above his head creates a bubbling cauldron of water around him. By now he is fifty feet below the surface. He ducks, fighting ferociously against the strong gravitational pull, as one of the rotors skims his left ear. Reaching the lake bed, he notices something.

'That's disgusting, someone has dumped an old bicycle in the lake - still, it could come in handy.'

As Jake emerges from the lake pedaling furiously, he sees a massive ball of flames and heads towards the plume of smoke emanating from it. As he rounds the corner he sees Sally, her hair tousled, clothes torn and dirty, standing outside a barn.

The house has been reduced to rubble. Jake drops the bags, jumps off the bike and races towards her.

'What happened?'

'My ejector seat bounced off the roof and landed here.'

Jake runs his hands over Sally's body. 'Are you hurt anywhere?'

'No.'

'Maybe I've missed a bit.'

Sally giggles. 'I think you were pretty thorough.'

'It's my medical training. I trained under Buddhist faith healers for a couple of years.'

'Never mind me, Jake. I saw the explosion in the lake. How did you survive that - and where did you get that bike?'

'It never fails to amaze me what some people will do, Sally. I found this beauty at the bottom of the lake – what a waste! A couple of new tires and a bit of oil and it could be as good as new.'

'Jake, why do you think the house caught fire, was it booby-trapped?'

Jake tries to reassure Sally. 'Of course not, in old houses like this it's normally a gas leak.'

'This house is all electric, Jake.'

'Really, it must be quite expensive to heat.'

'Yes, my aunt was always complaining about the bills.'

'Well, she won't have to complain any more. Have you got the attaché case, Sally?'

'I'm afraid it slipped out of my hands, Jake. It's on the top of the barn, can you see it?'

'Yes, I can see it. I'm sure I can climb up there.'

Jake is three quarters of the way up the rotting wood of the wall.

'There's a ladder in the barn, Jake.'

The plank that Jake is desperately grasping onto with his bare hands starts to split. Jake hangs on grimly and finds himself being hurled towards the large barn window - fortunately it's open.

Sally calls out. 'Are you okay, Jake?'

'I'm fine, Sally.'

As he dusts the hay off himself, he sees something glinting underneath a pile of old magazines. He rummages through the magazines before picking up the object.

'That's interesting - I wonder if Sally knows her aunt was into bondage.'

Jake finds using the ladder much easier. He picks up the attaché case and slides down to where Sally is waiting for him.

'Jake, if *we* saw these explosions, then someone else must have. Do you think we should get out of here?'

'That's probably a good idea, Sally, but when I was on the top of the barn, I saw an abandoned '59 Chevy in that field. One of my favorite cars. It might be a good restoration project. Can I just have a quick look at it?'

'If you must, Jake, but be quick. Oh, look, you've brought my makeup bag, how sweet! That wind played havoc with my hair. You can have ten minutes while I brush my hair and put my face on, okay?'

'Thanks, Sal.'

Jake is unable to control his excitement. 'I don't believe it! It's my favorite color. I'm just gonna leave it like this, the patina gives it character.'

He pops the hood. 'Just look at that V8 beauty!'

Moving round to the trunk he spots a few oil cans. 'Hmm...it wouldn't do any harm to have a little tinker.'

He finds a rag to wipe his hands and decides to have a quick look at the interior. After tugging vigorously at the door, eventually it opens with a massive grating, screechy creak.

'Nothing that a squirt of WD40 won't fix – hey, that eight-track still has a cartridge in. I wonder what it is?'

He wrestles it out of the deck. 'Little Willie John!'

Jake rushes back to Sally. 'We need to catch a train!'

'Where are we going?'

'Kokomo.'

'We can use my aunt's car. It's in the barn, covered in hay bales.'

'It's a long way to Kokomo, Sally.'

'Of course it's not, it's only a couple of hundred miles down the road. We can be there by nightfall.'

'Hey, that's my line.'

*Ten minutes later*

Sally has convinced Jake to let her drive. He didn't take much convincing really, that helicopter caper had been lively to say the least and the bicycle he rescued had no suspension or tires. As a result, even though he wouldn't admit it - even to himself - he was feeling a little rough around the gills. His main reason though, was that it would give him an opportunity to fully appraise Sally and he had to admit that driving her aunt's Cadillac, with her hair slicked back and her Wayfarers on, she looked pretty damned good. Sally is aware that Jake is watching her, she casually unhooks the catch of the soft top. Unfortunately, the wind catches it and it disappears into a ditch. Jakes looks back.

'Maybe we'll find it on the way back, I think there was a little split in it anyway.'

Sally switches the radio on, an advert blares out.

*'If you're coming to Kokomo - Yate's Motel is the place to go.'*

The jingle is followed by a message.

*'Hi, I'm Norma Yates, my father and I would love to welcome you to our luxurious motel. Normally we're fully booked, but we've just had a late cancellation, so if you're quick, you can experience our honeymoon suite, complete with its newly refurbished shower curtain.'*

Jake manages to tear his gaze from Sally and notices a cracked, discolored sign on the side of the road.

'Hey, look – the Yate's Motel is only a couple of miles up the road, what do you think, Sally?'

'The Honeymoon Suite sounds nice and I could definitely do with a shower.' She sniffs the air. 'And if I'm not mistaken, so could you.'

Jake checks in his pockets for his wallet - he finds it and takes it out, along with a fish. He looks sheepish.

'You're not mistaken...'

'That fish reminds me of Poisson Dating. I can't believe that only a few days ago we were...'

'Yeah, a lot's happened since then, Sally.'

Jake notices a neon sign flickering erratically. 'The turn off is on the left there, Sally. You stay in the car - I'll book us in.'

As Jake waits patiently in reception, he notices that Sally's car is the only one in the car park.

'Good evening, sir. How may I help you?'

The voice is that of the woman on the radio.

'Hi, I'd like to book a room for the night.'

'Certainly, sir. I'll just check to see if there's one available.'

Norma, if it is Norma, is not unattractive. In fact, she would be very attractive if it were not for her appearance. She peers out of the window.

'A room for one person?'

'No, two please.'

She stares out of the window for a much longer period of time and again consults her bookings diary.

'I'm not sure if...'

'Your ad on the radio said the Honeymoon Suite is available.'

'Which radio station was it?'

'I'm not sure. It was playing in my sec... er... wife's car.'

They both gaze out of the window.

'Is that the car you're referring to - out there?'

Since there was only one car in the car park, Jake thought that the question was unnecessary, but he was too far into the conversation to back out now.

'Yes, that's the car.'

'And is that your wife sitting in the driving seat?

' 'Yes, that's her.'

'She's very attractive, isn't she?'

Jake wasn't sure where this was leading.

'*I* think so.'

'Yes, very, very attractive. Will you ask her where she bought that jacket from? I'd like a jacket like that.'

'Of course I will.'

'And that lipstick she's wearing, will you ask her what shade it is? I think it would suit me.'

'Sure thing, now can I just ask, is there a room available?'

'I'll have to check, young man.'

Jake can't help thinking that he is probably the same age as her, he considers discussing it, but he is in no mood for small talk.

'Here we are. The only room we have vacant is the

Honeymoon Suite.'

'I'll take it!'

'My, my, you're very keen, have you two not had sex for a while?'

Jake knows there is no correct answer. He signs the register and holds out his hand, Norma scrutinizes the register for a while before eventually placing a key in Jake's outstretched hand, seductively stroking his palm with her fingers, as she does so.

'Thank you, Mr. *Bell* - end of the corridor, on the first floor - have fun.'

As Jake hurries out of the reception area, he hears Norma muttering to herself. 'Youngsters today, all they think of is sex...'

'Did you manage to get a room?'

'We are in luck, they had one vacancy – the Honeymoon Suite. I signed us in as Mr. and Mrs. Bell, I hope you don't mind.'

'Not at all, Jake - Mr. and Mrs. Bell, that has a nice ring to it.' Jake looks around the motel, the whole place appears to be deserted.

'This place doesn't look busy, Sally.'

'Perhaps the guests are out sightseeing. I bet this place will be really lively later.'

'Maybe...'

Jake thinks he sees the silhouette of a man's head in an upstairs window of the old house, but when he looks more closely there's no one there.

'What is it, Jake?'

'Nothing.'

Jake throws Sally the key and starts rummaging through the trunk. He finds his attaché case and slides into the passenger seat. 'It's that one up there – on the end. I won't be a minute, Sally.'

By the time Jake carries what remains of their belongings up to the room, Sally is lying on the bed wrapped only in a bath towel, watching Netflix. She offers Jake a chocolate.

'Compliments of the Yates Motel, I've left some for you.'

Sally blushes as Jake looks at the two lonely chocolates in the box and then at her hamster cheeks.

He laughs. 'If they're both here after my shower I'll share them with you.'

Jake is in the shower admiring the newly refurbished curtain and briskly lathering himself with the complimentary two-in-one shampoo and shower gel. He is halfway through a rousing chorus of *Born to Be Wild* when he notices a cover being slid open, revealing an eye. The eye looks familiar.

'Mr. Bell, is there anything you need?'

'I think I'm fine at the moment, Norma, thanks.'

'Perhaps your wife would like some more chocolates?'

'That would be nice, Norma.'

'Will I put a card in from you?'

'What a thoughtful idea, Norma.'

'To my darling wife from your devoted husband?'

'I couldn't have put it better, myself.'

'I'll do that straightaway. By the way, Mr. Bell, you need to rinse those suds off your cojones, sir. Otherwise, you could get an itchy rash.'

Without thinking, Jake directs the shower head towards his testicles.

'That's a reasonable attempt, but you need to open your legs a little wider - a bit more – that's it, much better, have a nice day, Mr. Bell.'

Jake dries himself and returns to the bedroom.

'I must say, the service here is second to none.' He hears the box of chocolates being slid underneath the door, picks it up with a flourish and offers it to Sally.

'For you, my queen.'

As Sally laughs and reaches for the box, her towel falls open, revealing her smooth, freshly-cleaned skin.

'That shower gel is nice, isn't it?'

'Yes, a little bit gives a lot of lather. My skin feels nice and soft, does yours?'

Sally giggles. 'That's for you to find out.'

Jake is just about to, when he hears Norma's voice over an internal intercom.

'There's a back entrance, Mr. Bell.'

Jake wonders if she has a videocam trained on them.

'What?'

'I'd advise both of you to leave from that exit – NOW!'

The tone of her voice is urgent.

'Why, Norma?'

'Some men have just pulled up in the car park. They're carefully inspecting your wife's car. I could be wrong sir, but they don't look like the type of men you want to invite to your honeymoon night. Ooh, wait, there's a woman with them. Nice legs, but personally I think that micro-mini skirt's a little too short for a woman of her age. I'll try and stall them for as long as I can for you, Mr. Be...'

Jake's not listening, he pulls on the first thing that comes to hand, throws his shirt towards Sally and grabs his attaché case from under the bed.

'Put this on and follow me.'

Jake sounds casual enough, but Sally notices the underlying sense of urgency in his voice. She frantically fastens a couple of buttons on the shirt and follows Jake towards the rear exit of the apartment. It's locked!

Jake slams his shoulder against it and then notices the key hanging from a hook on the wall. He rubs his shoulder, takes the key from the hook and unlocks the door. In a flash he has the door open and is climbing down the fire escape. The last part is missing so he jumps the last ten feet or so.

'Jump, Sally – I'll catch you.'

Sally jumps, but the shirt she is wearing snags on a rung of the ladder, leaving her suspended precariously above Jake. Only the tattered shirt around her neck holding her high above the ground. Jake looks on helplessly.

'I wish I could put something up there.'

'This is no time for that, Jake!'

Just at that, a huge man appears from around the corner.

'Climb onto my shoulders.'

Jake considers his options and quickly realizes he has no other alternatives, apart, of course, from leaving the woman he has grown to love, dangling naked and afraid, a few feet above this massive, powerful, rugged hulk of a man. He puts a foot out and the man lifts him effortlessly into the air. Jake reaches up and untangles Sally's clothing. She wraps her arms around Jake's neck and the man carefully lowers them both to the ground.

'My hero!'

Jake smiles proudly and turns towards Sally, only to realize she is feeling the toned, swollen biceps of the stranger.

'Come vith me if you vont to live.' He articulates in a strange guttural accent. Sally takes his shovel-sized hand and happily wanders off with him, the torn shirt flapping around her bare nether regions.

Jake ponders his next move. As Sally and the hunk round the corner they encounter two sharply dressed agents. The large man makes a lunge for one of them, but his bulk slows him down and he is pistol whipped by the other agent. As he lies groaning, the agent who didn't pistol whip the big man, pulls his revolver on Sally. 'Now then, what have we got here? How would you like me to put my gun in your mouth?' The other agent has his gun trained on the semi-conscious giant. He impatiently shouts at his colleague.

'Just get on with it, you have your orders – shoot her!'

'It seems such a waste, but orders is orders.'

He cocks his pistol and aims it at Sally's brow. Her whole body is shaking. With closed eyes, she puts her hands together and starts to pray.

# Chapter Thirteen

## The Great Escape

'I'm the one you want.'

Jake appears from behind the wall. The two agents smirk at each other.

'I don't think so, mate - did anyone say anything to you about killing a man wearing pink panties, Barney?'

'No, I'm pretty sure I would have remembered that, Clyde.'

There is a groan from the colossal man on the ground. The two gunmen glance at him – a fatal mistake. Well, not fatal - because Jake never kills anyone if he can help it, but certainly a serious mistake. Sally opens her eyes, surprised to see the two agents bound and gagged and Jake wildly slapping the face of the huge rugged, handsome, muscular man who helped them.

'I hope you're not jealous, Jake.'

'Of course not, darling. I knew you were only putting on an act when you held his hand and happily skipped along the lane, gazing fondly into his eyes. I'm not jealous at all, I'm just performing a proven method to revive someone who is dazed and defenseless.'

Sally reluctantly drags her eyes away from the man's thighs.

'Can I help? Perhaps if I rub his...'

'It's okay, Sally. It was kind of you to offer, but he's come to.'

Jake bends down and whispers in his ear. 'Thanks for the help, but I'll take it from here.'

He turns to the two men.

'Tell your friends Jake Poisson is back.'

A look of fear passes between them. Jake smiles, grabs Sally's hand and guides her towards a nearby cornfield. As they disappear, Barney turns to Clyde.

'Can you believe that was Jake Poisson?'

'He seems friendly enough.'

'Yeah, for a cold-blooded killer...'

As Jake and Sally zigzag through the cornfield they come across a scarecrow. Jake returns the pink panties to their rightful owner and pulls on the scarecrow's trousers. Sally admires his attire while he prepares a makeshift camp.

'They're a little bit short on the legs, but the bum's a nice tight fit.'

'Thanks, Sally - and I must say, those panties look better on you than they did on me.'

Jake opens his attaché case. He passes a protein bar and an energy drink to Sally and takes a few walnuts for himself.

'I've been wondering what you keep in that case, Jake. What else is in there?'

'It's just something I've been working on. I'll explain later, but first I need to know why they came after you and not me.'

'I think it's because I know too much.'

'About Blowman or Dan Corleone?'

'Both - they're interconnected now.'

Jake gives a low whistle. 'I was worried about that.'

'I'm afraid your fears have come true. A lot has happened in the last couple of years.'

'I just hope I've come out of it in time to save us.'

'It's not just us, Jake – it's the whole...'

Sally is interrupted by a burst of gunfire.

'Thank God I've got most of my faculties back.'

'I know, Jake. I've been watching you closely all this time - that's my job. I was beginning to think you were never going to recover. When did you start to get your memory back?'

'I started to get flashbacks after I was thrashed on my buttocks, then beaten senseless, then tasered, but it wasn't until I got that machine attached to my private parts that my recall really improved.'

'Jake?'

'Yes?'

'When that man pointed a gun at me.'

'Clyde?'

'Was that his name? I was too frightened to listen to anything he was saying.'

'You didn't look frightened, Sally – apart from the quivering and the tears and the pleading -oh, and the praying - no one would have guessed you were terrified.'

'That's nice of you to say so, Jake, but I was really, really scared.'

'It's normal the first time that happens to you, Sally.'

'Were you not scared of those men, Jake?'

'No, I was too busy assessing them for weaknesses. I am trained to react like that.'

'Well, you know what I was thinking, Jake?'

'No.'

'I was thinking I've never really felt your body next to mine.'

'That's easily fixed.'

Jake takes Sally into his arms.


*Three minutes later...*


'That was very nice, Sally, but they'll be sending out the helicopters soon.'

Jake jumps to his feet. There they are – zero-two-two point five.'

'Which direction is that?'

'North-northeast.'

Sally's eyes desperately scour the sky. 'Where?'

'Over there!' Jake points in the opposite direction to where Sally is looking.

'Oh, I thought that was a crow.'

'Above the crow, do you see it?'

'Not really.'

'It's an MV-22 Osprey, probably decommissioned from the Marine Corps.'

'How do you know?'

'I'm trained to recognize every type of military aircraft by the sound of its engine.'

'What are we going to do now?'

'We need to head for Nick's Café.'

'That sounds nice, Jake, but do you really think this is the time for a coff...?'

Sally is disturbed by the crackly and barely audible voice of a man emanating from a loudspeaker in the scarecrow. They both turn and notice its eyes are, in fact, concealed webcams.

'If you two have finished I would advise you to head one-five-seven point five degrees.'

A woman's voice butts in. 'That didn't take them long.'

'Hush, Norma - this is important.'

'I was only saying, for a couple on their honeymoon I would have expected...'

'Take no notice of Norma.'

Sally brushes the corn stubble from her body.

'What direction is that, Jake?'

'East-southeast.'

The loudspeaker crackles into life again.

'You need to take your clothes off and bury them, then rub

127

the corn husks all over your body, so the dogs can't track you.'

'They haven't got a lot of time, Norma.'

'It's worth it, besides the husks are a great exfoliator.'

'Are you sure about that?'

'Well, I've never had complaints about the way my skin feels - remember the local football team when they...?'

'Okay, Norma, point taken - just let me give them some last-minute instructions.'

'I'm only trying to help.'

'I know, dear – Jake, we are one click away from you. We'll be waiting for you, over.'

'I wanted to say over.'

'Okay, say it.'

'Over.'

Jake has buried the few clothes they had and now they are rubbing the corn husks over each other.

'Jake, how far is a click?'

'It's a kilometer, five eighths or naught point six-two-five of a mile. It shouldn't take us long, but we'll have to zig-zag through this cornfield to avoid leaving a trail.'

Sally stumbles and twists her ankle. She cries out in pain and Jake turns to her.

'Jump on my back, Sally.'

'I'll be too heavy for you, Jake.'

Jake appraises - her from top to toe.

'I'll manage - I'm trained to carry heavy loads.'

Sally reluctantly climbs on his back. Jake's time in the jungles of Borneo helps him to make good progress and he is even able to carry on a conversation whilst travelling over the exceedingly rough terrain with his secretary on his back.

'Sally, do you know when you said a lot had happened

during the last couple of years and that Dan Corleone and Blowman were interconnected, what did you mean?'

Five minutes later Sally decides that she will speak to him again.

'I'll tell *you*, if you tell *me* what you meant when you said you were trained to carry heavy loads.'

'I didn't mean you, honey. I meant massive backpacks with lots and lots of heavy things in them, I had to carry them for miles and miles. You are really light in comparison, in fact, if it wasn't for whatever that is rubbing on my back, I'd have hardly noticed anything.'

He hoped he didn't sound breathless.

'Are you sure, because I'd hate to think you thought I was too heavy for you to carry.'

'No, really, it's no hardship at all. That friction is keeping me nice and warm.' Sally is unable to stifle her moans.

'Are you alright, honey?'

'Ummmmm...'

Jake decides to drop the topic for the time being. Just when it seems he may falter, a flashing light gives him hope and renewed vigor.

'Oh-oh, we've come to a clearing – I hope we won't be seen.'

'What sort of grass is that, Jake?'

'It's rye grass - I think we're near, Sally.'

They hear Norma's voice from a distant speaker.'

'Keep going – you *are* near!'

'What's that noise, Norma?'

'Jake stood on a mockingbird - he almost killed it.'

'Wow, he nearly killed a mockingbird, where are they now, Norma?'

'They are in the grass. She's frightened they'll catch her in

the rye.'
'That's another story!'

Moments later, Jake feels the earth underneath him give way and the two of them slide down a helter-skelter, before landing bumpily on some rough matting. Norma is there to greet them. She is almost unrecognizable from the dowdy receptionist Jake first met. She takes Jake by his arms and lifts him onto his feet. Then she gently raises Sally from the matting. Stroking her hair, she whispers in her ear.
'There's a little piece of corn in it – there, that's better. Look at you, I told you that corn husk was good for your skin. You look a little bit flushed, though. It must have been awful for you running through that cornfield naked like that.
'Ummmmm.'
'You come with me - I'll look after you. Jake here can deal with the boring details.'
Norma leads Sally along a dim passage. As they disappear, he hears Norma reassuring her.
'You're perfectly safe here. Arnie is already here, he's that nice big, muscular hunk who rescued you from the fire escape.'
'Does he use corn husks on his skin?'
'Oh yes, that's how I found out about it, I've seen him exfoliating out in the fields on many occasions.'
'Ummmmm.'
'Sally, I've rescued all your luggage from the apartment. I took the liberty of trying out some of those lovely things in your makeup bag. I hope you don't mind – what do you think?'
'Of course I don't mind, that color really suits your eyes – and the lip gloss is perfect for juicy, full lips like yours.'

'Thank you, Sally, that's really nice of you to say so. We need to wash all that muck off you now, though and the shower's a bit temperamental - I'll need to get in with you to show you how to...'

*Inside the bunker*

'With all your training I knew you'd find me!'
Jake's attention is drawn to a man immediately behind him.
The man is wearing a hazmat suit. Jake instantly recognizes
him, even with his helmet in place.
'Pop!'
'Son!'
They hug each other tightly, then, as they both realize that
Jake is naked, they stand awkwardly, neither trying to take
their gaze from the other's face. Eventually Jake's father
takes a jacket from a peg on the wall and hands it to his son.
'Pops, you shouldn't! That's your old flying jacket.'
'Oh, I think I should – wrap it around yourself until Norma
gets your clothes for you. Then give it straight back to me.'
'Why are you wearing that hazard materials suit, Pop?'
'I'll explain later. We've lot to talk about, Jake - there are
some people I'd like you to meet, but first I'll show you round
our HQ.' The HQ, as Jake's father calls it, is really just a
rabbit warren of old tunnels. Many of the carved-out rooms
are empty, but one or two contain old machinery, fuel
canisters, dusty, unidentifiable tins of food and other
oddments.  During the 'tour', Fox quickly skirts past a room
with blacked-out windows and a Laboratory with a

*Top-Secret*

sign on the door, he tries to distract Jake's attention as he
does so, but Jake surreptitiously tries the door and finds it
locked. He makes a mental note of the shape of the integral
lock on the door handle.

'I haven't shown you the rest room. It's not quite completed yet, but hopefully you'll be able to visualize what it'll look like when it's finished.'

'Here it is Jake, our rest room.' The room is to the left and Jake's father pointedly guides him into it. The room is sparsely furnished, with only a couple of filing cabinets, a large table and a few old, wooden chairs. The only wall which isn't bare is the one which is facing them, on that wall there is a large, faded, black and white photograph. There is a long silence as Jake stares at the photograph and then turns to face his father. He utters only one word.

'Why?'

Fox searches for the right words, his lips are dry and he stares at the floor. 'Jake....I...'

'Your turn now, Mr. Bell.'

'We're a little busy at the moment, Norma.'

'You promised me I could do it.'

'Oh, all right, but don't be long, Jake and I have important things to discuss.'

'We'll only be a few short minutes.'

Norma winks at Jake then mutters to herself.

'If past experience is anything to go by...'

Norma leads Jake down the corridor.

'The first thing we need to do is wash that husk off you. The shower's a bit temperamental. I'll need to go in with you to show you how to use it...'

Three minutes later.

'I thought it wouldn't take long, but that was even quicker than I expected. I don't suppose many men can last as long as Arnie when he's exfoliating.'

'Who's Arnie?'

'You've met him, he's the one who rescued your bride from

133

the fire escape.'

'Is he your father?'

'Oh no, no, of course not. I wouldn't watch my father exfoliating.'

'But when I checked in, you said there was only you and your father.'

'I meant there was only me and my father running the motel. Arnie spends most of his time in the fields.'

# Chapter Fourteen

## Behind a Rock and a Hard Place

Norma watches Jake as he dresses – and curses her luck.
'If it wasn't for that bride of his, I'm sure with a bit of training, I would be able to...'
'Did you say something, Norma?'
'No, I was just thinking out loud.'
'I'm ready now, can you take me to my father?'
'Your father? Norma's face turns a dark shade of puce.
'I suppose so.'
'Thanks, Norma, we've a lot to talk about.'
'I'm sure you have!'
Fox is still in the rest room, staring at the photograph. He turns as he hears the two of them enter.
'How did the two of you get on?'
'Er, fine – there was a little more husk than I expected, but it didn't take long to rub him off.'
'Did Jake tell you I was his father?'
'No, he never mentioned that – not even a word. I'm sure I would have remembered something like that.'
Jake looks at Norma incredulously. Norma turns a darker shade of puce and then a greeny type of puce.
'It's news to me.'
'Well, I'm not his real father.'
'Phew, that's a relief!'
Norma's coloring begins to return to normal, but now Jake goes puce, he turns to Fox.
'You're not my father? - How can that be?'
Just at that point, Sally enters the room.

'Hi, Fox.'

'Hi Sally, that's good timing. I was just about to explain to Jake about how Gloria and I found him.'

'About how you *found* me? - Wait, you two know each other?'

'Sally's my wife.'

'Pops, you never told me, I would have loved to have been bridesmaid.'

'Pops? Norma, why are you calling Fox – Pops?'

'Because I'm her father.'

Looking around, Fox realizes that there are more shades of puce than he had originally thought.

'I think we all need to sit down and discuss this. I've made some coffee and I have some of Norma's home-made biscuits here.'

'A minute ago, I thought you were my father and earlier today I fu..., well anyway, I was very close to your wife and your daughter and you expect me to sit down with you over coffee and biscuits! I don't believe it - you must think I'm...'

Fox opens a biscuit barrel and starts pouring the coffee.

Jake notices the contents of the barrel.

'Are they ginger parkins?'

'Yes.'

'My favorites, perhaps I'll have just one, I haven't had anything since those almonds and it's been a busy day.'

Norma stares into Jake's eye, smiling sweetly as she hands him the biscuits.

'I'm putting two on your plate, they're my special recipe. I do hope you like them.'

'Thanks.'

'Let's all take a seat.'

'There aren't enough seats, Pops - since Mr. Bell is not your son, can I sit on his knee?'

'I suppose so.'

Norma snuggles into Jake's lap, overtly rubbing her bottom into his crotch and at the same time gloating at Sally.

'Mmm... - these parkins are really nice, Pops, er, Fox.'

Norma beams with pride and jiggles her backside even more suggestively.

'I'm pleased you like them, Jake. I can put my hand to almost anything.'

Jake is relieved when Fox distracts him from his thoughts.

'I know this must have come as a shock to you, Jake, but I'm sure that once I explain you'll understand.'

He looks at Norma and Sally. 'And I hope you two will too.'

Sally is glowering at Norma - Norma is still gloating. The more Sally glowers, the more Norma rubs her bottom into Jake's crotch. Jake notices and tries to fight his reaction. Fox doesn't seem to notice, he is too deep in thought.

'I have to go a long way back here, Jake. Way back until you were just three years old. Your foster mother, Gloria and I were living on that farm in Nantucket, miles from nowhere.'

'I remember it.'

'Yes, that's where we raised you until you were ten. Well, it was very quiet, nothing much happened there, but one day I went out into the barn and I noticed there was a large hole in the roof.'

'How large?'

'Oh, I'd say about six feet by six feet.'

'A meteorite?'

'I'm coming to that, Norma.'

'Okay, but hurry up, Pops – this is exciting.'

'Well, as I was saying, there was a large hole in the roof of the barn, so I went to investigate.'

'What did you find, Pops?'

'I'm coming to that, Norma. Underneath a pile of hay, I found a rocket ship.'

'I knew it, I knew it! It was aliens!'

Norma squirms around excitedly on Jake's knee. Jake tries to appear unmoved. He can handle the tale, but the squirming is another matter.

'No, it wasn't aliens. It was a toy spaceship, the kind you find on carousels.'

'Oh, that's a shame.'

'Well, that wasn't the end of it, Norma. The most unexpected thing about it was, that inside the toy spaceship was a little boy.'

'Who was it?'

'It was Jake, of course.'

'And you and Gloria brought him up as if he was your own?'

'Well, obviously we searched for his real parents, but we couldn't find them. Apparently, they worked in a traveling fun fair and they were worried in case they got prosecuted by health and safety, so they high-tailed it out of there. So, after a week or so we gave up the search.'

'It's just like the Superman comics isn't it, Pop?'

'I haven't read those comics.'

'Or the films!'

'I've never seen those films.'

'Now that you've explained it, Fox, it all makes sense to me, but I need to know what happened to my real parents.'

'Of course, but first I need to explain where I met Sally.'

'Fox, If I'd known Sally was your wife, I'd never have...'

Sally interrupts Jake, she tries to sound convincing, but the flatness of her voice shows her true feelings.

'I want you all to know that with Jake it was only in the line of duty. I never enjoyed one minute of it.'

'What about the other two?'

'Hush, Norma.'

'I was only asking...'

'I don't know if you remember, Jake, but I had a little workshop in that barn.' I remember it well, Po... Fox.' 'Yes, you used to help me in there, after school, didn't you?'

'I sure did. I learnt a lot in there. I can still remember how to stimulate a rat's brain by attaching electrodes to its cerebral cortex.'

'Yeah, unfortunately that was one of my most successful experiments and it led me into a whole world of trouble.'

'Was that why I had to move away with Mom?'

'One of the reasons, Jake, the other one was because I was banging Norma's mother like a drum – but that's another story.'

Jake, Norma and Sally look at each other in amazement as Fox casually carries on.

'So - where was I? Oh yes, my experiments with rats. I then moved on to other animals and eventually humans – that was fun. You've seen one of my successful outcomes already.'

Three expressions all change from amazement to incredulity. Jake is mentally scanning the room for escape routes. Sally can't hide the tremble in her voice.

'Who?'

'Arnie – you don't think anyone can grow as big and strong as that normally, do you, Sally?'

'I was hopeful...'

'At first, I thought he was a great success, but I soon realized there were side effects.'

'Such as?'

'Just little things at first, Jake. Dry skin, nervous

twitching...'

'Is that why he exfoliates so much? Sometimes I've watched him exfoliate as much as three times a day.'

'I agree that's a bit excessive, but I think he'll grow out of that, Norma.'

'How old is he?'

'I'm not sure, Jake. From his teeth, I would estimate he is around your age.'

'My age - surely not? He looks years older – he must know how old he is...'

'He has no recollection of his life before the fall.'

'What fall?'

'When I found him, he had obviously fallen from something because his head was badly bruised.'

'Where was he?'

'About ten yards outside the barn where I found you.'

'When did you find him?'

'About two weeks after I found you.'

'My God – you know what this means, don't you?'

'Wha...?'

The almighty crash, as the rest room door is kicked open, takes everyone by surprise - except Jake, of course - he is fully prepared. He has already maneuvered Norma into a more comfortable position, thus improving the circulation in his legs and he is now wiggling his feet up and down to loosen his calf muscles. He slides a hand into his attaché case and waits patiently, all his senses on full alert. He's like a panther ready to pounce into action.

'Hi Jake, fancy seeing you here...'

'Candice Virtue!'

Jake decides to delay his pouncing for a while.

'Mr. Bell, that's the woman I told you about. Now that I've

140

seen her close up, I think she can just about get away with
that skirt, despite her age.'

'And who are you?'

'I'm Norma, would you mind if I tried your skirt on, it's real
leather, isn't it?'

'Yes, it is, and since you've been so complimentary, I don't
see why not.'

Candice moves her fingers to her zip. As he anticipates
Candice removing her skirt, Jake's senses have been reduced
to one – his sight – in his distraction, he fails to notice a
muscular man enter the room.

'Not so fast!'

'Yeah, not so fast, do it slowly.'

'I didn't mean that, Mr. Poisson.'

'No?'

'No, I meant not so fast, we need to talk.'

'It's you – you were with my mother in the courtroom –
what unspeakable things have you being doing to her, you
fiend!' 'Jake, Gloria's not your real mother.'

'Fair comment – but she's your wife, Fox.'

'Ex-wife, Jake.'

'Fair comment.'

'Gloria never complained.'

'Fair comment - I suppose...'

'I know a lot about you, Jake, a lot more than you think. It's
a shame Miss Virtue wants to kill you.'

'I agree with you, but it would be a real shame to stop
Candice just before she's finished, if you can just hang on for
a few minutes I'll die a happy man.'

'Jake, you know I don't want to do this, but I have my
orders.' The two agents, Barney and Clyde have now entered
the room.

'Yes, orders is orders.'

Jake surreptitiously opens his attaché case and lets two tears drop from his cheeks. As the smoke disappears, the agents realize that, so too, have Jake and Sally. Sally looks lovingly at her rescuer. She reaches out to take him in her arms.

'I want you to know it was a marriage of convenience with Fox.' Jake strokes her hair reassuringly.

'That was close - luckily, I had some instant smoke mix in my case. I'm afraid it's just you and me again, Sally.'

They hear a breathless, excited voice behind them.

'And me! – I've brought your attaché case, Jake.'

Sally glowers at Norma. 'And your makeup bag, Sally.'

'Thank you, Norma, how sweet of you.'

They hear heavy footsteps running through a corridor and then shoulders being thrown at the heavy iron door, followed by loud cursing.

'Luckily for us, it opens inwards.'

'Maybe, Sally, but it may not take them long to figure that out.'

'Come vith me if you vont to live.'

'Arnie, what are you doing here?'

'I vos exfoliating.'

Sally looks down. 'I can see that - would you like me to get you a bigger corn husk?'

'Sally, eventually they are going to realize that the door is unlocked, we'd better move. You can watch Arnie exfoliating later.'

'Okay.'

'Can I watch you exfoliating, Jake?'

'Alright, Norma, anything you want, but - let's go!'

*One hour later*

Norma and Sally are lounging on the grass in a clearing next to a babbling stream, contentedly watching the two men exfoliate. Norma is idly stroking Sally's hair. They appear to have reconciled their differences.

'Why did you marry Pops, Sally? You could have had any man you want. You have lovely smooth, silky hair, by the way. Do you think I could borrow your shampoo and conditioner sometime?'

'Of course, - but your hair looks nice too and you have soft, silky skin, Norma.'

Sally leans over and fondles Norma's belly.

'And a nice taught stomach.'

Completely distracted, neither of them notice Arnie striding towards them. He is towering over them now, a certain part of his anatomy blocking out the sun.

'I'm zorry to disturb you two vimmen, but Jake says ve haf to go now.'

They look across and see that Jake is fully dressed and has a bow and arrow in his hand.

Sally turns to Arnie 'Do you have to get dressed Arnie?'

'Yes, vee haf only a few minutes. My rucksack is behind zat rock.'

'That's probably enough time, I'll just come with you to make sure you've washed all the husk off.'

Sally follows Arnie to the rock as Norma saunters up to Jake.

'Where did you get that bow and arrow, Jake?'

'I made them - I'm trained to make weapons out of almost anything.'

'That's a very good skill to have, Jake.'

Loud groaning noises can be heard from behind the rock. Jake strains his ears.

'What's that?'

'Probably wild boars, it's the rutting season round here.'

'Well, if one comes near us, I'll kill it easily with this.' He holds up his bow with a flourish.'

'Have you killed many wild boars, Jake?'

'No, I don't believe in killing any living thing, but I am trained to, I would only do it to protect you, of course.'

Norma slides her arms around him.

'Oh Jake, you're so sweet, do we have to leave immediately?'

'We've got three minutes.'

'That's probably enough time...'

Behind the rock, Arnie and Sally pause momentarily from their coupling. Sally strains her ears. 'What's that?'

'Probably vild boars, it's zee rutting season round here.'


*Later that afternoon*


The four of them have reached a small clearing in the heart of a forest.

'This place is well hidden, Arnie. I think we'll be safe here.'

'Yeah, I don't think anyone else knows about it. I come here when I need to exfoliate.'

'Ummm.'

'Are you alright, Norma?'

'What? Oh, yes – I think I just swallowed a little fly.'

Sally notices that Norma is looking worried, so she tries to cheer her up.'

'Jake's got a plan.'

'Have I?'

Jake sees Norma's disappointment. He's grown very fond of her in the short period of time that he has known her – sometimes it only takes three minutes to fall in love. He tries to reassure her.

'I mean – have *I* got a plan – wait until you hear it!'

Jake closes his eyes as if deep in thought, when he opens them, he sees three pairs of eyes staring intently at him.

*'I've even managed to convince Sally and Arnie, so that's a good sign, I suppose.'*

He closes his eyes again as if considering all the angles.

'Hmmm, yes, that will work.'

'What is it?'

'What's what?'

'The plan.'

'The plan, oh yes – I need to get into that Top Secret Laboratory.'

'Pops always keeps it locked.'

Jake pulls out a set of skeleton keys from his attaché case.

'I'm trained to open any lock. I'll go in under cover of the night.'

'Pops has a twenty-four hour alarm system.'

Jake pulls out a small black box from his attaché case.

'I'm trained to disable any security system. – If all goes according to plan, I'll be in and out of there in less than ten minutes and no one will be any the wiser.'

'Are you going to set off lots of explosives?'

'Why would I want to do that?'

'Well, they do it in all the films I've seen. They have those ones where they pull out a wire and wrap it around a pole or something. Have you not got any of those in your attaché case?'

Jake flips open his case. 'Let's see – almonds, moisturizer,

Swiss Army knife – the expensive one with a compass – no – no explosives in here. I must have forgotten to pack them.'
Norma looks hurt, Jake immediately regrets being so flippant.

'It might have been a good idea, Norma, but for this mission, stealth is the name of the game. I want to be in and out like a ghost.'

'That's a shame because I've got some fireworks left from the Fourth of July.'

'Hang on, that's a great idea, Norma. You could set them off to create a diversion.'

'That's what I was thinking!'

Jake is happy to see that Norma is now smiling. 'Shall we synchronize our watches?'

'That's another great idea, Norma. I don't know what I'd do without you.'

Norma can't help showing her pride, she snuggles up to Jake.

'Now all we have to do is wait until nightfall.'

Jake looks into his case. 'Is anyone hungry? - I only ask because I'm running out of almonds.'

'I haf some food in my rucksack.'

'That's great, Arnie, what is it?'

'Corn.'

Sally snuggles up to Arnie. 'My favorite, you're so clever, Arnie.'

# Chapter Fifteen

# Sally and Norma are Bonding

*Nightfall*

Jake is in the Top-Secret Laboratory, unfortunately he's not the only one, Barney and Clyde are on lookout duty.

'So, you thought you could infiltrate your father's Top-Secret Laboratory without us noticing, huh? Well think again, Jake Poisson.'

'He's not my father.'

'The doctor is not your father, but I thought...'

An almighty bang reverberates through the building, followed by a juddering as the door to the Top-Secret Laboratory is violently kicked open. A barrage of corn ears peppers the walls, deafening the inhabitants. Fortunately, Jake is trained to distinguish voices through very loud background noises.

'Arnie!'

'Come vith me if you vont to live.'

Jake willingly follows Arnie through the corridors of the building. As Arnie uses his boot to disintegrate the outer door, Jake turns to him.

'We need some kind of transport - they'll be all over Sally's aunt's car.'

'I haf a motor sickle.'

Jake is about to ask about the others, but as the door crashes to the ground and the dust settles, an exploding rocket whistles past their ears and ricochets off the walls of the corridor, another one lights up the sky, revealing a dark shape in the corner of the courtyard.

'A Harley Davison – now that's what I call transport.'

Sally waves to him from the front of the sidecar, she has a satnav in her hand.

'Where to?'

As he jumps onto the pillion seat he gives her the directions.

'Your aunt's, Sally.'

'Ve'll be there before nightfall.'

'It's already nightfall.'

'Nightfall tomorrow, zis motor sickle may look good, but it iz wery slow.'

Norma leans over to Jake and whispers sweetly in his ear.

'Jake?'

'Yes?'

'Can I put the directions in next time?'

'Of course...'

Despite all Jake's training, the combination of the Harley's blown baffles echoing into the night air and the fireworks detonating in the night sky, means he doesn't hear a frantic voice calling from the half-demolished building.

'Jake, come back – there's something you need to know...'


Despite having to use the backroads, they make good time and arrive well before nightfall the next day, in fact, dawn is just breaking.

As they approach the surrounding area Jake turns to Sally.

'I must say, your aunt's house is in a nice spot. If it wasn't for that burnt out shell, the view would be breathtaking.'

'Yes – and the house looked nice too, before the explosion.'

'I've been thinking about that. I didn't want to worry you at the time, but you could have been right about the booby trap.

Do you think your aunt could have been involved in this in some way?'

'Jake, there are some things you need to know about my aunt.'

Sally glances over towards the other two, neither appears to be listening, but she's not prepared to take any chances.

'I'll tell you later.' She mouths to Jake.

As Arnie switches off the engine and coasts to a stop, Norma opens her eyes and stretches her limbs. She looks over at Jake.

'Are we here already, I must have dozed off?' She looks around.

'I think I recognize this place, I'm sure I came here a few times with Pops when I was little. It had a big house though, so maybe it's not the same place.'

'There was a large house here until a couple of days ago, look - it was over there.'

'Wow, that's gonna be some repo job.'

'Can you remember anything about your visits, Norma? It might help me figure out how your dad got involved in this affair.'

Norma nods pointedly in Sally's direction.

'I'll tell you later.' She mouths.

Three of them are taking their time, trying to shake off the effects of the journey, but Arnie is already striding off in the direction of the barn, Jake notices and begins to follow him. The women are discussing toilet arrangements - after much deliberation they decide to head for a suitably quiet spot.

After a bit of beating around the bushes they almost stumble down a hole.

'Look someone's dug a pit for us already. That's handy, I'm bursting.'

'So am I!'

Seconds later, they are both startled by Arnie's booming voice.

'Vot are you doing up there?'

'Our hats blew off and we're looking for them.'

They both giggle with embarrassment.

'Vell, I hope you find zem soon, because it's starting to rain out zere. In fact, it feels like eet's peezing it down.

Quickly' pulling up their panties, Sally and Norma head for the barn. Jake is following Arnie through a tunnel.

'Arnie, how did you know this tunnel was here?'

'I alzo came here ven I voz leedel.'

'If you don't mind me asking, Arnie, how did you get that accent?'

'Vot accent?'

'I recognize this place!'

Jake turns round to identify the voice and realizes both women have said it in unison.

'Zis tunnel eez blocked. All zat rain must haf caused zee roof to cave in.'

Sally and Norma try to look innocent.

'I think it's stopped raining now.'

'Vel it voz some kind of tropical downpour, wery vet and wery varm.'

'The weather round here can be very strange, I noticed that when I used to visit my aunt. I think it has its own micro-climate.'

'And eet zeemed to come from two directions.'

'Yes, it does that as well, it's something to do with the Gulf Stream.'

Norma is impressed with Sally's ability to look so innocent while telling such whoppers. Jake is impatient.

'I think we should be investigating this place for clues.'
'Yes sir!'
Both women make mock salutes.
'I vill try and clear zis tunnel vile you haf a look round.'
'Good plan – we'll see what's in the barn.'
As soon as they are back in the barn, Jake's military training takes over. 'I'll bring the Harley in here and hide it – we'll need a lookout.'
'Can I be lookout?'
'Of course, Norma, you climb up that ladder into the loft. Sally, you search down here first.'

Jake wheels in the motorbike and sidecar, removes their cases and starts to cover the Harley with hay. As he finishes, he sees Norma sliding gracefully down the ladder towards Sally.
'Sally, tell Jake there are some men out there – and they've got guns!'
'What do they look like?'
'Kind of silvery metallic with long barrels and...'
'I didn't mean the guns - I meant the men.'
'They all looked very similar, black suits, white shirts, black ties and sunglasses. Oh, and there was one woman, I couldn't see her very well. She was wearing a very short skirt in a lovely pastel lavender color. I couldn't see her face, do you think it could be that woman, the one who was going to let my try on...?'
'Candice?'
'Is that her name? I think she's the same size as I am, I'm sure her clothes would fit me.'
'Actually, I think she's a bit slimmer than you, Norma.'
Sally smiles innocently, Norma juts her breasts out. 'In some

areas, perhaps.'

Jake can sense an argument brewing and he's wondering how he can defuse it. He's relieved when Arnie distracts them.

'Come vith me if you vont to live.'

'Quick, follow Arnie – I'll guard the rear.'

Arnie, Sally and Norma set off down the tunnel, Jake follows, carrying the cases. They quickly reach the point where the tunnel had been blocked. Somehow Arnie has managed to clear the blockage and shore the walls up with timber.

'Arnie, that's a brilliant job!'

'If I'd had more time I could haf done it better, but eet vill do, I suppose. Vee need to go in zis direction.'

The tunnel splits into a number of directions, but Arnie seems to instinctively know the way and eventually they see daylight.

'What is this place, Arnie?'

'It's vere the doctor did his experiments on me.'

He kicks a door open. 'That's vere I leeved.'

As Arnie heads for the exit, three faces peer into the darkness.

'Good God!'

'It vos not zo bad. If I stood on my tippy-toes I could see out of zat vindow.'

Sally is shocked.

'And to think I was married to that fiend!'

'How could my father do something like that?'

Norma has tears in her eyes, Jake tries to hide his.

'Don't forget, I thought he was my father too.'

Jake wishes he could explore this rabbit warren further, but he knows it won't be long before Candice and her agents catch up with them. He closes the door.

'We can't stay here any longer.'

Once all four are out of the tunnel, Arnie ties a rope around a couple of the props and, with a casual tug, the entrance collapses.

'Zere are horses over zere.'

'Ooh, I love horses.'

'I've got a better idea, Arnie, bring that rope, please.'


On the highway Jake is driving, Arnie's in the front passenger seat and the two women are stretched out in the back.

'This old Chevy's running sweet as a nut since I gave it that lube job.'

'Ya, this was my favorite weehickle.'

'You've driven it, Arnie?'

'Ya.'

Jake waits for Arnie to elucidate, but it doesn't look as if he's going to be very forthcoming, so he decides to check in the rear-view mirror.

'Well, it doesn't appear as if we're being followed, so that's a good thing. I wonder what the top speed of this thing is'

'This one has the three hundred and forty-eight cubic centimeters wee eight. It's capable of producing three hundred and fourteen horsepower, top speed around von hundred and thirty miles an hour.'

'No shit!'

'I vouldn't adwise it though.'

'Why not?'

'Zee brakes don't verk.'

Jake decides to keep his speed down, he checks in his rear-view mirror again.

'What's that you're reading, Norma?'

'I found it in the barn.'

'Is it good?'

'It's very interesting.'

Sally looks across. 'Holy sh...'

'Oh yes, I saw a pile of those the first time I was in the barn. I'm beginning to wonder about your aunt, Sally.'

The journey goes smoothly, Jake is enjoying the power of the V8, Arnie is cracking walnuts with his bare hands and throwing them back to Sally. Norma is deeply engrossed in her magazine.

'Uh-uh.'

'What is it, Jake?'

'There's a roadblock ahead.'

'I can't see anything.'

'It's three miles up ahead, not visible to the naked eye, but I'm trained to sense these things.'

'Oh yes, it's coming up on my cell phone.'

'Well done, Sally. It's always a good idea to get confirmation.'

'Vot are ve going to do?'

'I've got an idea. Sally, take off your clothes.'

'I hardly think this is the time or place, Norma.'

'Just do it, we haven't got much time. Look, I'm doing it.'

Norma starts stripping off. Jake is trying to drive with one eye on the road and one on the mirror, while at the same time use engine breaking to slow them down.

'Arnie, have you still got that rope you used to pull us out of the fields?'

'Ya, it eez in zee trunk.'

'Good if I just pull this seat down - yes, I've got it.'

'Can you cut it in half.'

'Ya.'

They all watch in amazement as Arnie bites into it.

'Vot next.'

By this time Sally and Norma are both naked. Norma takes the rope and passes half to Sally. 'Wrap it round you like this. When we stop let me do the talking.'

'I hope you know what you're doing because we're approaching the roadblock now.'

As they pull up, two portly cops approach them.

'We've got reports of a stolen '59 Chevy which matches this description.'

'Oh no, officer, this is a late '58. You can tell by the longer tailfins.'

'I see, my apologies. What are you doing in these parts, anyway?'

'As you can see, we are heading for the Annual Bondage Exhibition in Indianapolis. We are the organizers, can we rely of your custom, gentlemen?'

Norma and Sally both twiddle with the ropes. By now the two drooling officers have moved to the rear of the car to get a better look and Norma passes the magazine to one of them.

'Because if you are, I'll leave some tickets at the reception desk.'

'Well, strangely enough, me and Dale here, were just discussing that, weren't we, Dale?'

'Weren't we, what?'

Dale is going cross-eyed trying to focus one eye on Sally's near naked body and the other eye Norma's completely naked body.

'We was considering going to that bondage thing. Just out of a legal interest, mind.'

Norma realizes her rope has slipped, she rearranges it, but fails to hide any of her modesty.

'Of course, we get a lot of policemen, it's a great excuse for tying people up and beating the sh...'

Sally quickly interrupts the conversation.

'I'll make sure they're VIP tickets.'

'Well, thank you very much, Miss. Now, I suppose you'd better get on your way, you don't want to miss the start, do you?'

'No, we don't, otherwise we'll get a spanking. Thank you, officers.'

Sally blows them a kiss as they drive off.'

'What lovely young ladies, Dale – now turn that radio off while I read this magazine.'

*Further down the highway.*

'That was a close shave.' Jake glances back at Norma, she's engrossed with her rope.

'Have you tried this one, Sally? It gives you a lovely warm feeling on your...'

'Sorry to interrupt, Norma, but I think the two of you should put some clothes on. There's a fleet of Apache helicopters with heat-seeking missiles within fifty miles of us, we need to find somewhere to hide.'

'How many iz zere?'

'Four.'

'How do you...?'

'Jake's been trained to recognize the sound of every type of military aircraft, haven't you, Jake?'

'I have, Sally, but I must admit, on this occasion I've been listening to Barney and Clyde's communication devices. I have an earphone in each ear, so my aircraft engine recognition's not so good at the minute. Judging by the messages being sent, I think they're closing in on us. I'm afraid we've run out of luck this time.'

'Turn left von hundred yards down zis road.'

'Zis, I mean this, dirt track?'

'Ya – now head for zat forest.'

The forest track is narrow and dark with numerous twists and turns.

'This is a good idea, Arnie, but they'll still be able to pick us up on their radars.'

'Stop here.'

Jake remembers the brakes don't work so he pulls on the handbrake and the Chevy skids into a ditch.

'Shit!'

'No vorries.'

Arnie jumps out of the car and runs into the forest.

*'The son of a bitch!'*

Jake doesn't like to use bad words in front of women, fortunately he just thought it and didn't say it out loud – even more so, because Arnie returns after a couple of minutes and frees them out of the ditch.

'Drive between zose trees – through zere, ya.'

As Jake carefully steers through the undergrowth, he begins to realize they are entering some sort of tunnel.

'Vait here.'

Once again, Arnie jumps out of the car. The other three occupants watch in amazement as he drags a number of large bushes across the entrance of the tunnel to cover their tracks. As he climbs back into the car Sally leans forward and kisses him on his cheek.

'Oh, Arnie, you're so strong.'

'It vos nossink.'

Norma makes sure Sally is watching before leaning forward and kissing Jake on his cheek.

'Oh, Jake, you're such a good driver.'

'The four of us make a good team.'

'Ya.'

Jake lets the car slide down into the tunnel until he thinks they are far enough in to avoid any radar searches.

'Where is this place, Arnie?'

'Ven I vos younger I leeved here for a vile.'

'You lived in this cave?'

'Ya, it vos originally a gold mine, but I conwerted eet into liwing accommodation. Zere iz a bedroom along zat corridor weeth an en suite and further down eez another bedroom

158

and a family bathroom. I did zat in case I got guests.'
'And did you get any?'
'I haf now.'
He smiles at Jake. Jake feels the tears welling up inside him
again. One drop rolls down his left cheek.
*'Thank God Harry Pusey's not here to see this.'* He thinks.
'It must have taken you ages to build this.'
'Ya, it took over three weeks because I had to cut down all
the lumber myself by hand. Zere eez no Home Depot near
here.'

Arnie has waited a long time to entertain and he delights in
showing the others the smokeless barbeque, the chocolate
fountain and his supplies of tinned food. After their first real
meal in days, Arnie dims the paraffin lamps and pours the
drinks.
'It's getting late, what are the sleeping arrangements, Arnie.'
'Vell, Jake – I thought you and me could sleep in von bed
and the two vimmen in zee other.'
'Really?'
Arnie laughs.
'No...'

# Chapter Sixteen

# Family Resemblances

*Three days later*

Jake hears a knock on the door.

'Breakfast in zirty minutes, Jake, iz zat okay?'

'Sure thing, Arnie, thanks. I think it's safe to get out of bed now, Norma, they'll have given up the search by now.'

'Okay, I'll untie you, Mr. Bell.'

'You can call me Jake - I think we know each other well enough by now.'

'I suppose so, Mr. Bell – do you think your bride and Arnie will be on first name terms by now?'

'Norma, there are some things I've been trying to tell you.'

'I know, it's a shame we didn't have more time.'

'Yeah, well I don't want to get off on the wrong foot with you, Norma, so while you're undoing my bindings I'll tell you the most urgent things.'

'I'm all ears.'

Norma was busy untying the rope from Jake's ankles and as she bent over him, he could see that she definitely was *not* all ears.

'My name's not Jake Bell, it's Jake Poisson, but more importantly, Sally's not my bride, she's not even my wife. She is married to your father, remember?'

'Well, I thought maybe you do things differently in New York.'

'In the car you said you had something to tell me, what was

it, Norma?'

'Oh, it's probably nothing.'

Someone is tapping at the door.

'Arnie's washed and ironed your clothes, I'll leave them outside your door, he's cooking your breakfast now, it will be ready in ten minutes.'

'Thanks, Sally – we'll be there soon.'

Jake sees Norma's worried expression.

'Is it something to do with Sally?'

Putting her finger to her lips, she whispers.

'No, it's something I've remembered - I'll tell you later. Now, let's get showered together, it'll save time.'


*At the breakfast table*


'These eggs are lovely, Arnie, where did you get them?'

'I haf my own cowey ov grouses. Zey vere running vild ven I built zis place.'

'Wow, there's not many people who can say they have their own covey of grouse.'

Arnie beams with pride. Jake turns to Sally.

'Sally, do you know where your aunt is at present?'

'Which one?'

'The one who's house burnt down.'

'Oh, Auntie Rea, she could be anywhere.'

'But do you have any idea where she is *likely* to be, could you not phone her?'

'I suppose so.'

'Good, that would be a start.'

'What do you want me to say?'

161

'Just say you haven't seen her for a while, so you just
wondered what she was up to – just chit-chat, don't give
anything away.'
'What should I not give away?'
'Well, that her house has been burnt down, for a start, that
we found her underground dungeons, or whatever they are,
that we found her stash of bondage magazines, that we are
trying to find her whereabouts...'
'Okay.'
Sally picks up her cell phone.
'Auntie Rea? – Yes, I'm fine – no, nothing exciting – has it?
That's terrible – you're standing outside it now? – Must go -
bye, Auntie Rea.'
Sally puts her cell phone down and turns to Jake.
'Did I give anything away?'
'No, you were great, where is she?'
'She's outside the house we burnt down.'
'Well, strictly speaking, it wasn't us – it was the helicopter -
at least she's not far away - let's go.'

It only takes three hours for them reach what was left of the
house, Sally rushes up to her aunt.
'Ah, Sally, am I pleased to see you! As you can see, I'm
having to move into the barn until my house is rebuilt, can
you give me a hand with these fish, please?'
The other three dismount from the Harley.
'You've brought some friends with you, how nice! Are you
going to introduce us?'
'This is Ja...'
Jake grips Sally by the shoulder, being careful not to hurt her
in any way.
'Sally, step aside - I don't think I need to be introduced – say

your prayers, you've got one minute to save your skin.'
Jake takes the aquarium from Sally.
 'That's too heavy for you to carry, you must be tired after your three days in bed.'
He holds it up and studies the contents.
 'Charlie, you're not dead!'  He turns to Sally's aunt.
 'That swine Colonel Wilde thought he could break me by playing mind games, but I'm made of stronger stuff. I'm trained to deal with the mental torment of losing a favorite fish.'
 'Jake, have you gone mad? Why would you want to kill Auntie Rea – and why would she have your fish?'
 'Would you like to tell her Auntie Rea, or should I say – Georgette!'
 'Jake, I saw Georgette in court, I would have known if it was Auntie Rea.'
 'Your aunt is a master of disguise, only someone who is trained can tell. Besides, I've had intimate dealings with your aunt.'
 'Very intimate, how's your...?'
 'We'll not go into that just now, if you don't mind – although I can recommend an excellent ointment, if you ever...'
 'I hope I never need it, you do realize, Jake, I did it for your benefit.'
 'Well, I'm beginning to wonder, but you've got a lot of explaining to do – for a start I'd like to know where my Porsche is.'
 'I stored it safely in my garage.'
 'Where's your garage?'
 'Attached to my house.'
 'Where's your house?'
 'You're looking at it...'

While this conversation has been going on, Norma has been wandering in and out of the barn, nonchalantly depositing magazines into the sidecar.

'I'm just tidying the place up for you, Auntie Rea. You'll need a bit space for your furniture.'

'Thank you, my dear. *Is it?* - Could it be? *It is!* - I could never forget that beautiful, angelic face, it is you, isn't it?

'I'm Norma, I used to visit here with Pops when I was younger.'

Tears roll down Auntie Rea's cheeks, she holds her arms out to Norma.

'My baby, I've missed you so much, Fox told me we had lost you, he told me you'd wandered off into a corn field, never to be seen again.'

Jake is talking to his fish, he turns to Georgette.

'I understand how you feel, I felt that way about Charlie – come on little fishees, let's find somewhere nice for you. You like a nice view, don't you? – Especially you, Charlie.'

He heads towards the barn, carefully cradling the aquarium, Sally follows him, keen to see what Arnie is up to. Norma wonders why Auntie Rea is holding her so tightly.

'I've missed you too, Auntie Rea.'

Auntie Rea a.k.a. Georgette whispers into Norma's ear, her voice barely audible.

'You don't understand, Norma, I'm not your aunt.'

'You're *not* my aunt?'

'No and I'm not Sally's aunt either. I'm just a close friend of her mother, Sally's always called me Auntie Rea since she was little.

'Well – who *are* you?'

I'm your *mother* – shhh!... Don't say anything, I'll explain everything later – we can't trust anyone.'

'How can I be sure you're my mother?'

'Just look at you, you're beautiful, that figure, your bone structure, your style in clothes. I love that micro-miniskirt by the way.'

Rea lifts up her own dress to display her shapely legs.

'We are two peas in a pod.'

'We can't trust anyone? We can trust Jake though.'

'Especially not Jake – not yet!'

'But, we're lovers.'

'There you go, further proof you take after me – I've always liked cock too.'

Norma takes a step back. Now that it's been mentioned, she can see the resemblance, Rea is still an attractive woman, but she must have been incredibly beautiful when she was younger and the other thing – well, that explains a lot.

'What do we do now, Mom?'

'Just act like you don't know anything, like me.'

'You don't know anything either?'

'No, I mean I'm acting like I don't know anything.'

'But you know everything?'

'Not quite, I don't know who or what caused my house to explode, but I have my suspicions. I intend to find out – and when I do!'

Jake has placed the aquarium in what he thinks is the best vantage point for it, he returns to Sally and Georgette.

'What are you two up to, plotting something devious?'

'No, we were just talking about women's things, weren't we Auntie Rea?'

'Yes, fashion, sex, things like that.'

'That's nice. I have to tell you, I came here to kill you, Rea.'

165

Jake was bluffing, of course.

'But I'm slowly beginning to piece together what happened and as a result I'm rapidly changing my opinion of you, if you tell me what I need to know, I'll help you in any way I can.'

'How can you help me, Jake?'

'There are people who think you know too much. I can protect you from them.'

'And why would you do that?'

'Because I love your daughter and I would hate to see her lose her mother so soon after finding her again.'

Rea and Norma looked stunned.

'Don't worry, your secret is safe with me.'

'But, how did you...?'

'I'm trained to recognize family resemblances, that's how I know that Arnie is my brother.'

'That explains a lot.'

'What's that, Norma?'

'Nothing.'

'I'd like to help you, Jake, but it's too dangerous. I don't know who I can trust.'

'Georgette, there must be...'

'There is, I've written down what I know in Archi. All the information you need is in there. It's coded though, so you may not...'

'Just let me worry about that. Is there nothing you can tell me now?'

'You need to work it out for yourself, Jake. All I can do is point you in the right direction. You are the only one who can save us all, and only when you realize that yourself – do you understand?'

'I'm beginning to, but...'

'You must go now, Jake - I can give you one thing. When the

time is right you will know how to use it, come here.'

Rea pulls him towards her, loosens his belt and inserts something into his boxers, having a long fondle as she does so.

'Mom!'

Rea's face is a picture of innocence.

'I had to make sure the lanyard was secure. We wouldn't want it to drop out, would we?'

Norma looks down at Jake's crotch.

'By the look of it, you've strangled it.'

'I could loosen it off a little?'

'No, Mom. I think that's enough help for one day.'

'Talking of choppers, did you know Fox has one hidden in an underground hangar in that cornfield over there?'

'How did Fox get his hands on a chopper?'

'As you know, Fox likes a bargain and it was going cheap. It was a prototype, apparently only two of them were ever made, because no one could fly them.'

'Damn, that sounds perfect, but I would need the keys.'

'I have them, Fox had them put on a chain for me as a present after a particularly good session. The chain is around my neck, help yourself, Jake.'

Jake's hand is almost down Rea's blouse when Norma slaps it.

'Just pass it to him, Mom, that lanyard's giving him enough grief as it is.'

Jake takes the keys. 'We'd better go, look after Charlie for me, Rea.'

As they go to find the others, Norma whispers to Jake. 'Do you know what Archi is?'

'It's a language, spoken by a very small number of people.'

'Can you speak it?'

'Like a native, I lived with them for three months when our sub ran aground in the Caspian Sea.'
'What were you doing in a submarine in the Caspian Sea?'
'It was a sightseeing tour arranged by Club 18-30.'

# Chapter Seventeen

## Debriefing

*Three hours later*

'I wish we hadn't had to leave Auntie Rea on her own like that.'

'I know what you mean, Sally, but it's for her own safety.'

'Norma's right, Sally. If they knew we were there with her, she'd have been a target. Besides, Arnie is going to stay with her until the builders arrive – tomorrow, I think. If he makes good time on his Harley, he should rendezvous with us within the week.'

'Who are they, Jake?'

'I was hoping you might be able to help me there, Sally. For the past two years or so, I've been out of action, so to speak, I have my suspicions, but I need concrete evidence.'

Norma looks as if she's asleep, Sally whispers to Jake. 'I feel nervous without Arnie, can I sleep in the same bed as you two tonight?'

As Jake considers her request, he finds the lanyard cutting into him. He shifts in his seat to ease the discomfort, causing the helicopter to drop sharply. Norma opens her eyes, smiles and nods to Sally. Jake's eyes water with the pain, the chopper lifts sharply and Norma drifts off to sleep again.

'Sally, you know you said your job was to watch me?'

'Yes.'

'I want you to think back to when you were asked to do it, try and remember everyone involved and what each person said and did.'

'I can do better than that, Jake – I kept a diary.'

Jake is trying his best to maintain a degree of optimism. His dealings with Rea, Georgette, or whatever guise she was in, do not fill him with a great deal of confidence, but he is hoping that the combination of Auntie Rea's coded manuscript, Sally's diary and the fact that his memory is improving by the hour, will help him unlock the mysterious dealings of the Blowman Corporation and its relationship with the Dan Corleone Agency.

'Is it in a safe place?'

'Yes.'

'Buckle up, both of you, we're coming in to land.'

The hangar doors are partially closed so Jake slows down to five hundred knots, once inside he slams on the anchors, activates the parachute and reverses the engine thrust. As the women desperately huddle together, in an effort to shield themselves from what appears to be an imminent collision, the chopper screeches to a halt narrowly missing a reinforced concrete wall. Jake looks over at Sally and Norma's tightly entwined bodies.

'You can open your eyes now, ladies. The eagle has landed.'

As the women reluctantly untangle themselves, trying not to look in the direction of the wall, they glimpse Jake unbuckle himself, pull a tape measure out of his pocket, and effortlessly leap out of the cockpit. He makes a quick measurement.

'I must be getting rusty, I'm normally within three feet and if I'm right this tape reads one meter.'

His comment is wasted on Norma and Sally. They had both

agreed on how to spend their last moments together and the fact that Jake had somehow miraculously saved them from an untimely end, was not going to change their plans.

'Don't stop, Sally, it's so close...' Jake overhears the last part of Norma's plea.

'No, not really, I'm a little disappointed, another couple of inches and I'd be happier.'

Sally tries to stifle a giggle. As she reaches her destination, Norma tries to stifle a moan.

### Inside the base

Jake knows the layout of the base better than any other person alive, he alone, was responsible for designing the elaborate maze of secret passageways and hidden staircases. Leading Norma and Sally through the rabbit warren, he outlines his plans. Peering through a spyhole, he turns to them.

'That's the general's secretary – I'm going to interrogate her - I want to know who's responsible for sabotaging my chopper.'

'Can I interrogate her, Jake?'

'Are you sure, Norma, do you know what to do?'

'Yes - please, Jake - I've read up on it.'

Jake is reticent, but Norma's eager, pleading expression persuades him to change his mind – that, and the fact that has just spent three days in bed with her, convinces him that she is capable of anything.

Five minutes later, Jake beckons Sally towards a second peephole.

'There's your mark, I'll introduce you – you do the rest.'

Jake silently slides open a hidden panel enabling him and Sally to surreptitiously enter the room.

'Whaaa...'

His eyes wide open with fear, a bead of sweat runs down the General's face.

'Drum, what a pleasure. I didn't expect to see you so soon – and who is this lovely lady accompanying you?'

'You seem a little nervous, Snake, is there a reason for that?'

'No, no! – No reason at all – you took me by surprise – that's all!'

'Well then, you can relax, Snake. My secretary has something which I think you will enjoy. Meanwhile, I have something I need to do, I'll leave you in her capable hands. I'll be back in ten...?'

Sally gives a little shake of her head.

'Fifteen?' Sally nods.

'Fifteen minutes it is, then.'

Sally undoes the top buttons of her blouse, wiggling her backside provocatively as she does so. The general's body quivers with excitement as she opens her handbag and takes out the machine. By the time his pitiful, muffled screams reverberate around the room, Jake has long gone.

Jake backtracks through the passageway. He checks on Norma's progress. 'Does she know anything?'

'She knows which side her bread is buttered on, that's why she's with the general, but that's about all she knows. I've interrogated her thoroughly – we'll get nothing else from her.'

The girl is securely bound to a chair. Jake studies every inch of her naked torso very carefully, he can see no visible marks of any description, but there's no harm in checking a second time.

'Very impressive.'

'She is.'

'I meant your interrogation technique, Norma.'

'I've been studying auntie Rea's magazines. Sometimes you want to leave marks, sometimes you don't – I chose not to this time.'

Jake was impressed with Norma's aptitude for this line of work. He notices a half-filled wine glass on the desk, and takes a sip.

'I'm thinking melons, peaches, perhaps a little rosebud.'

'Yes, I thought so too – full-bodied, perhaps a little over-ripe, but in the right places.

'I meant the wine, Norma.'

'Me too,' she lies. 'I don't recognize her, what's her name?'

'She said she was Randy.'

'She certainly looks it.'

'No, that was the name she gave me, her full name's Randolph. She's only worked here for a short while. She started off as a clerk, but was rapidly promoted to personal assistant to the general – even though she can't type! Who would...'

Jake is deep in thought, his gaze firmly fixed on the girl's legs.

*'There's something about those legs...'*

And then it comes to him, he turns to Norma.

'We need to get out of...'

'Randy!'

'Well, I must admit...'

He turns, realizing that the voice came from the direction of the door.

'I see you've met my sister.'

'Well, only briefly, I was about to untie her when you

interrupted me, Miss Virtue - Norma, you must have misunderstood my instructions, I said I hoped you would bond *with* her.'

Candice strides towards her sister and places a gun to her temple.

'No matter, she has served her purpose.'

Randolph flinches in fear.

'I don't want to distract you from your work, but I must say that's another beautiful skirt, Miss Virtue, do you think it would fit me?'

'It's Norma, isn't it?'

'Yes, how clever of you to remember me.'

'Oh, I remember *you* alright. What was the exact expression? - "A woman *her* age"?'

Norma's eyes widen in surprise.

'Oh yes, I've seen the CCTV footage from your office.'

'You were some distance away, and the windows were dirty.'

'No matter, after I've killed my sister, you're next – if only because nobody should allow their windows to get that dirty.'

'Woah, let's have no talk about killing, that's not nice. Besides, you'll be saying I'm third on the list.'

'Well, that is rich, coming from Jake Poisson aka Major Thomas Tom aka Chief Ironheart Custer aka, need I go on?'

'How...?'

'I've read your file from cover to cover, it's the thickest one in the agency, but it's not as thick as your head!'

Jake looks puzzled.

'I could never hurt you, Jake.'

Jake looks even more puzzled. Out the corner of his eye he sees Norma and Randolph shaking their heads and rolling their eyes. Norma speaks first.

'How could you not know, Jake? She has the hots for you.'

Randolph joins in.

'Yep, for two years she's being banging on at me about how she'd like to...'

'Shut up you. When I want your opinion, I'll ask for it.'

'Just because you're my much older, less attractive sister doesn't mean you can boss me about. Mom wouldn't like it.'

'Keep our mother out of this, and anyway, I'm more attractive, aren't I, Jake?'

Jake looks from one sister to the other and then back again.

'Well, I've never seen you without any...'

'We can soon solve that.'

Candice whips off her skirt and tosses it on the floor. Jake realizes why he never discovered the color of her panties.

'Mom told you about that, she said never go out without...'

'Randy, you're not my mother and you never will be.'

Randolph shrugs her shoulders and turns to Norma.

'Do you see what I've had to put up with all these years?'

Norma nods and turns to Candice, who is now removing the last vestiges of her clothing.

'Do you mind if I try this skirt on?'

'Not at all, Norma. I think you'll suit that color.'

They all turn as Sally enters the room.

'Does anyone know who Applepieface is?'

'That would be me – what are you three laughing at?'

'The general is in urgent need of band aids.'

As Randolph unties herself and rushes off to tend to the general, Candice turns to the others.

'She never was a movie-goer.'

As Randy returns to the room, the three women are busy trying on each other's clothes. Jake is in the corner, desperately trying to loosen the lanyard.

'I see you've found the liquor cabinet. Hey, that's my dress, Candy!'

'Obviously – it's far too big for me! I just wondered if the color suited me. What do you think, Jake? I mean, I know it's too big and far too long, but what do think about the color, does it go with my green eyes?'

Jake looks up, grateful that Candice is finally wearing something. He's on his sixth glass of wine now.

'Definitely, you've got the greenest, green eyes I've ever seen.' He slurs, as he dashes towards the bathroom.

Randy isn't satisfied.

'Well, you could've asked me, Sis.'

'You weren't here!'

Sally tries to diffuse the situation.

'How is Snake?'

'It's just an old war wound - he'll be fine. I've given him a sedative, but I must say I've never seen it as swollen as that, it was like a massive cucumb...'

To Sally's relief Candice interrupts her sister.

'Who or what, is Snake?'

By the time Jake returns from trying to empty his bladder, the women are all trying hard to control their laughter, particularly Randy.

'That's not what he told me!'

Four heads turn towards Jake and four concerned voices ask in unison.

'Are you alright, Jake?'

'Does anyone have a pair of scissors?'

The following morning four semi-clothed females are scattered around the room, recovering from the events of the previous day. Jake is leaning back on the only office chair, smoking a dubious-looking cigarette. Candice appraises him through the early morning mist and the smokey haze. She has to admit, even with his unkempt hair flattened to his head and dressed only in a crumpled, stained pair of boxers, he still looks damned good.

'That was great, we must do it again sometime, perhaps when the liquor cabinet gets restocked.'

Jake inhales deeply.

'That's a good idea, Candice – hopefully Snake will have replenished his secret stash by then.'

Candice nods in agreement. 'But first I need to trace your father.'

A voice comes under the desk, followed by Norma's head.

'My father?'

'No, his father – Fox.'

'He's my father!'

'So, he's your brother! – That's gross!'

'I'm not her brother.'

'Well, you're certainly not her sister - after last night I can vouch for that!'

'It's a long story, Candice – Fox found me in a spaceship.'

'That must be some good shit, Jake – give me a pull.'

Jake obliges. Sally's head now pops out from under the desk. She nudges Jake and he falls off his chair. She gives him her iciest of icy stares, but Jake is oblivious to it.

'What Jake means, is that Fox adopted him after he found

him in his workshop. He is not his real father.'

Norma's forceful nudge fails to revive Jake from his stupor. She wraps her arms around him possessively.

'I'm sorry to disappoint you, Candice, I hope you didn't get your hopes built up last night, but me and Jake are an item – aren't we, Jake?'

Sally gets to her feet and raises herself to her full five feet.

'And you can forget about Arnie, he's mine!'

Randy's barely audible voice pipes up from a cupboard in the furthest corner of the room.

'You can have the General.'

'No thanks, I'm not having my little sister's cast-offs.'

The look of disappointment on Candice's face is obvious and Sally takes pity on her.

'There's always my husband.'

'Your husband?'

'Fox.'

'Holy shit, what do you...?'

'It was only a marriage of convenience.'

'Why would I be interested in Fox?'

'He's very intelligent.'

Candice is not impressed.

'And he's good in bed - for his age.'

'I thought you said it was a marriage of convenience.'

'You know what they say. "When in Rome".'

'What's that got to do with anything?'

'That's where we had our honeymoon.'

'Ooh, I've always wanted to go to Rome, even so - I don't think...'

'He's very rich.'

'I must admit, I've only ever caught the odd glimpse of him, but he did look quite distinguished with the light behind him.'

A shadowy figure has entered the room undetected.
 'Well, well, well, what have we here? Looks like I've caught you with your pants down, Jake - *Jake?*'
Jake's body shows no signs of movement.
 'And why are the three of you all almost naked?'
At that moment, Randolph falls out of the cupboard.
 'My mistake, why are the four of you almost naked?'
Jake has come to his senses.
 'I can explain – I was checking them for bugs, man'
 'And why is the general naked and tied to a chair with his penis covered in band-aids?'
Randolph attempts to crawl back into the cupboard.
 'I can explain that– his penis was bleeding profusely.'
 'And why was the general's penis bleeding profusely?'
Sally is endeavoring to climb back under the desk.
 'I can explain that – I forgot my machine was on the highest setting when I used it on him.'
The shadowy stranger appears lost for words, eventually he turns to Candice.
 'Goddammit, Virtue, I'll see you in my office first thing tomorrow morning.  Now get out of my sight – and don't forget to take your belt with you.'
 'That's my skirt.'
Norma gives Candice a warning look and passes her something from under the desk.
 'No! That's my skirt, this is yours.'
The shadowy figure calls to his two henchmen.
 'You two, bring *him* and make sure he's securely fastened. He's as slippery as an eel.'

'Can we bring the ladies too?'

'It's tempting, but you've met my wife. What do you think she would say if I turned up with those three in tow?'

'I think she'd say.'

"Why have you brought three very attractive, almost naked, ladies into my house?"

'I think she'd say.' "What have you been up to?"

'Thanks for your incisive and informative comments men, but it was a hypothetical question – now get Poisson out of here!'

The henchmen bind Jake tightly and lead him away. 'What was that big word the boss used?'

'I think it means when you gets really cold.'

'Yeah, I suppose they would be, since they was almost naked.'

# Chapter Eighteen

# Arnie Hits Town

*The next day*

The two henchmen lead Jake into a darkened room, where a shadowy man sits at a desk. Candice Virtue stands by his side.

'I must say, Jake I didn't think I'd get you this easily – no way José – not in a million years – not even if...'

'I get the picture, you're happy to see me, but have you asked yourself why it was so easy?'

'Miss Virtue here, tells me she did a good job tiring you out. Oh, you look so disappointed, Jake. Don't tell me you didn't know. That's all it was to her – a job, nothing more.'

Jake shows no emotion, he keeps his eyes firmly fixed on the floor. Candice, on the other hand, finds it hard to control her feelings. The big man doesn't notice, he's too busy gloating.

'You don't need me anymore, Boss, do you? - I have an urgent hair appointment, my split ends are...'

'No, you go ahead, you've done a great job helping me to bring in the great Jake Poisson, the man everyone said was uncapturable.'

Jake looks up.

'Who said that? I never did.'

'Everyone else.'

'Fair comment.'

Candice secretly gives Jake a little smile of encouragement as she leaves, but there's no acknowledgement from Jake, she fights back a tear.

The shadowy man continues.
'So, Mr. Jake Poisson, finally I have you to myself – you're going to tell me everything you know, you're going to talk like a parrot.'
'You expect me to squawk?'
'No, Mr. Poisson, I expect you to lie.'
'Then - why...?
'Ha, Mr. Poisson, you are so naive, what do you think I have here?'
The Shadowy Man holds up a phial of clear liquid.
'I'm hoping it's gin and tonic, but since I can't see any ice and lime, I think I'm going to be disappointed.'
'I prefer lemon.'
'Next time try it with lime, or even a little mint. You won't want to go back.'
'Hmm, I'll give that a try -ha-ha, very clever, Mr. Poisson. I see what you did there, but you cannot distract me as easily as that. I am a professional.'
The Shadowy Man injects Jake with truth serum.
'The first thing I want to know, Mr. Poisson, can I call you Jake?'
'No.'
'By the time we're finished you'll be begging me to call you Jake.'
'Why?'
'Well, because, I mean, er, well, surely, you've seen the films, they always say that.'
'What films?'

'The...er...spy films and that sort of thing.'
'Name one.'
'Look, Mr. Poisson, I can't just think of one off the top of my head.'
'James Bond?'
'Yeah, there must be one of those where he said it.'
'Which one.'
'Can't I just call you Jake, it would be much easier.'
'Okay.'
'Ha, the truth serum is working, now where was I?'
'The first thing I want to know...'
'Oh yes, the first thing I want to know, to satisfy my curiosity, is how you ended up in a room with four naked ladies?'
'It wasn't the way it sounds.'
'Goddammit, I certainly hope not – I mean, good heavens man, from what I heard one of them was your sister and another one, your mother-in-law!'
'She's not my sister.'
'Fox is her father, isn't he?'
'Yes, but he's not mine.'
'How come?'
'He found me in a spaceship.'
'Goddammit – this truth serum is wearing off. There's no point persisting with this charade, you obviously have a much higher tolerance than anyone I've ever encountered.'

No one seems to have noticed an even shadowy-er person in the corner, probably because that person was in the shadows.
'You were warned, number two. Take your belongings – your contract is terminated – and take those two goons with you!'

Left alone with the very, very shadowy person, Jake fights hard to shake off the effects of the truth serum.

'How long have you been here?'
'I've been here since the start, as I told you when you were a child – you need to eat more carrots.'
'What's my childhood got to do with you?'
'Everything, Jake – I'm your father, I know everything about you.'
Jake appears stunned. He'd arranged this meeting, even to the point of allowing himself to be captured, but now he has to fully convince this man in front of him, that he has fallen for his lies, hook, line and sinker – otherwise his life and the lives of all his friends are in grave danger.
'I don't believe you – and even if you are my father, why would I want to talk to you? Fox is my father and he always will be. That makes you no relation, do you hear me? – NOTHING!'
'Jake, it's natural for you to feel that way and I understand why. I can't ask for your forgiveness, but if you give me a chance to explain...'
'Why should I listen to your lies? My whole family abandoned me as a child!'
'Jake, it wasn't like that, please...'
'Please listen to your *lies*?'

Jake's captor takes a syringe from the desk and injects himself. That's truth serum, Jake – I can't lie to you. I knew you were telling the truth about how you were found – now, please let me explain the full story.

Now that the figure has come out of the shadows, Jake can clearly assess his features. The resemblance is striking – if it

184

wasn't for the scar, the beard and the glass eye, he'd be a dead ringer. Jake might have fallen for it – if it hadn't been for his training.

'It is *you*, father – isn't it?

Jake's voice is cracking, his eyes watering, his breathing labored.

'It is, Jake - Now, how about a couple of vodkas?'

'I'd rather have a gin and tonic?'

'With ice and lime?'

'Of course.'

'I'll just buzz my secretary.'

He presses a button on his intercom.

'Bring us a vodka on ice and a gin and tonic.'

'With ice and lime?'

'Of course.'

Five minutes later the secretary enters the room. Jake has his back towards her and, due to his bonds, he is unable to turn round. He can, however, smell her perfume as she clumsily places the drinks on the desk. The amiable veneer of Jake's captor slips.

'That will be all – be more careful next time, you fool!'

Jake is now absolutely certain of two things...


*Meanwhile...*


Captain Pusey is on one side of Officer Crockett's hospital bed, Lieutenant Columbo on the other. The captain speaks first.

'For goodness' sake, Crockett, that was a new taser, how the hell did you manage to get it in that shape and in that position? I would have thought it was a physical impossibility – well, Crockett? Speak up, man!'

'I'm trying to, Cap'n. The doc said I had made medical history – the first man ever to have a taser inserted so far into his...'

'Okay, Crockett, I get the picture – what about you, Columbo – how do you account for that baton? It looks like someone's bitten a chunk out of it.'

'That was me, Cap'n, the thing told me it would deaden the pain.'

'And did it?'

'I don't think so - he was crying.'

'How do you know, Columbo? You were runnin' away, man.'

'Not running away, Crockett, tactical evasion. Rule number one in the Enemy Confrontation Manual- isn't that right, Captain?'

'Let's not go into that now, Columbo. I want to know what this thing was – and how this fiasco started.'

'It's not fair, Cap'n – I only stopped it because I wanted a closer look at its Harley and sidecar. It's the only one I need to fill my I Spy Book of Unusual Vehicles.'

'That doesn't explain why I'm sitting by your bedside in this hospital.'

'Well, Cap'n, when I approached the vehicle, I noticed it had an unusual cargo.'

'What was that?'

'Corn husks.'

'And there was something in the sidecar rubbing them on its body.'

'Go on?'

'Well, it was too big and strong to be human, it must have

been some kind of robot or alien or something because even on full strength my taser had no effect on it.'

'And then?'

'Well, Cap'n – the thing took my taser off me and shoved it right up my...'

'That was your fault, Geordie – you wouldn't stop.'

'Okay, I admit that and I wouldn't have minded so much – but it left my taser switched on.'

'The batteries will run out soon, Crockett – dry your eyes.'

Suddenly, Gonna Fly Now - the theme from Rocky - fills the room. All three men search for their cell phones.

'It's me – who the hell's ringing me when I'm consoling one of my men who's going to have an operation with only a three per cent chance of success?'

Crockett turns green.

'Don't worry, I'm going to have words with this bas...'

Crockett is now turning purple.

'WHO IS IT?– Oh, hello Jake, good to hear from you, how can I help you?'

'And it's good to hear from you HP, I wouldn't be talking to *Captain* Pusey, would I?'

'You most certainly would, you old son of a...'

'I was just wondering, Captain – any luck with that flasher case?'

'Yeah, there were two of them. You wouldn't believe what those perverts were up to – the old lady ID'ed one of them. I don't know how though – one perps face was a right mess. He looked as if he'd walked into a wall. I've told Crockett about that bloody taser before.'

'Did you find out anything about their backgrounds?

'Strange thing was, neither of them could remember

anything about the last couple of years - before that their memories were fine.'

'Good.'

'What was that, Chief?'

'I mean, good God - is there nothing these monsters won't do? Great job HP, you're keeping our streets safe.'

'Thanks for that, Chief. My men and I appreciate it. Oh, by the way, just a word of warning there's a maniacal alien on the loose. It's driving around on a Harley Davidson.'

'With a sidecar?'

'Yes.'

'It didn't, by any chance, have any corn husks with it, did it?'

'Yeah, do you know what it is, Jake?'

'No, but you know what these Harley guys are like.'

'True.'

Jake is about to hang up as the very, very shadowy person's secretary re-enters the room

'Oh, I'm sorry to disturb you, I didn't realize you were on your phone.'

Jake still has his back to the secretary.

'That's okay, I was just finishing, Olga.'

Olga rushes to Jake's seat.

'Oh my God – I can't believe it, it's been so long, I thought I'd never see you again, Jake!'

She frantically tries to undo his wrists.

'We must get these straps off you before he comes roun...'

Jake stands up. 'No need.'

Olga grabs him and kisses him passionately on the lips, she pauses briefly for breath, then resumes her embrace.

Eventually Jake manages to loosen her grasp a little.

'How long will the sedative last?'

'I gave him a triple dose so we should be safe for a while, but how did you know it was me, Jake?'

'I recognized your perfume – it's the one I bought you on our first date – it hasn't been in production for ten years, so I figured...'

'You were right, Jake. I've used it sparingly – just in case I ever saw you again, but how did you know about the sedative?'

'I recognized the smell – it's the sedative you always gave me when you had a headache.'

The man opposite groans.

'Do you think your father will be alright, Jake?'

'He's not my father.'

'But he... but I heard him saying he was.'

'I am absolutely certain. My father would never have insulted you like that, I only went along with his charade because it suited me. I now have a much better idea who my real father is.'

'I want to help you, Jake, but I need to know – why did you abandon me?'

'I never abandoned you, Olga. I left you a note.'

'I kept that note, Jake.'

She passes him a crumpled piece of paper.

*6 Margaritas*
*4 Sicilian*
*Large garlic bread*
*2 Diet Cokes*

'That's not the note!'

He fumbles around in his back pocket.

'Aha – I have it here.'

## My Dearest Olga

*I'll be a couple of hours late.*
*I have a big order to deliver.*

*Love, Jake*

'Have you been wearing the same trousers all this time?'

'Er, no – I've been doing a lot of to-ing and fro-ing recently and I've lost weight. I just pulled on the first pair that fitted me.'

'Well, I waited for over an hour and when you didn't return, I thought you'd left me, so I went back to Norway, had twins – Hansel and Greta and elocution lessons. Have you noticed that I say six now, not sex?'

'Yes, your diction is perfect.'

'So is yours, Jake, although it may just be those tight trousers. Oh, and I almost forgot, I completed a part-time PhD in Electrical Engineering and Quantum Physics, when the twins were young.'

'Where are the twins now?'

'I left them in Norway with my parents. I'm not one to brag about my children, but they're doing very well. One travels the world by private jet giving lectures on how to save the world and Greta has her own McDonald's franchise.'

'How old are the twins now?'

'They are both twelve.'

'Wow – time passes quickly!'

'It does, it's exactly twelve years and nine months since I last saw you, Jake – what does that tell you?'

'It tells me you're good at remembering dates.'

The man in the chair groans more loudly.

'We need to discuss this somewhere else, Olga.'

'We could meet at mine later, Jake. Could you make it for sex?'

'Do you mean six?'

'No.'

Fortunately for Jake, before he is able to consider the proposition, his phone rings.

'Yes, I heard, give me an hour – I'll meet you there.'

Jake turns to Olga.

'I'm afraid I can't make it tonight - give me your number and I'll get back to you. You'd better get out of here, it's no longer safe for you.'

Olga tries to hide her disappointment. She writes her number on the back of his hand, gives him one more lingering kiss and then, hastily, they both head out of the office before the shadowy man who claims to be Jake's father comes round. As they leave Olga hands Jake something.

'My attaché case! Where did you get it?'

'One of that shady man's henchmen had it with him when they captured you, I knew you had been in the Boy Scouts, so I guessed it might be yours.'

'That's great, but remember, Olga, I wasn't captured – I was infiltrating.'

'Oh yes, sorry, I forgot. Have you checked the contents?'

'Good idea, let's see – almonds, moisturizer, Georgette's code book, some kind of electrical thingy that I found inside a pile of magazines.'

'Can I have a look at that, Jake, please.'

'Well, just a quick look, because I think it may be important.'

'What kind of magazines were they, Jake?'

'Well, they were – it's hard to explain, they had...er...pictures of...er...'

191

'Were they bondage magazines?'

'No, no - 'course not...'

'They were, weren't they?'

'How did you know?'

'When I was completing my PhD in Electrical Engineering and Quantum Physics, I specialized in devices which would produce pain – for medicinal purposes, of course.'

'Of course.'

Jake looks appreciatively at Olga. Five minutes ago, he was absolutely certain he never wanted to see her again, now he's not so sure.

'I have been experimenting with rudimentary devices, I have a friend who had been running trials with one of my machines as a means of losing weight, unfortunately someone stole it before she could properly evaluate it.

'How does it work?'

'You don't want to know, really, – but she said the effect on the one volunteer she tried it on was amazing – if you want to know more, I can introduce you to her, Jake.'

Jake is starting to wonder whether he was rash to lower his certainty level.

'That won't be necessary, Olga – my interest is purely academic.'

Olga twirls the device around in her hand, holding it up to the light.

'But this – this is much more advanced than anything I could ever have hoped to produce. This is capable of transmitting the electrical impulses wirelessly in all directions. It's a game changer – but in the wrong hands, Jake – I couldn't begin to imagine!'

Jake hears a noise from the adjoining office.

'Neither could I!' He lies.

He takes the device from Olga and carefully returns it to his attaché case.

'Change of plans – you're coming with me – let's go!'

# Chapter Nineteen

# The Stakeout

Even though he'd been bound, blindfolded and gagged after he was taken from the general's office, Jake had sensed that they were heading towards Manhattan. Now that they are out on the street a cursory glance confirms his suspicions.
'Do you have a car, Olga?'
'No.'
'Good, follow me.'
Jake heads into the back streets of Chinatown, opening the door of a small shop, he ushers Olga inside.
'Wait here, Feng Shui will look after you – I'll be back in a minute.'
Jake disappears into the back of the shop. He bows to the owner and takes the out the device out of his attaché case

'Tai Chi, wǒ de péng you  nǐ kě wú kě yǐ bang wǒ zuò shí gè？'

Tai Chi studies the transmitter.
'I've never seen one as advanced as this, it may take longer than usual.'
'Two hours?'
'Certainly, since it is for you, my honorable friend.'
'Can you deliver them to this address?'
'With pleasure.'
'Duō xiè.'
Jake hurried types a message into his cell phone, bows to Tai Chi once more and returns to Olga. A young boy enters from the rear of the shop.
'Father, who was that?'

'That, Shar Pei, was the Gay Dragon.'

'The Gay Dragon, father – the man who...?'

'The very same one, my son.

'Father, may I please go and enter this momentous occasion into my diary?'

'You may, my son, after you have helped me make ten of these transmitters for that illustrious gentleman.'

Jake is back on the street again, moving swiftly and effortlessly. Olga is struggling to keep up with him.

'Jake, can you not slow down a little bit? I need to catch my breath.'

Slowing the pace, he turns to her.

'Tell me, Olga – how do you come to be working for that man.'

'Three months ago, when I got back here, I went to visit your mother.'

'Gloria?'

'Yes, I drove to her house to ask her where you were, but at the last minute I lost my nerve.'

'So - what did you do then?'

'I was about to drive off when your sister...'

'Liz?'

'Yes, she came out of the house with a man – the way she kissed him, I reckoned it was her boyfriend.'

'Not necessarily, what did he look like?'

'The bearded one off Scooby Doo – what's wrong, Jake, you look disappointed?'

'Nothing, I just got my hopes built up – that's all.'

'Oh, so anyway, they drove off and I followed them.'

'And what happened then?'

'He dropped your sister off and then he went into that man's office.'

'What is that man's name?'

'I never knew, everyone just referred to him as 'The Boss', I hardly ever saw him. I just got the job there a week ago in the hope that I would find you. I had tried other ways – someone mentioned something about Poisson Dating, so I signed up there, as an alias, of course, but I had no luck.'

.'I can get you a discount.'

'No need to – I've found you, silly!'

'Oh look, Olga, we're there – down here!'

Jake leads her down some stairs and onto a subway platform. They make it onto the train just as the doors close. Three stops later, he whispers to Olga.

'I'm getting off at the next stop – don't get off until the Brooklyn Bridge – City Hall station. Wait under the mosaic.'

'Which one?'

'The one which says Brooklyn Bridge – do you know it?'

'Yes.'

Olga grabs Jake's arm. 'I'm frightened, Jake – there were some nasty looking men working for him, will you...?'

'I'll be fine - *I hope!*' Jake thinks to himself.

Jake is off the train now. He waits until Olga is out of sight, then dials a number on his cell phone.

'The bait has been taken - you know what to do.'

## Thirty minutes later

Sitting on the bench reading a newspaper, the man seems like any other bored traveler, apart from his habit of occasionally looking up towards the far end of the platform. He is doing just that when an attractive young woman bends down in front of him on the pretext of picking up something she has dropped. One minute later, she is at the end of the platform and he is sleeping peacefully, oblivious to the hustle and bustle going on around him.

Meanwhile, Olga is waiting nervously beneath the Brooklyn mosaic. Suddenly she feels a hand gripping her arm tightly.
'Come with me – don't look back!'
'Whaaa...!'
'Jake sent me.'
Olga couldn't resist, even if she wanted to – the grip was too strong, the woman's stride too urgent.
'Where are we going?'
'All in good time – relax, just act as if we are on a shopping trip.'
'Are we?'
'Well, there's a nice pair of shoes in Bentley's that I wouldn't mind trying on, but I don't think Jake would like it – perhaps we could go there on Saturday.'
'Will it not be busy at the weekend?'
'Umm, it could be, maybe we should leave it until next week.'

The shared train ride is short; with the two women laughing and chatting as if they were old friends, as they step onto the platform and hurry to the escalator, they are unaware of the commotion behind them.

'Call the guard, I think he may have had some kind of seizure, he just seemed to collapse.'

'He might have hit his head when he fell.'

'There's no blood, maybe, he's just fainted.'

'Did you see it happen?'

'No, I didn't see anything.'

None of the five or six observers noticed a man with an attaché case strolling nonchalantly towards the stairs.

*Fifteen minutes later*

Jake greets the two women as they enter the room.

'Come in Olga, let me introduce you to the others.'

Although Jake appears casual and carefree, he is watching the reactions of every single person in the room.

'This is Norma and those two over there are Lars and Sven – and of course, you've already met Candice.'

Olga just nods, but Jake is aware of her uneasiness because he is trained to recognize furtive glances.

'I'm afraid we need to search you, Olga. I'm sure you understand – it's for your own protection.'

'Of course - are you going to do it, Jake? – Where's the bathroom?'

Norma looks indignantly at Olga and then expectantly towards Jake.

'Jake...?'

'Of course, Norma.'

He turns to Olga.

'Norma performs all our searches; she's trained in ABSP.'

'What's that?'

'Advanced Body Search Procedures.'

Norma beams with pride, Sven and Lars pat their pockets as if there may be something in them. Norma smiles and shakes her head.

'Not this time, boys.'

Jake surveys the room for the first time, after giving it a once-over he phones Sally.

'Sally, I must say what a brilliant idea it was to rent this office above Starbucks. It's safe for you and Arnie to come up now – any chance you could bring coffees? I know they won't be as nice as yours, but these are desperate times – oh, and...'

'Bagels?'

'That would be nice.'

Sven and Lars wait expectantly for Jake's instructions.

'Okay, Sven, you keep an eye on the entrance to my office – Lars, you set up the surveillance equipment. By the way, it's great to have you back. I must say, you both played your parts brilliantly.'

'It's good to be back. We both had MESH and that was bad enough, but we knew that you would be the only person brave enough to go through MESH+ - that must have been hell. Was it as bad as when you had to drag the two of us five miles through that minefield?'

'It wasn't particularly nice - I must admit and it's taken longer than I expected. But I'm almost fully recovered now and I've got you two and Sally and Candice to thank for that - oh, and someone who goes by the name of Georgette. Have either of you met her?'

Both Sven and Lars look sheepish. Sven pretends to be checking on the proceedings outside and Lars appears to be engrossed with the lens of his camera.

'It's all set up, Jake. I have sight and sound and I'm recording every moment.'

'Good work, Lars – by the way, you never said whether you've met Georgette.'

'Oh look, here's Sally and Arnie with the coffees – bagels, too! Could you bring mine over here please, Sally? I have to adjust this lens.'

Jake takes a tray off Arnie who is carrying one in each hand and one in his teeth.

'Wow, that's a nice selection of bagels, Sally – and what's that strapped to Arnie's leg?'

'Corns, Arnie found out that the grocery store next door just throws them out if they're past their sell by date, can you believe that?'

Jake can, but he doesn't like to say, neither does he want to mention the teeth marks on the tray. While the rest of them tuck into the coffee and bagels, Arnie strips down to his boxers and starts rubbing himself down with the corn husks.

'Zees are wery gut, nice and rough.'

Norma rejoins them. 'Do we have any, ooh, can I borrow some of these leaves please, Arnie? – You wouldn't believe how rough Olga's skin is.'

'Can I have zem back after you haf finished?'

Lars looks at Arnie pleadingly.

'Can we have one too?'

'Vitch iz eet, von or two?'

'One will do, we'll split it.'

'Okay, I like you two, you haf nice names, Swen and Larz. I am Arnie – I am Jake's brudder.'
Sven and Lars look stunned.
'It's a long story, I'll explain later. Just keep your eyes peeled.'
'Gotcha, Jake, what are you going to do?'
'I suppose I'd better check on Norma and Olga.'


*Fifteen minutes later*


Jake returns, his face covered in a mixture of water and sweat.
'That took a while, but it was worth it.'
He holds up a small, shiny object.
'A tracking device, Jake?'
'Yeah.'
'That's bad news.'
'Yep, but the good news is Olga's skin is much smoother – I've kept what's left of the leaves for you.'
He throws one at Lars, who promptly splits it and hands half to Sven, the rest he gives to Arnie.
Jake watches Sven and Lars both sniff theirs and lovingly place them in the pockets of their jeans. He turns to Arnie who is vigorously rubbing his bare torso with his supply.

'WHAT THE...!'

As if in slow motion, Sven and Lars are thrown against the wall. There is a space where the door was and a door where Arnie was. Arnie has been shunted a few inches back, but he

201

seems unruffled – apart from a few splinters in his hair and a couple of leaves laminated to his chest.

'Vot vos zat?'

'They're on to us, Arnie – we've had it.'

'Not yet, bro!'

Arnie steps out of his Y fronts. Placing a cob inside them, he fires it down the stairs. A loud scream echoes from the stairway, followed by a series of thuds and then a chorus of groans. Arnie darts down the stairs and returns with a comatose body under each arm.

'Drop them in that corner please, Arnie. I'll interrogate them later.'

Hearing the commotion, Norma rushes in, closely followed by Olga, who is clad only in a towel.

Olga makes a beeline for Arnie.

'I don't think we've been introduced.'

'I'm Arnie – Jake's brudder.'

Olga appraises Arnie from head to toe and back again - but not going up as far as his head on the return viewing.

'Hmmm, I can see there are some similarities. You seem to have some debris on you, let me rub it off.'

'I'll do that!'

Sally whips the towel off Olga and starts cleaning Arnie.

'Do you have any debris on your body, Jake?'

'I don't think so, Norma.'

'Well, if you find any, can I wipe it off?'

'Of course.'

'I think you can give Olga her towel back now, Sally – Sven and Lars, are you two okay?'

Neither man pays any attention, they are too busy supervising.

'Wait, Sally - there's a bit left on his left shoulder, it's only small but it could aggravate.'
'That's true, Sven.'

'And there's a little sliver under his chin.'
'Well spotted, Lars.'
.'Are you two monitoring any coming and goings?'
'Of course, Jake we're professionals – remember?'
'Then why is that camera pointed at Olga?'
'Oh, I didn't realize, it's okay though, it's only a backup.'
'That's alright then, but keep an eye on that pavement – these two have regained consciousness, I need to deal with them.'

Candice has been sitting filing her nails and practicing crossing her legs provocatively.
'Hello! – I'm over *here* – anyone remember *me*?'
'I'm so sorry, Candice, there was a little bit of a distraction going on there. Would you like a bagel?'
'Yes please, but that's not why I'm trying to attract your attention.'
Jake takes a tray of bagels and coffees over to Candice. Instinctively Jake knows Candice wants to convey something to him privately. He leans towards her with the tray, keeping his voice low.
'I recommend the sprouted grain.'
'I know how to deal with those men.'
'Yes, a wise choice, Candice, an espresso will complement the flavor perfectly.'
Jake places the tray on a desk and addresses them all.
'We don't have a lot of time. Sven and Lars, you two take it in turns to keep watch for anything unusual going on out there. Sally – go down and into our office and do a last-

minute check on the monitoring equipment and then, once Olga is dressed, help Arnie watch over her, I don't expect we'll have any more visitors, but you never know.'
Jake gestures towards the two men in the corner.

'Candice and I will take care of these two.'
Jake notices the look of disappointment on Norma's face.
'Norma, when you've finished helping Olga, would you practice your search techniques on Sven and Lars? If things go as I expect, we will need all your expertise very soon.'
Jake notices the beaming smiles all round and compliments himself on his diplomacy. Then he reminds himself.
*'Don't get too complacent, Jake, you've a long night ahead of you.'*

Just as Jake and Candice are leading the two men to the interrogation storeroom there is a knock on the door – at least there would have been if the door had been in place.
'You get it, Jake – I'll start the interrogation.'
A young boy bows respectfully to Jake.
'O illustrious one, I am Shar Pei, my father Tai Chi has ordered me to deliver this package to you.'
'Thank you Shar Pei, tell your father I am honored to call him a friend.'
'Oh no, legendary one, it is us who are honored, but I would ask a favor if I may?'
'Anything, Shar Pei.'
'I have taken the liberty of bringing a permanent marker with me, would you indulge me with your autograph on my person?'
'Sure thing – where?'
'On my forehead, then I will never wash my face again.'
Jake takes the pen and starts writing -

'I've run out of brow, come back when you're older and I'll finish it off.'
Shar Pei bows again and takes his leave, glowing with pride.

As Jake reaches the storeroom, he can see that Candice has already started. Both men are spread-eagled over the desk, their trousers round their ankles. Candice is testing out the flexibility of a variety of straps, rods and canes, carefully bending them and swishing them through the air.

'As I'm sure you already know, Jake, the only way to remove the effects of the mind control is by applying fear and pain. That's why it took so long to free you. You have no fear, do you?'
Jake is wondering where Candice's line of questioning is leading.

'And you don't feel pain either, do you?'
Candice swishes a particularly thin metal rod. Jake is now *worrying* about where Candice's line of questioning is leading.

'Nope, definitely no point trying that out on me. It would be a complete waste of time, I don't know what pain is - if you feel that these men need it, though...'
As Candice pulls her arm back and takes aim, Sally opens the door. Her eyes widen in amazement.

The interruption puts Candice off her stroke and the rod crashes down onto the desk, narrowly missing the quivering buttocks of one of the men.
'Jake, can I speak to you?'
'Of course, Sally - I'll be back in a minute, Candice.'

Jake joins Sally outside the storeroom.

'I've brought my diary for you – oh, and I have my machine.'

'Thanks, Sally.

Jake knocks on the storeroom door.

'Yes?'

'I'm coming in – hold your fire!'

Jake is relieved to see that Candice has not yet started her interrogation.

'I can save you some effort, Candice. I have a machine here that will perform...'

'It really is no trouble – besides, I need the exercise.'

Candice brings the rod down swiftly on left buttock of one man and the right buttock of the other one, both scream in unison.

'See? I could go on like this all day.'

.'That's impressive, but is it effective?'

'I'll check.'

She prods the rod up the nearest man's backside.

'You - what is your name?'

'Aaargh - I don't remember!'

The other man desperately, but unsuccessfully, tries to avoid the rod.

'His name's Curly, but I've forgotten mine. Does that mean I'm cured?'

Jake shakes his head.

'I admire your evasive tactics, but I'm not convinced, besides I need to try out this machine, go and get Olga for me, please.'

'I'm sure that if I had a couple of hours...'

'You're probably right, Candice, but, unfortunately, we don't have that much time.'

As Candice heads off to find Olga, the two men plead with Jake.

'Please, Jake, set us free – we were only obeying orders.'

'Who gave you those orders?'

'We can't tell you – we'll be killed.'

'In that case I can't help.'

'Wait...wait...it was...'

At that point Candice returns with Olga.'

'Tell me!'

'We don't remember, do we Curley?'

'No, we has forgotten.'

'We'll see – Candice, flip them over.'

'That's my machine, where did you get it?'

'I have my sources, Olga - what I want to know is, can you get these things to work together?'

Jake shows her the machine and the transmitter.

'I can try, but I can't guarantee the safety – if there's an overload anything could happen.'

'If it doesn't work, we can always revert to Candice's method.'

Candice flexes one of the canes, Olga's face lights up.

'Maybe we should use Candice's method first.'

Both men groan, Jake's buttocks clench spontaneously, as he remembers his first meeting with Georgette. He shakes his head and offers her the equipment. Olga reluctantly takes them, deftly attaches wires from one to the other, twiddles a few knobs and returns the equipment to Jake.

'It's ready – just press that button.'

'This one?'

'Yes -oh *yes*!'

Candice and Olga stand back in admiration, Jake turns to

face the wall.

'Is it possible to reduce the range?'

Lars bursts into the room.

'Jake – target identif...ayee...yeed! What the ...?'

'Okay, Lars, man your station – I'll leave the ladies to finish off here.'

'Thanks, Jake.'

'No problem, Lars.'

'Jake, are you coming?'

'Not quite yet, I'll be along after I've finished reading this notice.'

'The one that says – *Please switch off the lights*?'

'Yeah - interesting, isn't it?'

Jake snakes along the wall and sidles up to the window.

'That man with the crutches is just the caretaker, but keep an eye on him. Is everything working, do we have sound and vision? – I've just brought this large notepad in case I need to write anything down.'

'Will those two men in the storeroom be writing anything down, Jake?'

'Possibly ... possibly, Lars – now let's all concentrate on our positions – you two keep watching and recording my office, I'll watch the stairs.'

Jake heads for the stairs.

'Randy!'

'Randy?'

'Yes, Lars, this is Randolph, Candice's sister – how did you get in here?'

'I walked up the stairs – I was going to knock on the door, but...'

'We're making some alterations - most offices are open plan

nowadays – how's...?'

'Jake, I've left Snake – he was a fake.'

'Yes.'

'You knew too?'

'He told me a whopper, he was the one who sabotaged my chopper. The swine poured wine into the fuel line. He'll serve time for his crime.'

'Lars, Sven, you two men - I'm going to take Randy to see Candy, her experience will make her very handy.'

As Jake leads Randolph to the storeroom, both men give up any pretense of watching anything over the road, they turn to each other.

'Are you thinking what I'm thinking?'

'Yep – poetry in motion...'

# Chapter Twenty

# The Bells Are Ringing

*Thirty minutes later*

Jake returns to the observation area.

'What have you been doing, Jake?'

'I've just been showing Candice and Randolph around our new HQ, the store...er... interrogation room, the kitchen, the bathroom, and so on.'

'Yes, Jake's made a really good job of it.'

'I can't take the credit for it, Candice, I just provided the cash. It was Norma and Sally who decided on the designs for the bedding and towels and so on.'

'I used to manage a motel, you know.'

'You can tell, Norma. I love your choice of colors.'

'Thank you, Randy.'

'I picked the crockery, though - it's important to have the right coffee cups.'

'I noticed those cups, Sally – I nearly bought some of those from Macy's, but they are so expensive.'

Somehow, Jake manages to maintain his smile. Norma grabs his hand.

'Jake told me nothing is too good for his friends, didn't you, Jake?'

Jake looks at Sally.

'If there's one thing that all this has taught me, it's that friends are worth much more than money.'

Sally's expression is a mixture of astonishment and admiration.

'Besides, when I got my memory back, I remembered where I'd put my secret stash.'

Norma gives his hand a tight squeeze and kisses him on the cheek. Jake colors, Lars and Sven chortle to themselves.

'Well, Norma, we've got things to discuss, let's leave the others to their work.'

As the two of them wander off, Candice approaches Sven.

'That looks like a very intricate camera. Look at all those knobs and dials. You must be very good with your fingers.'

'Would you like me to demonstrate, Candice?'

'Later, perhaps – I'll just stand here and watch, if you don't mind?'

'Of course I don't. There's a spare camera over there if you want to play around.'

'Naughty boy!'

Meanwhile, Randolph has been chatting to Lars.

'Wow, they look like very powerful binoculars!'

'Would you like to have a look through them?'

'Yes please.'

'Phew, I didn't realize they would be so heavy, could you help me please, Lars?'

Lars stands behind her, to steady the binoculars, he feels the heat of her body against him.

'Ooh, Lars, it makes things much bigger, doesn't it?

*Sometime later*

'Any more movement, men?'

'Nothing to report, I'm afraid, Jake.'

'That's disappointing - it'll be getting dark in a couple of hours - I suppose we should hit the mattresses.'

Lars is addressing Jake, but looking pleadingly at Randolph.

'Good idea, Jake. I've done a quick calculation and I've worked out that there are exactly twice as many people as mattresses. That works out at one mattress for every two people.'

'Lars was my financial advisor - he's very good with figures.'

'Well, I'm not sleeping with my sister, so I guess this is your lucky night, Lars. I can't remember if I introduced myself – I'm Randy.'

'So am I.'

*The next day*

Jake is sitting in the attic checking his cell phone as Candice walks in.

'Here you are, Jake!'

Jake looks proudly around the room.

'What do you think of our conference room?'

'Ouch!'

'Mind your head, the rafters are a little low in places, you're a little early - did you get my text'

'There's something I need to tell you before the meeting, Jake.'

'Oh, okay – do you like the furniture?'

'It's lovely, Jake.'

'Take a seat.'

'On this crate?'

'Yep, pick any one.'

Candice plonks herself on the nearest crate trying to avoid Jake's gaze. She is hesitant, unsure of how to broach the subject.

'There's something I need to tell you, Jake, but I'm frightened I may hurt your feelings.'

Jake isn't really listening, he's too busy wondering how Candice can sit on such a low object without...'

'Jake – are you listening?'

'Of course.'

'I know you are, Jake. I'm sorry - you're so sensitive and caring - I realize how hard this must be for you.'

'I am – it is.'

Jake feels pleased at the way he is handling this.

'Jake – you swine! You're making this really hard for me – why are you always so nice? I don't deserve it!'

Jake isn't sure if there is a correct response to this, he tries to hedge his bets. Studying Candice's face carefully he tentatively continues, not sure whether to make his response a question or a statement. He tries both.

'You don't?... You don't.'

One of them must have worked because Candice crosses her legs and carries on.

'My dearest Jake, I know I may have given you the impression I am available and I know how strong your feelings are for me and I'm sorry to have to break it to you this way, but I've fallen for Sven, so you and I are going to have to cool our relationship – at least for the moment.'

'Er...okay, Candice.'

'No hard feelings, Jake.'

'As long as you're happy, Candice.'

'Oh, Jake, that's what I love about you – you would do anything for me. Come here and give me one last kiss.'

Jake almost falls into her lap as she drags him off his crate.

'And don't be too down-hearted. If it doesn't work out, I'll get back to you. While you're there - perhaps just one last feel … mmm … yes … keep it warm for me.'

Candice blows him a kiss as she leaves. A couple of seconds later she makes a fleeting reappearance.

'Oh, by the way, Sven's asked me to marry him and he wants you to be his best man.'

Jake looks at his watch.

*'Good, I've still got time to…'*

'Hi, Jake.'

'Oh hello, Randolph – you're early.'

'I came here to tell you something – nice place!'

'Thank you, mind the…'

'Ouch!'

'Rafters – take a seat.'

'One of these crates?'

'Any one.'

'There's no easy way to say this, my dear Jake, so I'll just come straight out with it.'

Jake glances at his watch.

'Good.'

'Oh, Jake, don't be so nice about it – you're just making it harder. Before I start, just promise me you won't cry. I don't think I could take that.'

'Okay.'

'Oh God, Jake why are you so perfect?'

Jake shrugs his shoulders.

'I'm not going to look at you, Jake. The way you move sends shivers down my spine.'

'Okay, I promise I won't move.'

'You promise?'

'Yes.'

'Alright, here goes – Jake, I know you thought I'd come here to take up where we left off – I mean, it was obvious to any fool there was a strong physical attraction between us, but I want to be straight with you from the start.'

'Okay.'

'Lars has asked me to marry him and I've said yes, so this will be our last kiss.'

Randolph drags Jake towards her.

'Mmmm...maybe not, I'll get back to you on that one – must dash, wedding plans and all that.'

Randolph narrowly avoids the rafters on her way out.

'Oh, by the way, Lars is going to ask you to be best man, so try to act surprised – that's it, that expression is perfect.'

Jake stares at his watch.

*'Now, where was I?'*

'Hi, Jake.'

'Oh hello, Sally – you're early.'

'Jake, there's something I need to tell you before the meeting – wow, you've done this out nicely – I love the retro furniture.'

'Thanks, Sally - take a crate.'

'That's what I love about you, Jake – you're so creative, imaginative, caring...'

'You're going to marry Arnie?'

'How did you...?'

'Just a guess.'

'I hope you understand, dear Jake, I know it could have been great, but it's just that Arnie is so big and strong and rugged and – well – big!'

'And Arnie wants me to be his best man?'
'I don't know, he hasn't said.'

'Oh, okay, I suppose you want one last kiss?'
'Nah, see you later, Jake.'
As Jake returns to his planning, his phone rings, he is thinking out loud as he answers it.
'You can't win them all...'

*'But you can win this one!'*

'Georgette – is that you?'
'None other, Jake. I'm just phoning to tell you that Fox and I have got back together, it was all a misunderstanding. You can tell Norma, I'm sure she'll be pleased that her parents are reunited. From what I've heard, it looks like you could be one of the family soon.'
'Really?'
'Don't pretend you're surprised - you make a lovely couple. Can I just mention though, since we still have a little time left, Monday afternoons are best for me?'
Jake thought back to his first meeting with Georgette.
'I don't think I could...'
'Don't worry about anyone finding out, I'm the soul of discretion – oh, by the way, how are you getting on with that codebook I gave you?'
'I haven't had the time to study it in great detail, but I think I've cracked the code.'
'Be very careful, Jake, do not divulge the information in that book to anyone – the safety of the free world is at stake - must go, got things to do.'
'I wo...'

Jake carries on the conversation until he realizes he's talking to himself. He takes the codebook out of his pocket and thumbs through it.

*'The precedent of the untied snakes, the prone monster of grain bittern.'*

He closes the notebook triumphantly.
'A snake is an animal and a bittern is a bird, which is also an animal – this obviously has something to do with animals.'
'What's that, Jake?
'Oh hi, Norma, I didn't realize I was thinking out loud.'
'What was that you were saying about presidents and prime ministers?'
'You must have misheard me, besides, it's top secret. I can't tell you - it would put you in danger.'
'Okay, Jake.'
'Norma, can I just ask you, do you know any Archi?'
'The language - yes, one of our guests spoke it - why?'
'Oh, no reason, really.'
'He didn't speak any English, so he used a phrasebook.'
'You wouldn't...?
'Have it? - Yes, he left it in the drawer of the bedside cabinet. I've kept it in my handbag ever since.'
'That's handy.'
'He was a very handsome man.'
'That's nice.'
'And he was very good with his hands, very good.'
'That's interesting.'
'He was very imaginative – very.'
'Okay – give me the book and you can go.'
'Jake – you're jealous!'
'I'm not – why would I be jealous over an extremely

handsome man who used his hands in an exceptionally imaginative way and who probably wrote the Kama Sutra?'

'He didn't write it - he translated it. That's why he had the phrase book.'
'Your mom phoned.'
'Rea?'
'Rea, Georgette – whatever you want to call her.'
'Did she want to talk to me?'
'Yes, but she couldn't wait.'
Jake notices the look of disappointment on Norma's face.
'She had things to do. She wanted to tell you she was back with your father, so you're now one big happy family.'
He reaches for her hand.
'Norma – your mom tells me that I might be...'
'Hi, Jake.'
'Morning, Jake.'
'Jake, has the meeting already started?'
Jake pulls his hand away from Norma's.
'Not yet, Lars – we are all here now though, so we may as well begin.'
As he glances towards her, he sees Norma wipe a little tear from her eye.

# Chapter Twenty-one

# The Meeting

'First of all, I'd like to thank you all for coming at such short notice. You may have noticed that Sally and Arnie are missing.'

Jake looks around and sees a roomful of blank expressions.

'Or maybe not - if you are interested, Arnie is escorting our two intruders to the nearest underground station, Sally is directing him. On their way back they will be picking up coffee and breakfast.'

'Yum, yum.'

'I'm starving.'

'Me too.'

'I could kill for a cappuccino.'

'That's maybe a bit harsh, Lars.'

'Yeah, a latte, perhaps – but not a cappuccino.'

'Alright men, you can fight over the coffees later, but first we need to get down to business.'

'Sure thing, Jake.'

'Yeah, what's the plan of action? This reminds me of when we were in 'stan, you ladies weren't there, but if you had been, you would have loved it.'

'I'm not sure about that, Lars – they weren't all good times.'

'Jake's right, Lars, what about that time Jake peed into that bottle and told us it was prosec...'

'Okay, Sven – I'm sure they're not interested in...'

'I am.'

'So am I.'

'Me too!'

Jake tries to distract them.

'As you know, for the last two years I have been trying to discover who is behind a ruthless, dangerous and mysterious organization. Namely, The Blowman Corporation and also what the connection is with The Dan Corleone Agency.'

Jake waits for this revelation to sink in.

'Did you drink any of it, Sven?'

'Too right I did! Over there you had to eat and drink anything to survive and I'm telling you, Candice, if you ever get the chance...'

'You wouldn't let Candice drink it, would you, Jake?'

'No, Norma – only you.' Norma beams with pride.

The expressions on Candice, Randolph and Olga's faces indicate that their thoughts are elsewhere, but Jake relentlessly perseveres.

'So, as I was saying, our task is to identify the men at the very top of these organizations and I am sure that with your help and the information contained in these two documents which have recently come into my possession, we should easily be able to do so.'

Jake seriously doubts that, but he doesn't want to dash their hopes too much. He picks up Sally's diary and reads the first entry to himself.

*Started a new job today looking after some miserly skinflint – nothing on television, so I think I'll wash my hair.*

He quickly closes the diary and places it under Georgette's codebook.

'I'm sure that will contain a lot of useful information.'

He turns to see Candice mouthing to Sven.

'What did it taste like?'

Jake breathes a sigh of relief as Sally and Arnie enter the room.

'Oh, great, it's Sally and Arnie with breakfast. Tuck in everybody and then me, Lars and Sven will go over last night's recordings.'

*Thirty minutes later*

'Okay men, Norma, Candice, Randolph and Olga have gone shopping, so that leaves us with a bit of time to look at the surveillance cameras for last night – Arnie will be joining us after he's finished exfoliating.'

'He's a character, that Arnie – I can't believe he's your brother, Jake.'

'Well, he is, I can assure you of that, Lars.'

'I've never known any man with that amount of stamina, he was at it all ni...'

'Okay, Sven – I think we can keep my brother's private life out of this – have you got the cameras ready for playback?'

'Ready to go, Jake. I set the motion sensor to pick up all the action.'

'Let's go then.'

Sven presses the playback button.

'I had to recharge the batteries this morning so there must be plenty of action.'

'Great, well done, Sven.'

The three men are all intently watching the screen as Arnie enters.

'Nice timing, Arnie – pull up a crate. I think you'll find this interesting.'

Now the four of them are intently watching the screen.

'It's blank.'

'That's because the motion sensor hasn't picked anything up yet – wait, there's something.'

'It looks like a cat.'

'Yeah, it's a cat – oh, oh, the screen's gone blank again.'

'There must be no motion – wait, it's on again.'

'That cat's come back again.'

'Is it the same cat?'

'I think so – anyone know anything about cats?'

'My auntie has one.'

'What color?'

'I don't think the color of Sven's auntie's cat has any significance here Lars – wait, it's gone off again.'

'No motion.'

'Okay, can we fast forward it?'

'Yep, here goes.'

'Cat.'

'Gone off.'

'Cat.'

'Gone off.'

'What's that?'

'It's a different cat.'

'Gone off.'

'There's nothing else.'

'The batteries must have run out.'

'Well, that's a little disappointing, we didn't learn much there.'

'We learnt zare are lods ov cats around here.'

'That's true, Arnie, I suppose we should always look on the

bright side. Wait, let's check through the other camera – just in case.'

All four men are now intently staring at the screen of the other camera.'
'That's Olga.'
'Oh yes, I remember, the blast accidently turned the camera round when the door was blown in.'
'It must have automatically zoomed in as well, Lars.'
'That's right, Sven – these cameras are very sensitive.'
'Can we fast forward it?'
'We can, but we might miss some valuable information.'
After five minutes the screen goes blank, much to the dismay of Sven and Lars.
'Fast forward it to see if anything else has been recorded during the night.'
'Whoa! That's Olga again - she never had time to pick up any nightwear. What's she doing up in the middle of the night, I wonder?'
'It looks as if she's texting someone or maybe surfing the net.'
'Well, I suppose we learnt that Olga didn't have any more bugs secreted about her person – it looks like she's gone back to bed, may as well switch it off.'
Just as Lars is about to turn it off, Jake notices something.
'Just leave it here for now, Lars – you lot can chill, I'll be down later.'

## That same evening

Jake and Norma are riding on the Metro.

'Ooh, Jake, I can't wait to see your apartment – I'm so happy I'm the only one you've asked.'

'Well, you were my first choice. I only asked the others out of politeness. Surprisingly, they were all happy to stay and sleep on those mattresses. All apart from Olga – who apologized for having urgent business to attend to. I'm pleased really, because my apartment only has two bedrooms.'

Norma tries to hide her disappointment.

'I suppose you're still a bit jealous about...'

'Who - that very handsome guest who was very good with his hands and very imaginative?'

'Yes, him – the one who translated the Kama Sutra.'

'Why would I be jealous about him – I've forgotten all about him.'

'Good – and I've forgotten that you didn't invite only me.'


## A long, ten minutes later

'Did you buy anything nice when you were out shopping?'
'Yes, thank you.'

## Another five minutes later

'Were you disappointed you didn't find anything out last night, Jake?'

'A little, but I am getting closer to solving the mystery.'

'I'm so happy for you, Jake – that guest meant nothing to

me, you know – nothing happened - well, nothing much. Tell me what you've found out – it's exciting!'

Jake stands and gently helps Norma to her feet. She melts into his arms and they kiss passionately. As the train stops their bodies are jerked apart.
'I'll tell you later – this is where we get off.'

*Back at the stakeout*

The men are playing cards while their partners try on their purchases.
'SNAP!'
'Do you know any other card games, Arnie?'
'No – zis iz zee only von – vie play anozer?'
'Well, it's just we are frightened to put our hands down in case you crush them with yours.'
'Yeah, Arnie – you don't know your own strength. Besides, you've won all twenty games now.'
'Lars is right, Arnie - why not poker?'
'Should vee not vait until vee go to bed?'
'It's only eight o'clock, Arnie, we won't be going to bed for at least an hour.'
'Vie not?'
'Well, for one thing, Jake said he'd be checking in with us to make sure we're keeping watch, besides, poker is a card game, it's not something you do in bed.'
'Oh, I am zorry, I meesonderstood.'
'Hey, it's not your fault, Arnie – I guess you've lived a sheltered life, yeah?'
'Yes, in a shelter I built myself.'
'If you boys have finished your card game, we'd like to show

you what we've bought.'

Candice is standing in the doorway wearing a new negligee, she is joined by Randy and Sally, both of whom are wearing similar outfits.
 'I'm with Arnie here - time for bed. Set the motion sensor for the cameras.'
 'Agreed, Lars.'
 'Vot about Jake?'
'That's what voicemail's for.'
Sven is busy altering a few settings on the cameras, by the time he looks up the room is empty.

# Chapter Twenty-two

# Justification or Just Fabrication

*The foyer of Highclere Apartments*

Norma hesitates as she and Jake enter the building, Jakes takes her hand and leads her in.

'Jake, I'm a little nervous, this place is so...'

'There's more to life than Bocote wood flooring, Norma – besides I prefer the understated chic of the Yates Motel.'

Norma laughs and tightly squeezes Jake's hand as they saunter through the foyer. As the elevator doors close Jake pulls Norma to him.

'I'd better warn you, Norma. I had to leave the apartment in a hurry, so I'm afraid it's in a bit of a mess.'

'Oh, Jake, you idiot – I wouldn't care if you lived in a cave. I just...'

Jake unlocks the door to his apartment, nudges it open and turns to watch Norma's reaction.

'You liar!'

'I am?'

Jake peeks over Norma's shoulder.

'I am! – What the?'

The apartment is back to its pristine condition. Jake glances around the room, he relaxes once he realizes there are no naked cleaners in sight. It's hard to tell who is the most impressed. Norma lies back on the Italian leather sofa, while Jake marvels at the fully stocked fridge.

'It's been a long day, Norma – how about I fix you a drink

while you have a shower?'
'Mmm... that sounds great, Jake - where's the bathroom?'
'There's a master bathroom through that...'
Jake notices the bedroom door is missing.
'Through there.'


*Ten minutes later*


Jake and Norma are lying in bed enjoying a post-coital drink.
'Jake, I can't believe my father is a bad man.'
'I don't think he is, Norma, I think he's just been unlucky.
His scientific genius has been his downfall.'
'What do you mean, Jake – are you just saying that to make
me feel better?'
Jake takes Norma's head in his hands, in the dusky light her
big, brown, saucer-like eyes remind him of a frightened bush
baby.
'We've both been through a lot during the last couple of
weeks, Norma – and I've grown very fond of you. It would be
tempting to say things to protect your feelings, but in this
case, I promise you, I'm not.'
'Jake's right, Norma.'
'Pops!'
'Fox!'
'Hello, Jake – I see you are getting to know my daughter.'
'You could have knocked, Dad.'
'I would have, if there'd been a door. I wasn't expecting you
so soon, I took the door off to have it repaired. Crocodile said
it shouldn't take long. I've done most of the other jobs. - It
must have been one heck of a party.'

228

'I'm sure Jake doesn't want to go into that.'

'Mom!'

'Hello dear. It's lovely to see you again. I'm sorry I didn't have time to talk to you yesterday, but your father and I wanted to make this place nice for Jake to return to.'

'Well - you've done a good job - I must say.'

'Thanks, Jake - we had a bit of help.'

'Hello again.'

' Who the fu...?'

'Jake – not in front of my parents!'

'Sorry, Norma.'

'I think we need to explain some things to you both.'

'Well, that's very nice of you, Fox, but could we put some clothes on first? And I think the three of you could change into something more appropriate – those PVC outfits don't look very comfortable.'

'Of course, Jake - as Fox said, we weren't expecting you back so soon.'

'Obviously not, Georgette.'

'You can call me Rea - Georgette is just my professional name.'

Jake and Norma are already sitting on the Italian leather sofa, when Fox and Rea enter the room, Jake directs them to sit on the opposite sofa. He has placed a number of drinks for them on the Louis Kazan crystal topped coffee table. Fox pours a couple of glasses of water and passes one to Rea, who feels an explanation is necessary.

'We've both been abstinent for a couple of days now – it's done wonders for our sex life, hasn't it darling?'

Norma squirms on her seat.

'Mom! I'm sure Jake doesn't want to hear about what you and Pop get up to in your private moments.'

'Norma's right – maybe some other time...'

Noticing Norma's disapproving glance, Jake quickly changes the subject.

'Besides, Norma and I have lots of questions to ask.'

'Fire away, Jake – I've been waiting for a long time to explain my side of the story.'

'Well, you can start by explaining how you managed to get here so quickly, Fox.'

'After you escaped from my complex, I was able to sneak away while my captors were watching the fireworks, I made it to my hidden underground garage, took my DeLorean out of storage, and a few days later I managed to get to Rea's house – what was left of it, that is. Some vandal had burnt it down, if I ever find out...'

'Carry on – how did it take you so long?'

'I had converted it to run on solar power, you don't get much of that in an underground garage. After a few miles the batteries went flat and I had to hide it behind a billboard until morning, I charged it by day and took the back roads during the night - do you know how much attention you get when you pull up in a DeLorean?'

'I can imagine.'

'Anyway, after a few days – I don't remember exactly how many - I managed to reach Rea's house. I could have cried, it was just a shell, if I could get my hands on the hooligan who...'

'So, then you drove the DeLorean here?'

'No, that would have taken far too long. I hid it next to a completely burnt-out Porsche – some poor devil must be wondering what happened to his prized possession.'

Jake stifles a cough, Rea colors and looks down at her feet.
'So how did the two of you end up here, in my apartment?'

'I had a stroke of luck - I was about to start hitching a ride to the airport when you all returned. I really wanted to reveal myself to you, but I didn't want to compromise your safety. Also, I needed time to explain things to Rea.'
'Well, that must have taken a while - you sure had a lot of explaining to do.'
'Rea took it quite well, didn't you, my darling?'
'I suppose so.'
'So, the two of you made it up and decided to come here for a second honeymoon – I bet you couldn't wait to tell us the good news?'
'Yes and no – Rea booked the next available flight, leaving me to make my own way. You just needed to sleep on it, didn't you, my angel?'
'I suppose so.'
'And you took a later flight?'
'I would have, but Rea had inadvertently picked up my wallet and credit cards, but then I had another stroke of luck – I noticed Arnie packing up his sidecar, when he'd finished, I hid in the back of it.'
'For *three* days – what do you eat?'
'Arnie had a habit of throwing the cobs of the corn into the sidecar after he'd used the husks to exfoliate.'
'You ate them?'
'Yep.'
'What did you drink?'
'Sweetcorn is seventy-five per cent water.'
'Good point, you can understand our suspicions though, Fox.'

'You don't believe me, why ever not?'

'Well, for years you pretended to be my father, you enjoyed threesomes with Gloria and another man, you told Rea that Norma was dead, you carried out illegal experiments on Arnie, you...'

'Everyone's entitled to the odd mistake, Jake.

Fox pours Rea and himself a couple of gin and tonics.

'It's getting a bit heavy, let's chill a bit.'

'Pop's right, Jake – I'm sure he has a perfectly good explanation for all of this.'

A large, muscular man, naked apart from a gimp mask, enters the room.

'Georgette, could you help me with this?'

Jake rushes to cover the man's private parts with a cushion.

'Oh, I'm sorry, Georgette – I didn't know you guys had company, I thought these two would still be in bed – it didn't take them lo...'

'Why's he calling you Georgette, Mom?'

'I always use my professional name with clients.

With a sharp tug and a loud shloppp sound, Rea manages to remove the mask from the stranger. Jake drops the cushion in surprise.

'This is no client – THIS IS MY FATHER!'

'Jake, you have no idea how long I have waited to hear you say that – may I give you a hug?'

'Well, I'd prefer it if you'd put something on first.'

'Of course, of course – and this is Norma - my, you've grown – I'm so happy to see you!'

'I'm happy too – very happy. Do you want to give *me* a hug?'

'Perhaps after I've had a shower, Norma – I'm a bit sweaty.'

Norma's eyes carefully follow the large, muscular, naked man as makes his exit.

'What a nice man your father is, Jake.'

'Oh yes, Norma – we're one big, happy family here.'

Fox turns to Rea.

'Well, that went better than I expected.'

'Agreed, but I think we may need a bigger size mask for Jake's dad next time.'

'I didn't mean that, Rea - I meant Jake's reaction, the treatments seem to have worked. Have you regained all of your memory?'

'Yes, I remember everything.'

'You remember why you went through MESH+ ?'

'Everything, but that.'

Jake's father returns, fortunately this time he is fully dressed, Norma looks a little disappointed.

'I'm sure Norma's getting a little bored with all this - Rea, why don't you take your daughter shopping, I'm sure you have lots to talk about.'

'That's a great idea, Fox – I've been dying to buy my little girl a dress to show off her lovely figure, ever since I found out she wasn't dead.'

Fox takes a gulp of his drink and sheepishly stares at a spot on the floor.

'I managed to get a perfect match for those broken floor tiles – don't you think, Jake?'

Norma looks puzzled as Rea hurries off to get her coat.

*Ten minutes later*

'I know we have a lot of explaining to do, Jake – but how did you know Wes was your father?'
'You trained me to recognize family resemblances, Fox – remember?'
'I knew that would come in handy sometime.'
'It's not the first time I've met you recently, is it, Wes?'
'No.'
'I met you in the courtroom, you were there with Fox's ex-wife, Gloria – the woman I thought was my mother and her partner, Charles.'

At the mention of Charles' name, Wes puts on his best emotionless, inscrutable face, but Jake notices a tell-tale flicker in his eyes. Jake sits back, waiting for any further reactions - there are none, but he has learnt enough to confirm his suspicions.
Eventually, after a long, uncomfortable silence, Fox speaks.
'Did you realize that Wes was your real father at that meeting?'
'No, but I had a strange feeling about him.'
Wes nods knowingly to Fox.
'You were right, Fox.'
Fox pours Wes a drink, tops up his own, and turns to Jake.
'We've been waiting a long time for this day, Jake, you must have lots of questions, we'll do our best to answer them all for you.'
'Well, you can start by telling me how I come to be sitting opposite a man who I *thought* was my father and a man who

*is* my father – both of whom have abandoned me at important times during my life.'

Fox sits up straight.
 'I can explain, Jake. As you already know, Gloria and I found you in a model spaceship in our barn, we asked around, but couldn't find out who your parents were, so we took you in and treated you as our son. A few days later we found Arnie, we realized that the two of you must have been left abandoned by circus performers, but despite hours of searching our efforts were fruitless.'
 'Did you know Arnie was my brother?'
'I had my suspicions, but I had no definite proof. The DNA test was only a ninety nine percent match and as a scientist I look for certainty.'
 'Fair comment, but the fact remains you left us – abandoned us! - To shack up with Norma's mother – I hope it was worth it.'
 'You've experienced her special skills, Jake, I'm sure you...'
'Let's forget about that for the minute, my physical wounds have healed, but I still bear the mental scars – anyway, where does Wes come into this?'
Jake and Fox look over at Wes, who is lying back on the sofa enjoying his third drink.
 'He can explain that to you better than I can, but I want you to know – I had no choice but to leave you and Gloria. Word had got round and there were some very unsavory characters skulking around the farm. It was quite a wrench, but then I met Rea and...'
 'You've already told me – you were banging her like a soldier's drum.'
 'I needed some consolation, besides, I made sure that you

235

and Gloria were in safe hands – didn't I, Wes?'

Wes has just drained his glass.

'You sure did – any more of this?'

Fox heads for the self-defrosting, fully integrated Sub-Zero fridge freezer.

'Did you notice I've restocked your fridge?'

'Yes, I did, thank you and while you're there you can get me another drink – I have a feeling I'm going to need it.'

Wes stretches his large frame out on the sofa. Jake can't help thinking that his father is an impressive-looking man.

'What about my real mother, where is she?'

'I'm not going to lie to you, Jake - you may find some of the things I'm going to tell you a little distressing.'

'Are you going to tell me she's hiding behind that door waiting to...'

'No, Jake – she's dead.'

Jake is stunned. Wes hands him a creased, faded photograph. As Jake studies it, he has a flashback. He can see a woman smiling at him, encouraging him, as he spins round and round, then her look of horror as he is catapulted towards her.

'I remember now – it was me - I killed her!'

'No, Jake! - It was an accident – a million to one, freak accident - I didn't want to have to tell you like this, but you need to know the truth.'

The only time Jake had ever really cried in his life was after a visit to a carnival. Now he feels tears rolling down his cheeks, it's a strange sensation and he doesn't know how to cope with it.

'I ... My God, what's wrong with me – I'm a grown man for goodness' sake.'

Fox returns with the drinks and sits next to Jake. Putting his arm around him, in an effort to console him.

'Jake – just let it out. I've tried to protect you from this moment for most of your life, but I always knew deep in my heart that one day it would come.'

All three men are now sobbing their hearts out.

*Ten minutes (and a few drinks) later*

Fox is searching through the Jonathan Adler Op Art drinks cabinet.

'We've only got crème de menthe left.'

'That'll do.'

Fox pours each of them a glass, Wes drains his in one go.

'Good stuff, that - refreshing, with a bit of a kick to it. Now that you've had a chance to recover, I'll explain what happened, Jake – if, after you've heard my side of the story, you decide you never want to see me again, I'll walk away.'

'That seems fair.'

Wes holds his glass up and Fox refills it.

'Here goes - as you already know, Jake, Fox found you in a spaceship, rocket ship, whatever you want to call it. It had come loose from a fairground ride and, as it did, it hit your mother and brother.

'Arnie?'

'Yes, your mother was decapitated and died instantly, your brother was brain damaged. I was working at the fairground, but I was away on business at the time, searching for bearded ladies and two-headed llamas. It was a fruitless task, by the way, taking much longer than I expected - I'd been told there was one in Nebraska.'

'A two-headed llama?'

'No, a bearded lady. Anyhow, to cut a long story short, by the time I returned the carnival had moved on, so I returned to the scene of the accident. I searched for you for days before finding you and by that time, Fox and Gloria had taken you in. I asked around and found out that Fox was a respected man in the community, a scientist specializing in health and well-being and Gloria was known by a lot of the men, who all said she was very good. I knew I couldn't look after you as well as they could. I thought he could help your brother, that's why I went back a few days later and left Arnie near the barn.'

'And that was it – as easy as that – abandon your kids and just walk away?'

'I was living a life on the road. I came to see you whenever the carnival was in your area. I even got Fox front row seats at a discount price one year. Remember the masked knife thrower who invited you on stage, and the clown who gave you a balloon? – They were both me.'

'I didn't enjoy it.'

'That's why I gave you the balloon – to stop you crying.'

'I had nightmares for a week.'

'That wasn't bad - most people had them for months, mind you, that was before I cut down on the booze.'

'That still doesn't explain how Gloria comes into this.'

'Well after a few visits I got to know Fox and Gloria quite well. Life can be lonely out there on your own, traveling from town to town.'

'My heart bleeds for you.'
'Thanks, son – that means a lot to me.'

Wes pours himself another glass of crème de menthe.
'Anyway, where was I? - Oh, yes – it's lonely out on the road.
I know there are lots of desperate young widows and bored
wives, eager for hot, sweaty one-night stands with a
handsome, virile roustabout, but after a few hundred of
them, the novelty wears off and you search for something
deeper and more meaningful. Fortunately for me, that was at
the time when Fox had to leave Gloria, he asked me to find
out about how you and Gloria were doing and report back to
him. The fact that Gloria was, and still is, a very attractive
and passionate woman was just the icing on the cake.'
'I'd rather not hear about the sex life of the woman I thought
was my mother, if you don't mind.'
'Okay, I can see you're a very sensitive person, Jake – I'll
skip over the juicy bits.'

'How kind of you.'
'So, everything was going fine. Fox had found a way of
treating your brother's brain damage, by injecting him with
experimental concoctions.'
'I hope you went through the proper medical trials, Fox.'
'Of course, I tested them out using a human volunteer first.'
'Who?'
'You.'
'*Me?*'
'Remember those iced drinks I gave you?'
'Those weird tasting Slush Puppie type of things?'
'Yes, among other things.'
'I'm not happy about...'
'Jake, you don't think the abilities you have are normal, do

you?'

'What abilities?'

'You have powers you don't even know about yet.'

'Such as?'

'Observation, for one. There's a ladybug on that banana plant over there - how many spots does it have?'

'Seven.'

'You didn't even look at it, so how could you possibly know?'

'I'm not sure, I must have noticed it, somehow – how did you know it had seven spots?'

'Good question, Jake - I must admit, I had a few slurps of the mixture myself, just to test its effectiveness, of course. It tasted quite nice, actually, considering one of the main ingredients was skunk's urine.'

'And Arnie had the same treatment?'

'Arnie's blend was different because of the damage to his brain. I had to travel to Sweden to get the finest pickled herrings – we didn't have Amazon Prime back then.'

'Is that why Arnie has a Swedish accent?'

'Hmm, I hadn't thought of that, it could be – I used to read the labels out to him before feeding him.'

Jake knows that constantly changing the subject is a useful weapon in the art of interrogation.

'Wes, do you know an Olga Oggblom?'

Wes almost chokes on his drink.

'Olga – I haven't seen her for years – why do you ask?'

'Oh, no real reason, I just happened to bump into her the other day.'

'Olga's back? Well, I never!'

'When was the last time you saw her?'

'Oh, I don't know – it must be over ten years ago.'

'Could it be exactly twelve years and nine months ago?'
Wes's cool exterior cracks.
'It could be, I, I suppose...'

Up to now, considering the circumstances, Jake's manner has been quite affable. Suddenly his demeanor changes completely.
'As you both are probably aware, my memory has completely returned and I can tell you that from what I have recently discovered, the current situation looks pretty dire. Wouldn't you agree?'
Both men quickly sober up and sit up, nodding their heads in agreement.
'So - listen very carefully because I think we only have one chance to get this right and if we don't...'
Wes and Fox look despondently at the empty bottles on the coffee table.
'We know – curtains!'
'I've just had a text from Norma, they are on their way back so you had both better answer my questions quickly.

'Iwilllcantalkveryquicklywhennecessary.'
'SocanI butnotquite asquickly as him.'
'Sven and Lars were both given MESH, why was I given MESH+?'
'It was costly developing my treatments, that's why I contacted the Blowman Corporation - for financial help. Unfortunately, they wanted to use my research not to repair and enhance a person's brain, but to control it – they became very good at that.'
'What were their methods?'
'Injections, tablets and so on – once ingested they had complete control.'

'How?'

'Suggestions implanted into music, DVDs, videos, social media – you name it, they can do it. Wes and I created the Don Corleone Agency to try to stop them, you and your team were appointed as our undercover agents.'

'I remember, it's coming back to me – go on.'

'We thought that erasing parts of a person's memory would be able to stop them from using their mind control techniques. Lars and Sven volunteered – under your guidance, of course.'

'That's right.'

'What we hadn't - couldn't have – known, was that they had a backdoor. When we discovered that, you knew there was only one way we could possibly defeat them - you created MESH+ - a total mind wash with replacement of only vital memories. It was your baby and it worked incredibly well – too well, in fact – we couldn't get you back.'

'What about the others – Sally, Norma, Candice...?'

'Have you ever tried to persuade a woman to change her mind?'

'Point taken, but why is it so urgent now?'

'Blowman have gone global, all hell has broken loose. You must have seen the news.'

Jake remembers Rea's diary. He now realizes the importance of it.

'How did you solve the problem of the backdoor?'

'We couldn't, but we found that emotions such as love and, especially, pain could, to some extent, override their mind control techniques.'

'How did you find that out?'

'It was quite accidental, Rea and I always enjoyed, er – how

should I say it? - Experimentation – Rea, under the guise of
Georgette, was the one who realized that it could reset Sven
and Lars resistance. They were given regular treatments.'
'I understand now, Sven and Lars were there to look after
me, weren't they?'
'Yes, alongside others, including Sally and James, the
concierge. We helped set up the dating agency because we
thought it was a good way to contact you, if necessary.
Poisson Dating was your brainchild.'
'And the Blowman Corporation were closing in on me,
weren't they?'
'Yes, we believe they are in the process of developing
bacteria capable of spreading their mind control power at a
previously unheard-of rate. The whole planet could be
infected in months. Everyone knew that you were the only
person capable of stopping them.'

Fox pauses to assess Jake's reaction.
'Fortunately, Rea – as Georgette – was able to get to you
first. She found it almost impossible to break you down, but
she was able to do enough to convince the Blowman
Corporation you were no longer a threat. I must say, Sally
played a great role in that deception – as, of course, did you.'
Jake didn't have the heart to tell Fox that he wasn't acting.
'But what can I do?'
'We have never been able to ascertain who the head of the
Corporation is. Cut the head off the snake and the body will
die too.'
'But...'
'You must think hard, Jake. When you were working for the
Dan Corleone Agency, you were onto something – think

back, remember everything you can. You are our only hope, Jake – our *only* hope!'

Jake senses movement outside, a few minutes later the others hear the door opening. Jake closes the conversation. 'Here come the ladies - good timing – I've left some equipment under the bed - I'm sure Georgette will be able to work out how to use it. We'll rendezvous at twelve hundred hours tomorrow.'

# Chapter Twenty-Three

# Meeting Adjourned

*Fifteen minutes later*

Jake and Norma are on their way back to the stakeout.
'I had a lovely time shopping with Mom. Did you have a
good time with our fathers? Your dad seems like a really nice
man.'
'It was informative.'
Norma waits for Jake to expand on his answer, but he
doesn't, so she changes the topic.
'It will be lovely to see the others again.'
Jake laughs.
'We only saw them this morning.'
'I know, I suppose it's because I lived quite a solitary life
before I met you. – What do you think they'll be doing?'
'What time is it?
'Eight fifteen.'
'Knowing them, they'll probably be in bed – I hope so, it'll
make our job a bit easier.'
'How?'
Jake grins.
'You'll find out soon enough.'
'Mmm... - that sounds mysterious – Mom bought me some
very exciting things. I'm dying to show them to you.'
Jake thinks back to his last encounter with Georgette and
feels a twinge in his buttocks.
'Anything to do with horses?'

'Of course not, why would you think that?' 'No reason, we're here - it *seems* quiet enough.'

As Jake parks the car, Norma reaches over her shoulder to pick up her shopping.
'This has a lot more room in it than a Porsche. Is that why you chose it?'
'It's a long story.'
'There's a package under the seat, do you know what it is?'
Norma passes it to Jake, as he opens it an idea comes to him.
'What are they?'
'These may just be the answer to all my problems.'
Norma glows with pride as she snuggles up to Jake, happy that he's happy.
'I need to get these to Tai Chi immediately.'
'Can I come, please?'
'Of course, Norma - you'll like his wife, Feng Shui, unfortunately she can't speak English, but she makes a lovely cup of tea.'

As they head towards Chinatown, Norma glances across at Jake.
'There's something I want to ask you, Jake.'
'Go ahead, Angel.'
'I watched you write your name on that boy's brow.'
'Yeah, Tai Chi's son.'
'I noticed you wrote Gay Drag.'
'That's right, I was working undercover going by the name of Sergey Dra...'
There is a screech of brakes as Jake pulls the car to a sudden stop at the side of the road.
'What's wrong, Jake - are you alright? – You look as if you've

seen a ghost.'

'I have – a ghost from way back in my memory, I can't believe I didn't make the connection before now.'

'What connection, Jake?'

'There's so much to tell, Norma – I'll hold a meeting tomorrow and tell everyone.'

Jake sees the look of disappointment on Norma's face.

'But I will tell you something now that I won't be revealing to them.'

Norma's expression lifts.

'I was going by the name of Sergey Dragoni – an alias - to infiltrate a gang of criminals who were trying to take over Chinatown, somehow it got shortened to Gay Dragon – I've never told anyone else – you are the first.'

Norma beams with pride.

'When you have the meeting tomorrow will you tell them that I helped you remember something important?'

'Of course.'

Norma nestles happily into her seat as Jake expertly maneuvers the pimpmobile through town.

'That's two things I've helped you with, isn't it?'

'It sure is, I don't know what I'd do without you.'

'It's nice of you to say that, Jake. I don't know what...'

'This is it, Tai Chi's store – look, there's Feng Shui, I'll introduce you to her.'

Jake grabs the parcel and leads Norma into the store, he speaks in fluent Cantonese to Feng Shui. A rough translation follows:

'Greetings, Feng Shui – this is my friend, Norma'

'I think she is more than a friend, Gay Dragon – rarely have I seen such a strong chemistry between two people– but I must warn you, I can sense there are many men after such a woman.'

'As always, your intuition is correct. It is true that there are others in pursuit of this lady, but, unfortunately, some mean to do her harm and that is why I need the help of your husband.'

'As always, my husband is at your command - I shall minister to your lover while you attend to your business.'

Jake heads into the back of the store. A few minutes later he returns, minus the parcel. They thank Feng Shui and leave, as they drive back to the stakeout Norma turns to Jake.

'Jake, are we in danger?'

'What makes you think that?'

'What you told Feng Shui about people meaning to do me harm.'

'You speak Cantonese?'

'We get a lot of visitors from overseas - I seem to be able to pick up their language easily.'

'And you're fluent in it?'

'Well, the family did stay for two nights.'

'Norma, when you were little, do you remember Fox giving you weird tasting Slush Puppie type of things?'

'Oh yes, my favorite was blueberry and...'

'Hmmm, he must have made some improvements to the flavors.'

'Jake, while you were in the back of the store, Feng Shui told me that you had single-handedly taken down a whole gang of hoodlums who had been terrorizing their neighborhood.'

'I didn't do it single-handedly, a make-up artist helped me with my disguises. That's how I was able to infiltrate them so easily. Unfortunately, I now realize that the kingpin evaded

me.'
'Is that why we are in danger?'
'He's one of the reasons.'
Norma looks worried.
'How many reasons are there, Jake?'
'Oh, no reason for you to be concerned, Angel, not when you've got me and the rest of the team to look after you.

As they reach the top of the stairs to the stakeout Norma turns to Jake.
'What's that sticking out of your pocket?'
'It's Candice!'
Norma giggles. 'She wouldn't fit in your pocket, silly.'
'No, I mean Candice must be using the machine.'

A quick glance around the empty room confirms Jake's suspicions.
'They've obviously decided to have an early night.'
'Judging by your affliction, Jake, I think we need to do the same. Should I put on one of the outfits that Rea bought me?'
'Somehow, I don't think you'll need to...'

The next morning it's business as usual. Sally and Arnie have brought the breakfasts and they're all seated around the table.
'Jake, can I tell them that it's great to see them all again?'
'Of course, Norma.'
'It's great to see you all again.'
'It's good to see you too, Norma – even though it was only yesterday when we last saw you.'
'Thanks, Lars.'
'Okay, that's the formalities over. I'm sorry to rush you, but I'm expecting some important visitors in an hour and I've got

a lot of new information for you.'

'Are you going to tell them how I helped you, Jake?'

'Yes, I am. I'm also going to tell them what our fathers' roles were in all this – and your mother's, Norma.'

'Rea?'

'Yes, or maybe I should call her by her working name – Georgette.'

Sven and Lars both suddenly look queasy. Jake quickly puts them at ease.

'Oh, by the way, men, I appreciate everything you've done to protect me through these difficult times. From what I've heard it was over and above anything a normal person could be expected to go through.'

Candice and Randy look puzzled, Sven and Lars faces turn from green to red. Norma is first to ask.

'What did...?'

'We'll just draw a line under that now. Knowing the two of them as I do, I'm sure they were both unwilling participants.'

Sven and Lars nod and try to look convincing, although the thought of Georgette dressed in her mask and leather gear, expertly using her ropes, chains and bulldog clips to exquisite effect, is secretly exciting both of them. Jake looks up.

'Where's Arnie?'

'He's...'

'Exfoliating?'

'No, after he'd finished fu... , well, after we'd finished, well, before we went to sleep, he said he no longer felt the need to exfoliate.'

'That's brilliant news – the treatment must have unexpected beneficial effects. So where is he now, Sally?'

'Last I saw of him, he was searching the freezer for ice cubes.'
The men study each other carefully.
'Don't look at me, I left some.'
'Well, I didn't use the last of them.'
Jake looks sheepish.
'Sally, go and tell him that a packet of frozen peas will work
equally well.'
'How often will we need the treatments, Jake?'
'I'm hoping that it will only require a couple of goes, Sven –
possibly followed by an annual booster. By the way – and
this is entirely coincidental – there was a lightening deal for
K-Y jelly. I can't resist a bargain, so I ordered a case.'
'Thanks, Jake.'
'Yes, a very thoughtful gesture, Jake.'
'You're welcome, men. Ah, here's Arnie.'

Jake looks at the pool of water collecting under his chair and
wishes he'd thought of the peas earlier. He waits until the
crinkling sound of Arnie's packet subsides before continuing.
'I know it's only been a short while since our last meeting,
but I've got some very interesting news.'
Norma is fidgeting.
'So have I!'
'What is it, Norma?'
'My mom bought me some lovely outfits for, shall we say,
night-time wear?'
'You mean...'
'Yes, for the bedroom. I tried one on for Jake last night, it
seemed to work.'

Jake picks up his sheet of notes and tries to hide behind it.
He makes a valiant effort to change the subject.
'There's a lot to explain so I've made some notes.'

'Where did you get them?'

'I wrote them.'

'No, I was talking to Norma – where did you get the outfits?'

'They were in the sale at Azaleas in the East Village, Candice
– fifty percent off! – I'll show you them later.'

'Can I see them?'

'Of course, Randy – with your hair color, you'll really suit
the red one.'

'Can I...?'

'No, Sven – none of them would suit you, besides, they don't
do them in your size, now can we get back to the matter in
hand, we have a lot to discuss.'

'Okay, Jake – I was just thinking it would make a lovely
present for Candice for our wedding night.'

'Sorry about that, Sven, I misunderstood what you were...'

'That's okay, Jake – it was an easy mistake to make.'

'I wish I could spend longer discussing Norma's outfits, but
as I said, we haven't got a lot of time, so I'll just crack on if I
may?'

Jake doesn't look up, hoping that no one will interrupt. He
carries on, ignoring the animated miming going on between
Sally, Norma, Randy and Candice.

'Yesterday I had a very informative meeting with Fox, Wes
and Rea, which I think will be of great interest to you all.'
Sven is engrossed in Norma's descriptive movements, he
senses from her expression that she is heading towards a
climactic moment.

Jake waits for a reaction, after a while he turns to Sven.

'I think Sven could explain better than me, the importance
of finding out what the three of them know – isn't that right
Sven?'

Sven manages to pull his gaze away from Norma's now pulsating body.

'What? – Oh, yes, I'm a bit hazy – who are these people again?'

'Fox is Norma's father, Rea is Norma's mother and Wes is my father and Arnie's father.'

'Whoa – this is all getting a bit complicated, Jake!'

Jake looks around, fortunately the ladies are not interested in the slightest – for some reason Norma is pushing up her breasts and wiggling her backside, while the other three nod in agreement.

'They are the bad guys?'

'Not exactly, Lars.'

Jake is happy at least one person is listening.

'So, they are the good guys?'

'Not exactly, Sven.'

Jake is even happier that he now has the attention of two of them. Arnie has been sitting quietly in the corner, suddenly he jumps up.

'So! - You haf met my farter?'

Norma stops her wiggling - she turns to Arnie.

'Yes, he's a nice man. He's older than you, of course, but he's kept himself in good shape, really good shape. he has a fabulous bod... '

'Arnie will be meeting him soon, Norma, I'm sure he...'

There is a knock on the door, Arnie rushes to answer it.

'My farter, I haf been vaiting so long to meet you – I must gif you a hug!'

After a few minutes he opens his huge arms and the crumpled body of a man falls to the floor.

'O illustrious one, I am sorry to disturb you. I have brought your items, I hope they meet your requirements.'

'I'm sure they will Tai Chi, I thought your son would be delivering them.'

'I must apologize for his absence, but since you signed his forehead he has been extremely busy making Tik Tok videos, he has thousands of followers now.'

'That's very good for him.'

'Yes, I am very proud of him, although I am a little uneasy about him borrowing his mother's clothing without asking her consent.'

'I can see how that might be a concern.'

Jake reaches into his pocket and passes Tai Chi a wad of notes.

'This should get him a few outfits of his own, the way he's going he'll be able to afford his own soon.'

'You are too generous, illustrious one, Shar Pei will be eternally grateful.'

Norma bows to Tai Chi

'Dōng cūn dùjuān huā yǒu tèjià.'

Tai Chi returns the bow to Norma, then turning and bowing again, he hands Jake a parcel.

'My wife, Feng Shui, told me your lover was very wise and beautiful, but her description could not possibly do her justice. You are a very lucky man.'

Jake bows as he takes the parcel.

'Thank you, my friend.'


As Feng Shui closes the door, Candice turns to Norma.

'What did you say to that man?'

'I told him about the sale at the store where I bought my

outfits.'

Jake laughs.

'Yep, that should put Shar Pei's followers up into the millions.'

'I meant for his wife...'

Jake glances at his watch.

'Wow – we haven't got much time before the others get here so I'm afraid I'm just going to have to read out the notes to you, if there's anything you want to discuss we can do that later, okay.'

'I could photocopy the notes for you to save your voice.'

'Good idea, Norma.'

'How many copies would you like?'

'Let's see, there are eight of us, so if you wouldn't mind doing seven copies, please - that would be great.'

Norma hurries off to copy the notes, after she leaves the room Sally turns to Jake.

'Have you set a date yet?'

'What for?'

'You and Norma, of course.'

'What do you mean?'

'Your wedding! – We could have a joint ceremony, all eight of us – can you imagine that!'

'I don't think that's going to happen, Sally. I'm happy for all of you, but the sort of life I lead isn't suited to marriage, besides I'm sure Norma wouldn't want to...'

'But, Jake – can't you see, she's...'

Norma returns, proudly brandishing a handful of sheets.'

'I've done them – shall I hand them out?'

'Yes please, Norma.'

'What would I not want to?'

'What? – Oh nothing – Sven was just asking if I was going to take you skydiving, we used to do it on a regular basis, didn't we, Lars?

Lars wonders how he managed to miss so much of the previous conversation, but the one thing he has learnt from Jake is to how to think on his feet.'
'We sure did, I remember that time we did that jump for the Orphaned Llamas Charity. Sven and I both misjudged the landing - we were hanging from the top of a tree and you glided down with your legs outstretched like a praying mantis.'
Sven takes over the tale.
'Yeah, Lars grabbed one leg and I grabbed the other.'
Norma hands Sven a sheet.
'What happened then?'
'By the time we got to the ground Jake's trousers and boxers were round his ankles – it wouldn't have been so bad, but the entire Old Indianapolis City Counsel were waiting there to greet us.'
Jake ignores the giggles.
'Okay, moving on - you all have a sheet in front of you. Arnie can you read it out for us?
'Eet says how, vere, voo, ven, vot, vy?'
'Excellent, Arnie, thank you for that – have I missed anything out?'
'Not really.'
'No, I don't think so.'
'I think that says it all.'
'It's all there, short and to the point.'
'Couldn't have put it better myself.'

Norma hands Jake his sheet.

'You wouldn't mind if I popped out to the mall for a couple of hours with Candice, Sally and Randy, would you, Jake? - It's the last day of the sale at Azaleas.'

Jake makes a half-hearted attempt to dissuade them.

'Well, it is just a discussion document and we do have a lot to talk about, but I suppose that's...'

Jake is searching for something to add, but looking up, all he sees is the rear view of Norma as she closes the door. He turns to the men.

'I think you'll be pleased with their purchases guys - I know I was.'

'From vot Norma vos telling the udders, I'm sure vee vill.'

Jake glances at his watch and makes small talk about the weather, the football and the latest gas price. He glances at his watch and waits...

# Chapter Twenty-four

# It's a Family Affair

*'Any minute now...'* Jake thinks.

The huge bang shocks everyone except Jake. The man who claimed to be Jake's father stands in the doorway, framed by two of his heavily armed henchmen. He enters the room, followed by Olga.

'Eventually, finally, at last, this time I have you where I want you, Jake –he snatches a sheet off the table - and what is this? – A-ha your cunning plan! Let me read it'
"How, vere, voo, ven, vot, vy?" – is this some kind of code?'
'Vot do you mean, it's wery obwious!'
'I wasn't talking to you - assho... - oww – oooh!
Arnie is now on his feet.
'What I meant was – I didn't mean to disturb you - you looked so comfortable sitting there, please sit down and take that massive weight off your plates of meat, sir.'
'Who iz zis man, Jake?'
'Arnie, that man is your uncle.'
Arnie grabs the man in a huge bear hug.
'I haf an oncle, zat is amazing! – Vot iz your name?'
A voice booms from outside the room.
'His name is Viggo- and I thought he was dead.'
'Wiggo – vot a vonderful name.'

Jake sees Olga's reaction to the sound of the voice and smiles to himself. Viggo isn't smiling though, his expression is one of pure fury. Sweat dripping from his throbbing temples, desperately struggling to free himself from Arnie's enthusiastic embrace, he pats frantically at his pockets in an unsuccessful attempt to find his Smith and Wesson.

Jake spreads his arms out in a welcoming manner.

'Come in Wes and meet your son Arnie.'

Wes effortlessly pushes the goons aside and steps through the splintered doorway. Jake's attention is still focused on Olga. Viggo collapses into a heap as Arnie loosens his grip. Arnie rushes towards Wes.

'You are my farter?'

Not quick enough to defend himself, Wes gets the bear hug treatment.

'Arnie...Argh...Aarghhh!'

Wes looks imploringly at Jake.

'Arnie, I think our father is a little tired after his exertions last night.'

'If he isn't, he should be – that machine of yours works wonders.'

'Rea - I'm so pleased you could make it - and Fox, is he here?'

Viggo is lying in a crumpled heap, ignored by the others because their eyes are on Rea as she enters the room wearing what can only be described as an indescribable outfit. She is aware of the effect she is having on the men and smiles seductively at each one in turn.

'If I'd known there were going to be so many hunks here, I'd have made more of an effort.'

'I think I speak for all of us here, when I say you look radiant.'

'Thanks, Jake, but I think I look as if I've just got out of bed.'

'You have.'

'I know that, Wes – but they don't need to know that - I was just using it as an expression, besides I've already apologized for leaving the machine switched on.'

Rea's eyes search the room.

'Who is this gorgeous creature, and where is my daughter, Norma?'

'This is Olga, Norma has gone to Azalea's with her friends – it's the last day of the sale.'

'Now, to answer to your question about Fox, he had to go abroad in a hurry – China, I believe, something about some kind of an outbreak - Now, I'm sure that you studs have lots to talk about and we have some serious shopping to do.

Linking arms with Olga, Rea hurriedly escorts her out of the room.

'I can't wait to show you a little black number I saw last time I went shopping with my daughter, Norma. It was made for someone with an exquisite figure like yours – you will look divine, I promise you!'

The men part like the Red Sea and watch open-mouthed as the two of them glide gracefully through the doorway and down the stairs.

As Viggo and Wes use the newly freed up space to embrace each other by the throat, Arnie turns to Jake.

'Voo is all zees peoples?'

'I know what you mean, Arnie – this might help.'

Jake grabs a pen and starts scribbling on his pad.

'I'll draw you a Diagram of relationships.'

A few minutes later Jake scrunches the sheet into a ball.

'Maybe later...'

He congratulates himself as he hits the wastepaper basket from five yards.

The room has been quiet during the two brothers struggle for supremacy, eventually, as both their faces turn purple through lack of oxygen, their grips slacken. Viggo breaks the silence.

'You son of a bitch, Wes – I'm gonna kill you, then torture you, then....'
'Is that any way to speak to your brother? Every day since you went missing, I have lit a candle for you and prayed to the Virgin Mary for your safe return. My prayers have been answered. I'm happy - you should be happy.'
'HAPPY? - Happy to find the man who ambushed me and left me for dead? If that raccoons' nest hadn't broken my fall, I'd have ended up as flat as a well-worn flatiron.'
'I had nothing to do with it, Viggo, I swear – why would I try to kill my own brother?
'You mean that wasn't you driving your car?'
'That wasn't my car – somebody must have copied my plates.'
'What about the phone calls and the messages threatening to kill me?'
'An impersonator, for three months before your accident I was out of the country - I couldn't have made those calls.'

'Where were you?'
'I was exploring an uninhabited forest in Tibet, looking for white pandas – the children love them.'
'Did you find any?'
'No, I had to make do with a couple of polar bears – and they're not easy to find in a forest.'

261

'You could have phoned.'

'I couldn't get a signal - a congress of baboons had eaten the phone masts.'

Viggo's expression softens.

'Seems reasonable - I should have realized that my brother wouldn't have...'

'You've always been a bit of a hot-head, Viggo, but you're my elder brother and I wouldn't ever take sides against you.'

The two brothers release each other's throats and embrace each other tenderly, tears of joy in their eyes.

Jake waits until he feels enough time has elapsed and enough tears have been shed before interrupting them. His tone is measured, his words forceful.

'Now where were we? – Oh yes, Viggo, you were saying that eventually, finally, at last, this time you have me where you want me.'

'Did I?'

'Yes, you did, Boss'

'That's right, Boss, I definite...'

'Guys, I don't... wait, what's this? - A fifty-dollar bill - it must have dropped out of my pocket when my favorite nephew gave me a hug. Pop down to that coffee shop and get us some coffees, please. It's time to celebrate.'

'And vee vould like bagels...'

The two men head down the stairs muttering to themselves.

'Did you see the size of that big guy. If he'd been green, I'd have sworn he was the Hulk.'

'Well, I sure as hell ain't gonna paint him to find out.'

'Me neither – make sure you don't forget those bagels.'

Wes and Viggo are standing in front of Jake like two naughty schoolchildren. Viggo speaks first.

'But if it wasn't you, Wes, who was it?'
Jake indicates for the two of them to sit down
'I have my suspicions, but unfortunately I can't divulge my findings just yet.'
Wes casually sits opposite Jake, Viggo is a little more reticent and moves to the edge of the table.
'Let me introduce you to my colleagues, Sven and Lars.'
Jake nods first to Lars and then to Sven. Immediately they understand his coded signal.

'I think we have time for another drink before your colleagues get back with the coffees – what were their names again?'
'Vladimir and Rasputin.'
Jake's mind is whirring, images are flicking through his brain like a Rolodex at full speed. He stops at a mental photo and focuses on the description under it.

Vladimir Parton aka Vlad the inhaler due to his habit of sucking the air out of his victims, ex KGB, ex PVC. His mind is whirring again. He stops...

Rasputin Rotten aka Rasputin, The Mad Punk due to his love of the Sex Pistols, Ex JVC ex DDT.

'How long have they worked for you, Viggo?
Jake notices a little bead of sweat on Viggo's temple so he subtly changes the subject.
'You're probably like me – hopeless with dates. The last two years have been a blur, I can hardly remember anything.'
On hearing this Viggo's body noticeably relaxes, he grunts as a sign of agreement.

The circular table is almost fully occupied and a casual observer would get the impression that this was an ordinary, run of the mill, business meeting. To the trained eye, though, it is clear that there is a great deal of tension in the room. Viggo's good eye darts from side to side, Wes keeps shifting his position in an unsuccessful attempt to make himself appear relaxed, Arnie is waiting patiently for his bagels. Sven and Lars feign indifference, but each one is acutely aware of their particular role in this gathering. Jake is the only one who is inscrutable. In truth, he is enjoying the proceedings, he has been in circumstances like this many times before and he is now on autopilot. He casually contemplates the two men in front of him, knowing that either one or both of them could be an enemy, on the other hand, none of them could be. He wracks his brain wondering if there are any other possibilities - before deciding that there probably isn't.

He recalls some of the things his Harvard professor said to him.

*"If it seems probable then it might be, but if it seems improbable then it possibly could be."*

*"A thirsty mind needs to think not drink."*

He remembers why he started skipping those lectures. Thankfully, he is distracted from his thoughts by the return of the henchmen.
'Ah, Rasputin and Vladimir.' He rises from his seat. 'Here, let me give you a hand.'
'We got a selection of bagels, Mr. Poisson – was that right?'
'That's perfect, Rasputin, thank you very much.'
'And I got some extra coffees in case anyone is extra thirsty and extra milk and extra sugar.'

'How considerate of you, Vladimir.'
Beaming with pride, the two men carefully place the trays on the table and return to the doorway, giving Arnie a large berth.
'Uncle Viggo, this is family business. It doesn't concern your colleagues, perhaps you could give them the afternoon off.'

It was more of a statement than a question and Viggo, realizing that he cannot refuse without incriminating himself, reluctantly accepts the suggestion. Besides, he knows that the two of them would be no match for Arnie – or Jake, for that matter. As the two henchmen leave, Jake turns to Viggo.
'We should never tell anyone outside the family what we're thinking, should we?'
Viggo glances quizzically at Sven and Lars.

'These men are like brothers to me. Besides, one is my peacetime consigliere and the other is my...

He pauses, pointedly waiting for Wes and Viggo's reactions.

...*wartime* consigliere.'

Jake points to the food on the table.
'Relax – enjoy – we have much to talk about.'
Viggo looks at his brother as if to say - '*we may as well go along with him.*'
Jake notices, but says nothing.

*Ten minutes later*

As Arnie finishes off the last of the bagels, Jake takes a bottle of JD out of the drinks cabinet and pours two fingers into several cut crystal glasses. Handing each man a glass, he offers a toast.

'Salut!'

'Salut!'

Wes downs it in one. 'Nice, but you haven't got any of that crème de menthe, have you?'

*Five hours, four bottles of JD, and*

*three bottles of Crème de Menthe later*


The shoppers return.

'Where are the others?'

'I sent Wes and Viggo off in a taxi, I told them they could stay at my apartment for the night – Wes had been staying there anyway. The rest of us are still here.'

'That's wight, I iz still here – I sink.'

'Me too.'

'Me three.'

'Rea and Olga you're welcome to stay here if you don't mind sharing a bed, but I can order a taxi for the two of you, if you think that would be better.'

'Looking at you lot, I think that might be a good idea. What do you think?'

Olga watches Sven slide off his chair and fall at her feet. She takes a napkin off the table and wipes his saliva from her shoe.

'I'm finding that proposition more enticing by the minute.'

Jake takes hold of a jug of water and pours himself a glass which he then empties over his head.

'That's better – how did your shopping trip go?'

Candice bends down to inspect Sven and in the process accidently dislodges Lars from his seat.

'It was great, we bought some lovely outfits.'

She picks up the jug and pours the rest of its contents over Sven. Clutching her bags to her chest she storms off, with the other girls following.

'But you lot won't be seeing any of them for a while.'

Arnie gingerly lifts up his head.

'Vot vent vong, brudder?'

'I don't know, Arnie, sometimes I just don't understand women - I suppose we'd better call it a day, you take the table, bro' – I'll join the others on the floor.'

# Chapter Twenty-five

# A Dingo in New York

*Ten a.m. the next morning*

Ten people are sitting around the table, not quite enough to form a jury - which is probably just as well because if there were, the men would all be guilty and the women would be wearing black hats. Jake tries to ignore the atmosphere.

'Good morning, everyone, I hope you all slept well.' He tries to ignore the groans.

'I know most of you know a lot of what I'm going to say, but I need to go back to the start so that Olga and Randy in particular, fully understand the great danger we are in.'

There is a knock at the door.

'Oh great - room service.' Four smartly-dressed, heavily-laden waiters enter the room and begin to distribute the mouthwatering food, but for some reason no one seems hungry. Jake's rolodex is whirring in his head.

Just as the waiters are about to leave, he takes a device out of his pocket and switches it on.

'Just a minute, follow me please.'

All four men stop dead in their tracks then follow Jake into the storeroom. Jake turns to the others.

'Enjoy your breakfasts, this shouldn't take long.'

'Vot vos that all about?'

'I recognize some of their faces, do you, Lars?'

'Yep, Sven – knowing Jake, he'll have something up his

sleeve.'

'Or down his twouzers.'

The three men shift uncomfortably in their seats, the women mysteriously regain their appetites. By the time Jake returns all the food has gone. Jake is happy.

'It works!'

The atmosphere in the room has changed completely and Jake feels confident enough to continue the debriefing.

'First of all, I need to apologize for last night. We were using interrogation techniques which Sven, Lars and I developed in 'stan.'

'That's right, Jake – we recognized the signal when you mixed up our names.'

'And what did you find out, Sven?'

'Er, I can't remember much after that.'

'How about you, Lars.'

'I remember struggling to get my tongue out of that crème de menthe bottle.'

'Okay, maybe we'll get back to that.'

Jake picks up the last sausage.

'Mmmm... – that's the nicest sausage I've ever had.'

By the grins on the faces of the others, he feels sure that they agree. He rubs his tummy and begins.

'As you all know, some time ago I underwent a procedure known as MESH+, my colleagues, Sven and Lars, here, were given a slightly less invasive version called MESH – short for Memory Wash.'

Randy is confused. 'Why weren't any of us given it?'

'I think Rea can answer that, Randy.'

'The short answer is that we didn't need to.'

'That's right, apparently the Mind Infiltration Control Key

doesn't work on women.'
'The mind infil...?'
'MICK for short.'
'What's that?'

'That's what I'm trying to find out, but first I must explain
how this all started. When I was little, I killed my mother and
smashed my brother's head in.'
Jake waits until the rest of them have finished moving their
chairs back.
'Good God, Jake!'
'I didn't do it on purpose, of course, I was riding on a
carousel when the spaceship I was in came loose and
decapitated my mother and caved in Arnie's skull.'
'That's tragic.' Norma reaches out to him, a tear rolling
down her cheek onto his hand.
'I know, it was only recently that I found out, myself.'

The room is in absolute silence as Jake continues., He
addresses Arnie, in particular.
'Anyway, to cut a long story short, our father – the man you
know as Wes, left us with Fox because he thought he could
look after us better.'
Rea takes over.
'And he did – I can vouch for that, he did everything he
could for both of you – and you too, Norma – we both did.'
Norma dabs her eyes with a tissue.
'I know that, Mom.'
Jake pats Norma's hand and continues.
'So do I, and at first it went very well. Fox's brilliance helped
him to produce a serum for Arnie – you just have to look at
him to see how successful it was.'

Arnie glows with pride as the others nod their agreement.
Jake turns his attention to Rea.

'By testing his concoctions on me and then on Norma, he found out that they had other benefits.'

'And that made Fox very happy, Jake. He loved you and Arnie as if you were his own.'

'I know that, Rea, but, unfortunately the wrong people found out what he was doing and realized that these serums could be used for mind control.'

'Do you know who?'

'I have my suspicions, but obviously I need to be absolutely certain. Fox became aware that something was wrong. He contacted me and with Lars and Sven's help, The Don Corleone Agency made some progress infiltrating The Blowman Corporation, but they were very cunning, constantly changing their modus operandi. There was always the possibility that we would get MICKed.'

'How do they do that?

' 'I begrudge saying it, but they have cleverly improved it over the years. Originally, they could only do it by injecting the serum directly into the victim, but now they can use subliminal messages.'

'How?'

'The messages are hidden in social media video clips. I don't need to remind you of the consequences – you only need to watch the news bulletins - you've seen the outcomes yourself.'

'Ya, now I onderstond vot eez going on, but vot can vee do?'

'Well, we've made some inroads, thanks to discoveries by Rea, in her guise as Georgette. Perhaps you'd like to explain, Rea?'

271

'I found that strong emotions such as pleasure and pain could have an effect on MICK particularly if the two were combined, that is, if the person found the pain to be pleasurable.'
'I can't believe anyone would...'
Rea gently strokes Olga's hand.
'You'd be surprised, my dear. It has to be done correctly, of course – by an expert'
'But how did you find all this out?'
'Quite by accident. I ordered an annual subscription of *Crocheting With A Purpose* and by mistake they sent me *BDSM Can Be Fun.'*
'So that solved the problem?'
'Obviously not, Olga – where have you been all this time?'
'I was in Sweden.'
'Oh!'

Jake breaks off from reading a text.
'The problem is, we can't go around stripping and beating every Tom, Dick and Harry just to prevent their minds from being infiltrated. Some people wouldn't like it.'
'I could do it discretely, and I could teach my girls here, Candice already knows how.'
Jake looks at a sea of nodding heads.
'It would take too long, besides, with Olga and Tai Chi's help I have found an easier way - which reminds me, I'd better go and check in the storeroom. Rea, can you bring everyone up to speed on recent developments?'

As Jake heads for the storeroom, Rea continues the briefing.
'We had underestimated the effect of MESH+, Sven and Lars were fine, all they needed was regular maintenance from me to ensure that they could not be MICKed.'

Lars and Sven's eyes remain firmly fixed on the floor.

'We knew that Jake was the only one who could get us out of this mess, but we couldn't get his memory back in one piece. When we found out that the Blowman Corporation had contacted Jake we needed to work quickly - that's when I issued a Code Red to get him back. I must say you all did a brilliant job – Candice, you even had *me* fooled!'

'Thanks Rea, I have to admit I quite enjoyed it.'

The conversation stops as Jake escorts the four men out of the storeroom and down the stairs. On his return they look questioningly at him.

'It worked!'

'Where are they now?' 'I put them into taxis, they're heading for their parents' houses, totally oblivious to where they've been for the last couple of years.'

'That's great, Jake – what's our next move?'

'Well, Lars, my plan is to try it out at Fox's daughter's wedding in two weeks' time.'

They all look stunned.

'I'm sure you'll all play your parts well. I've got lots to organize so I would advise you to take the rest of the day off and enjoy yourselves.'

Norma's face is beaming, she can hardly talk with excitement.

'Jake you are so clever, keeping it from me, but is two weeks enough time to organize our wedding?'

'Our wedding?'

'You said Fox's daughter – that's me.'

'Oh, yes - of course you are, but I meant Fox's other daughter, Liz. She's getting married to her fiancé, Ernest.'

Silent tears stream down Norma's face, but her pride won't let Jake see them. She rushes from the room, making an excuse about having to water her cactus. Sally, Olga and Randy follow her, Rea storms after them.

'And to think you might have been my son-in-law. I consider this to be a lucky escape.'

Candice is the only female left, as she leaves the room she glowers fiercely at Jake, mouthing 'Idiot!', as she slams the door behind her.

Jake looks puzzled.

'Scissors!'

'Rock - I win – you ask him.'

'Okay – Jake, you know that me and Sven will do anything for you, don't you?'

'That's nice, Lars.'

'Und me bro"

'Thanks men, it's good to know I've always got you three to back me up.'

'And you know we would follow you across a desert with only our own urine to drink.'

'I would always let you have some of mine.'

'We know that, and that's what makes it so difficult to tell you.'

'Tell me what?'

'We think you're wrong on this occasion.'

'About what?'

'About Norma.'

Sven and Lars are ready to vacate their chairs, but surprisingly, Jake is calm.'

'You'll have to trust me on this one, I have my reasons.'

One hour later Jake is sitting on a park bench next to the usual drop off point, wondering if the squirrel is still in the hole. He decides to risk it, but just to be on the safe side he snaps a fallen branch in half and pokes a piece of it in the hole. Not finding anything, he gingerly eases his hand into the opening and withdraws a damp package. He sniffs it.

'Damned squirrel!'

He opens the package carefully, shaking his head as he reads it.

'Damned Dingo!'

He presses #1 on his speed dial.

'You sure HP?'

'As sure as I can be with The Dingo, we got a tip off from the Head of the Italian Security Services that he'd flown in under an alias.'

'What was it?'

'Deano Martino – they were suspicious because that's the name of the chief of police's husband.'

'So, what made them suspicious?'

'The Head of Security was in bed with the real Martino at that time.'

'What time was it?'

'Three in the afternoon – Monday.'

'It's now Friday, why did it take so long?'

'Apparently, they didn't like to disturb him when he was at work...'

'Do we have any idea of Dingo's whereabouts now?'

'After the tip off I put two of my best men on him.'

'Are they still tracking him?'

'Unfortunately, he gave them the slip.'

'How?'

'They followed him into an all-night diner. One of my men occasionally sets off the alarms due to having the remnants of a taser being stuck up his ar...'

'And that raised The Dingo's suspicions?'

'No, apparently The Dingo didn't seem to notice.'

'So, what alerted him?'

'The manager had my men arrested due to an altercation about a lack of stodgy cake or something.'

Jake now has a much clearer understanding of what happened.

'Could that have been *stottie cake*?'

'Yeah, that sounds about right - I'm sorry I can't be of more assistance, my friend.'

'Not at all, Captain – you've been a great help.'

'Jake, I must warn you though - word is, he's got a contract out on you. He's no match for you though, is he?'

'The Dingo has never failed, when he gets a contract, he carries it out. That killer is around here somewhere. You can't make deals with him. You can't try to reason with him. The Dingo doesn't feel any sympathy or regret and he's not afraid. He's a monster and he will not stop until he kills me– nothing can change that – that's why he gets paid so much.'

'How much does he get?'

'I don't know exactly, but it must be a lot.'

'Why you?'

'He's never liked me since I beat him three times in a row at pogs in sixth grade.'

'You went to the same school? You must know what he looks like.'

'He's a master of disguise.'

'Remind me - what does his file say about his appearance, Jake?'

'Believed to be in the area. Description: Average height, average weight, nondescript, no distinguishing marks, no recent photographs, in fact no photographs whatsoever, hobbies – nothing out of the ordinary.'

'Heck, Jake – what are you going to do?'

'I have a hunch.'

'That's great, - your hunches have always worked in the past, but I've seen his file and this time I think you'll need more than just a hunch. This guy's wanted on eight continents.'

'I thought there were only seven continents.'

'He's wanted in places that don't yet exist. He can shoot a flea's testicles off from a hundred yards, swim half a mile under water, he's a tenth dan in every martial art that's ever been invented and he holds the world record for limbo dancing.'

'Okay, Harry - what do you suggest?'

'I've got a Bible in my desk drawer – I always read it in times of great trouble, it may help you.'

'Thanks for that advice, HP – oh, by the way – after my discharge from the army, I spent some time in a convalescent home in Newcastle upon Tyne. In an effort to wean me off pot noodles, they fed me on ham and pease pudding stotties.'

'Sounds horrendous, did it work?'

'Almost, I occasionally need a top up, so I'd be obliged if you could ask Crockett if he had any luck in his search.'

'Ask Crockett?'

Harry Pusey's hands shake as he reaches for his drawer.

'Damn, where's that Bible?'

Jake's phone goes dead, he re-reads the file contents, studying every word. Deep in thought, he's pondering his next move, when...

'Don't I know you, young man?'

'No, it was someone else who got bitten by the squirrel.'

'My dog is barking. He never forgets a face or any other part of a man's anatomy. Neither do I, for that matter and I've seen thousands of men's anatomies - I definitely think it...'

Jake throws the other part of the stick into the distance.'

'Fetch!'

Jake considers setting fire to the file, but after his last experience with a bin, he decides against it. Tucking it into his jacket, he heads off for Gloria's. Later that afternoon Sven and Lars are trying to show Arnie how to play Rock Paper Scissors.

'Bomb!'

'No, Arnie, you can only choose rock or paper or scissors.'

'Arnie looks around.

'Vare iz zee udders?'

'Jake didn't say where he was going, the rest must still be in their bedrooms.'

'Somevon needs to go and look for zem.'

'I'll do it.'

Lars wanders off in search of the others.

'Here you are, Rea, what are you all doing?'

'We are helping Norma pack.'

'Why?

' 'Why? ... Why? ... Why do you think? – To get away from that beast of a man with a heart of ice.'

'Who do you mean?'

'Jake – you idiot – who else would it be?'

'I just wanted to make sure.'

'Why are men so stupid?'

'I think it's because...'

'It was a hypothetical question, Lars – know what I'm gonna do? – After I've waved goodbye to Norma, I'm going to train my girls, you will be our first volunteer.'
Lars heads back to Sven and Arnie.
'Everything okay, Lars?'
'I think so.'
'What are you doing?'
'I'm just checking the freezer.'
Arnie breaks off from his game of Rock Paper Scissors with Sven.
'I haf just had a text from my brudder, he vill not be back today, he sez if zere iz anyzing vee need, to let him know.'
Lars is still staring into the freezer.
'He could bring some frozen peas...'

*Later that day in Gloria's house*


'Jake, where have you been? I've been worried about you, what have you been up to?'
'Nothing much.'
'Well thank goodness you're safe.'
'There's nothing to worry about, Mom, I live a very boring life these days.'
'I'm pleased to hear it.'
'Mom, are you on your own?'
'Yes, son, Charles has had to go away on business and Liz and Ernest are making last minute preparations for their wedding – have you got your speech prepared?'
'I've got a few notes jotted down - have the invitations been sent out yet?'
'They're on the sideboard there, ready to go.'
Jake feigns disinterest.

'I've brought you some of those herbs for your new meatloaf recipe. I shouldn't say it, but I've missed that meatloaf nearly as much as I've missed you.'

Gloria laughs and kisses Jake on the forehead.

'I'll start right away.'

Jake listens to Gloria's slippered feet padding down the passageway. In a split second, he is at the sideboard skimming through the pile of invitations. Happy that he's memorized them, he pockets a handful of spares, then joins Gloria in the kitchen.

### Three a.m. (the next morning)

Jake picks up a packet of frozen peas from the all-night store. He freewheels with his headlights off as he approaches the stakeout. Most drivers would have crashed into a lamppost or something with no power steering or brakes, but Jake has been trained to narrowly avoid obstacles by millimeters. He knows where to step to avoid any creaking stairs and within seconds he is inside the stakeout - removing and replacing the memory cards of the surveillance cameras.

A few short minutes later, Jake is parked in an underground car park studying the videos.

### Three p.m. (the next afternoon)

Jake is stealthily stalking a man who is hobbling along on crutches. He waits until he is only ten yards behind him then yells -

"Dingo – DINGO -DINGO!!!" at the top of his voice.

*A little later (the same day)*

Jake is showing Sven and Lars a very blurred photograph of
a mass of people who all seem to be running from something.
'That man there, you can't really see the crutches.'
'Who is he?'
'The Dingo.'
'My God, The Dingo's here – where?'
'He was heading for the Two Hands café in Nolita.'
'Isn't that where there are lots of Australi...?'
'Hmm... that might explain the panic. Unfortunately, I lost
him when the crowd stampeded.'
'That's a shame.'
'It is, Sven, but the good news is - I now know for certain
that he's deaf – oh, I also know where to get a great
mushroom latte.'
'Mmm, sounds delicious.'
'The bad news is - he's got a contract out on me.'
'You know what they say about him, Jake?'
'That he has never failed?'
'No.'
'That when he gets a contract, he carries it out and nothing
can change that?'
'No.'
'What do they say about him?'
'That he carries a doll of his next victim around with him
and sticks pins in it.'

Jake bends down. 'Ouch – I must have hurt my back in that
wild scrimmage.'
Lars and Sven look knowingly at each other. Jake heads for
his bedroom where he unexpectedly finds Rea, dressed only

in her lacy underwear, putting some of her clothes into an empty wardrobe. Jake averts his eyes.

'Oops – sorry Rea, where's Norma?'

'Where's Norma? – WHERE'S NORMA? – You may well ask where my daughter is – she's gone and she told me not to tell you where she's gone.'

'Why did she leave?'

'To get away from that beast of a man with a heart of ice.'

'Who do you mean?'

'You – you idiot – who else would it be?'

'I just wanted to make sure.'

'Why are men so stupid?'

'I think it's because...'

'It was a hypothetical question, Jake – know what I'm gonna do? – Now that I've waved goodbye to Norma, I'm going to train my girls, you will be our second volunteer.'

'Who's the first?'

'Lars.'

Jake wishes he'd bought two packets of frozen peas.

'I suppose I deserve it, Rea.'

'You do, but looking on the bright side – I still have my Monday afternoons free – what do you think of my new underwear?'

A little later that day Jake is studying the surveillance cameras again. He stops and rewinds the video a few times then dashes out of the stakeout and across the road into the Poisson Dating office. He boots up the system and quickly scans through the new applications.

'Gotcha!'

He opens Georgette's profile and selects Match before returning to the stakeout. This time he knocks on his bedroom door before entering.

'Come in.'

Rea is sitting on the bed reading a book.

'Oh, it's you!'

'Who were you expecting?'

'I've just ordered some new underwear from Amazon Prime, that last lot were a little too staid, don't you think?'

Jake thinks back, he can't remember much about them because there wasn't much of them to remember.

'I didn't notice, I only have eyes for Norma.'

'Well, you can knock that on the head – after the way you treated her.'

'When's she coming back?'

'Jake, you have some admirable qualities, I know - I've experienced some of them myself, but understanding women is not one of them I'm afraid.'

'So, when is she coming back?'

'I'm trying to tell you, in the nicest way I can, that she won't be coming back. You had your chance and you blew it.'

'I have my reasons, Rea.'

'I'm sure you do – name one.'

'I don't have time at the minute, but that's not why I came – I need your help.'

'Why should I help the man who has single-handedly destroyed my daughter's life?'

Jake takes a package out of his bedside cabinet.

'I got these for Norma as a surprise. I don't suppose she'd take them now. You two are about the same size...'

'Ooh, black, my favorite color – there's not much material here - just the way I like them, I wonder if it's too late to cancel my order.'

283

Rea opens the package and holds the diaphanous garments up to the light.

'Okay – what do you want me to do?

# Chapter Twenty-six

# The Budgie Smuggling Olympian

*Two days later*

Rea, in the guise of Georgette, is quietly sneaking out of a man's apartment. She leaves the door slightly ajar, nods to Jake as she passes him in the corridor, then swiftly makes her way to the elevator. A couple of minutes later, Jake is holding a gun to the man's head, all his senses are telling him to pull the trigger, but for some reason he is unable to.

'Go on, Jake, it's you or me – you won't get another chance.'

The face in front of him bears no relation to the schoolboy he once knew - plastic surgery and excessive Botox have seen to that. Jake manages to hide the tremble in his trigger finger, but his adversary still senses his predicament.

'You're too soft, Jake. Do you kill a deaf, cripple and have it on your conscience the rest of your life or do you take the risk that I'll finish the contract?'

'You're no cripple, Dingo – those crutches are hiding your rifle.'

'Maybe, but the way my backside feels at the minute – I doubt whether I'd be able to walk without them.'

Jake admires Georgette's professional approach to her job.

'You'll recover - and I'm speaking from experience - I'm finished here, Dingo, but before I go, I want to know -why me, Dingo?'

'I could say it was for the million dollars – which is half my usual fee by the way, but I'd be lying. I've wanted to kill you

ever since you beat me at everything in eighth grade.'
 'I was going to let you beat me in the ninth grade, but I enlisted and was posted to 'stan.'
Jake's conscience gets the better of him and he walks away. As he bends to fasten his lace a shot rings out – leaving telltale wisps of smoke wafting from the bottom of one of the crutches. The bullet narrowly misses Jake's head and lodges itself in a hot water pipe.*

*Some people might call that luck, but Jake has a heightened sense of danger which has saved him from harm on numerous occasions.*

Jake's head is surrounded by a halo of gushing steam, The blurred image of which, triggers something in The Dingo's memory - his mind is back in 'stan. Deafened by a tremendous explosion, he is lying semi-conscious, amongst rubble and debris - just as he takes what he thinks will be his last breath, he sees a hand reaching out for him. The hand is followed by an arm, the arm by a face and he feels himself being yanked to safety.
 'My God, it was you – *you* saved my life!'
 'It was all in the line of duty.'
 'How... how can I possibly repay you?'
 'A simple thank you will suffice– oh, and if you wouldn't mind canceling the contract?'
 'In the circumstances I think that's the least I can do.'
 'Thanks, Dingo.'
 'You can call me Clarence, Jake – but don't tell anybody else.' Jake laughs.
 'Okay, Clarence.'

*Two days later*

Jake rounds the corner of the garden of the Yates Motel carrying a small jewelry box and a massive bouquet. Wearing a huge smile on his face, he feels so happy he would love to burst into song, but, realizing that would spoil the surprise, he goes into stealth mode. On his hands and knees, he crawls silently through the undergrowth. He sees Norma heading towards him, wearing a bikini which fits where it touches - he's about to jump out and surprise her, when he hears a man's deep voice booming from the other side of the garden.

'Hallo, Norma – I'm over here, I have the camera.'

'Is this outfit suitable?'

'It'll do for a start.'

Jake turns and sees the owner of the deep, gravelly voice. He's not quite sure whether the man is wearing budgie smugglers or whether he's just had his genitals painted. His ego deflated - Jake is about to beat a hasty retreat.

'Jake – JAKE!'

Jake stands up and looks around and then points at himself as if to say. *'Me?'*

'It *is* you! Are those flowers for me? – And what's in that box – it isn't, is it?'

'Er, no – these are for a Miss Watt – I've got a job working for 1.800 Flowers. I think she's staying here.'

He looks at the card and tries, but fails, to surreptitiously slip it into his pocket.

'Oh no – I've misread it, she's staying at the Vates Motel.'

'I've never heard of that one, Jake.'

Ignoring her, Jake carries on.

'Who's your friend?'

'Oh, I'm sorry, I should have introduced you to each other –
Jake meet Maximillian – Maximillian meet someone I used
to know – Jake Poisson.'
'Pleased to meet you, Jake – so you're a delivery boy?'
Jake tries not to take the bait.
'Among other things, what do you do?'
'Max was an Olympic gold medalist.'
*Synchronized love-making, I suppose.'* Jake thinks.
'You'd probably assume it was weightlifting or gymnastics,
looking at him, wouldn't you, but no, it's fencing – for a big
man, he's got great rhythm and balance.'
Jake attempts a joke.
'Probably good at lunging and thrusting, eh.'
It falls flat.
'Oh well, I must go - otherwise Miss Watson will be
disappointed.'
'Watt.'
'What?'
'You said Miss Watt.'
'That's right - Miss Watson-Watt – she has a double-
barreled name.'
'Don't you want to stick around and see how the photos turn
out? – Max is taking a set for a magazine, a natur...'
As Jake beats a hasty retreat around the corner, he calls
back.
'I'd love to, but I wouldn't want to get in the way of your
sword swallowing.'

## Two days later

'Where've you been, Jake – we've been bored without you?'
'I thought you were teaching Arnie how to play Rock Paper Scissors.'
'He kept cheating.'
'I vosn't.'
'He was, so we moved on to Truth, Dare or Forfeit, but if we didn't do the dare, he would dangle us both out of the window by our legs.'
'Yes, zat vos zee four feet, eet vos a gut game – vot haf you been doing, brudder.'
'Not much.'
Jake tries to change the subject.
'We thought you were hiding from the Dingo, Jake.'
'He won't be bothering me again, Sven.'
Lars and Sven nod at each other.
'That's the Jake that we know and love.'
'Thanks men.'

Lars clears his throat.
'Arnie thought you might have been visiting Norma, because Rea said you'd given her some lovely underwear in exchange for her whereabouts.'
Jake strokes his chin, as if in thought.'
'Norma ... Norma...? Oh, that Norma ... Oh, yes, I did pop in to see her, but only because I needed to give the chopper a spin, I may be needing it soon – and I had some business down there, anyway.'
'That vos a coincidence.'
'Yeah, I suppose it was.'
'Did you gif her an inwitation to the vedding?'

'Damn - it slipped my mind!'
Even though Jake is trained to stay calm in every possible situation, he is starting to feel a little hot under the collar.
'Has someone turned up the heating in here?' Lars shakes his head.
'We have no heating, it broke down.'
'What about hot water, I could do with a shower after all my traveling.'
'We have no hot water, besides, Rea says cold showers are good for us.'
'Where is Rea?'
'She's gone somewhere with her step-daughter.'
'Liz?'
'Could be, we didn't ask.'
'What about the others?'
'They've gone with her – they won't be back for three days.'
'That's the day before the wedding. Did they say where they were going?'
'They weren't talking to me or Sven.'
'Why not?'
'Said we were your friends and they never, ever wanted to see you or talk to your friends again and if they saw you soon it would be too soon and even if it wasn't soon, it would still be too soon. Isn't that right, Sven?'
'You missed out the "... and no matter when it was, it would be too..."'
'Okay, I get the picture. I wonder where they've gone.'
'They told Arnie - he was the only one they'd speak to.'
'Arnie, did they tell you where they were going?'
'Zey said zey vonted to get as far avay from you as possible so zey vere going to dance with some chickens in wegas.'
Jake scratches his head. 'Do you mean they've gone on a Hen

party to Vegas?'
'That's vot I said.'
'You let them go – just like that?'
Sven and Lars protest.
'We were being dangled out of a window at the time.'
'Zat iz a gut game.'
'There's no need to worry, I'm sure they'll start talking to you when you and Norma get back together.'
'Somehow, I don't think that's ever going to happen.'

Jake's mind is elsewhere, in fact it's in the garden of the Yates Motel.
*'That's right, Norma, darling, just pull them down a little and smile at the camera ... yes ... perfect. Now bend over while I adjust my sword.'*

Jake's mind is whirring, during the past week he has almost been assassinated, the love of his life has spurned him for some hunk of a sportsman with a big sword and a pair of trunks four sizes too small – and now he is excommunicado, along with half of his team. What else can possibly go wrong?
'Someone called Ernest is comming to wisit you.'
'When?'
'At von o'clock.'
'It's five to one now.'
'Hello, future bro' in law, long time no see.'
'You're early.'
'Only five minutes – give me a hug, bro' in law.'

Jake considers passing Ernest to his brother, but after seeing the dejected look on Arnie's face he decides not to.
'What's wrong, Arnie?'
'I am wery sad.'

'So are we, Jake. We thought the only reason you hadn't proposed to Norma was because your life was in danger from the Dingo – now there's nothing to stop you.'

'Zat's right - besides, I vont to be my brudder's beast man and Sally vonts to be a teasmaid.'

For a moment Jake wonders where Arnie has been all these years, then he remembers.'

'Oh no, Arnie, that was never an option.'

Jake pushes the engagement ring box further into his trouser pocket in an effort to make it less conspicuous.'

'If I ever get married though, Arnie, I will be proud to have you as my best man.'

'So, this is your brother, Jake?'

'How remiss of me not to introduce you. Ernie - this is my brother, Arnie. Arnie, this is the man who is marrying the woman I thought was my sister.'

Ernie looks shocked.

'You thought...?'

'I don't suppose you'll want me as your best man now?'

'Of course I do, after all I've heard about you, who wouldn't want the great Jake Poisson as their best man?'

'What have you heard about me?'

'Er ... nothing.'

'Who said it?'

'Er ... no one.'

Ernie's behavior confirms Jake's suspicions.

'Actually, Ernie - I'm pleased you've come.'

'How so, future bro' in law?'

'It'll give me a chance to try out the modifications I've made to that machine you sold me.'

# Chapter Twenty-seven

## The Wedding

*Four days later, the wedding venue*

During the last few days, Jake's preparations have gone reasonably well. Ernest responded brilliantly to his treatment - before passing out - and he now seems capable of at least staying conscious during the ceremony. There is still no sign of the bride or bridesmaids, but at least all the guests Jake personally invited have turned up.

'They're all in place, like you said, Jake – one on each table.'

'That's great, Sven.'

'Here's the seating plan, you, Lars and Arnie – second thoughts, just you and Lars – direct the guests to their seats after the service and make sure no one leaves before my speech.'

'Sure thing, Jake – this reminds me of when we were in 'stan, you always planned things down to the last detail. That's why you never lost a man under your command.'

'Thanks, Sven, but I owe it to having men like you and Lars.'

'We would have waded through a river of shit for you, Jake – still would if you asked us.'

'Let's hope it doesn't come to that, Sven – at least not before the meal.'

'Oh, there's one other thing – a man's been asking to see you.'

'What did he look like?'

'Average height, average weight, nondescript, no distinguishing marks.'

'That could be anybody. I'd better go and see what he wants – where is he?'
'I left him with Arnie.'


*Two minutes later*


'Arnie, was there a man looking for me?'
Arnie points towards a coat rack. One of the coats appears to be moving.
'He vould not haf a conwersation vith me.'
Jake lifts the coat.
'Jake, am I pleased to see *you*! I've become very proficient at lip reading, but I'm afraid I couldn't understand the doorman here.'
'Iz zat an insoolt?'
'It's okay, Arnie – this is a friend of mine - I'll deal with it - could you make sure Ernest is still chained to his chair?'
Arnie mutters something under his breath and wanders off.
'Do you know that guy, Jake?'
'He's my brother.'
'Holy shit – I'm glad I've retired from my line of business!'
'He's very protective towards me.'
'I can see that.'
'Anyway, I'm pleased you could make it, Clarence.'
'You saved my life, Jake – I would wade through a river of billy goat's puke for you.'
'Let's hope it doesn't come to that, Clarence – at least not before the meal.'
Jake wonders if the view across the East River from his apartment will ever have the same appeal to him. He takes a

flower out of his coat pocket and pins it on Clarence's lapel.
'You're one of the family now.'

Clarence is unable to hide his delight, he contorts his face into what Jake takes to be a smile. At that moment Jake's heightened powers of awareness indicate that the bride's entrance is imminent.
'That's very kind of you, Clarence – there is one thing you can do for me.'
'Anything.'
Jake surreptitiously glances towards one of the tables.
'Do you recognize any of those faces?'
'In our line of business, you know that we see lots of faces.'
'Agreed.'
'And you know that even if I could definitely confirm one of those faces, for example the one with the moustache, was the one who put the contract out on you, absolute secrecy and confidentiality would prevent me from confirming that.'
Clarence taps his nose with his finger and winks.
'Understood - I've sat you in the corner where you can keep an eye on things for me. It's close enough for you to lipread the speeches.'
'Thanks, Jake – you think of everything.'
'I have to go now, Clarence – enjoy yourself and try not to shoot anybody.'

Jake pauses momentarily to check on the machine on table three, he smiles to himself as Dragoni, Featherstonehaugh and Hannon nearly choke on their wine. Making sure that all his men are in position, Jake heads for Arnie and Ernest. He checks that Ernest is secure before taking his brother to one side.
'Arnie, you know that man you threw into the coat rack?'

'Ya.'

'If he makes any suspicious moves - disarm him.'

'How vill I recognize him?'

'You've just seen him, what did he look like?'

'Awerage height, awerage veight, nondescwipt, no distingwishing marks.'

'I see what you mean – just remember, he's wearing a red carnation, ours are white.'

'So heez bumhole eez red?'

'Buttonhole, Arnie – that's right - and all ours are white.'

'I onderstand – mine's a leetel pinkish.'

Arnie wanders off, laughing at his own joke.

Satisfied that everything is in hand, Jake undoes Ernest's cuffs.

'The bride and bridesmaids will be here soon, just relax, Ernest.'

'Are you getting married, Jake?'

Jake had used Ernest as a guinea pig for his voice activated memory wash machine. The result had been impressive, but with a subject like Ernest there was always a danger of unforeseen complications. Jake hands Ernest a small object.

'This piece of amber was given to me by a Tibetan monk. It dates back to prehistoric days, can you see anything inside it?'

'Yes, there's some kind of creature – it's staring at me.'

Jake relaxes, knowing the stone is doing its work.

'Who is that woman in white?'

'That's Liz, she's your bride to be, she's beautiful, isn't she?'

'She wouldn't be my first choice, what about the one in pink?'

'She's a bridesmaid - just keep staring at the stone, Ernest.'

'The one in blu...?'
'He's an usher – don't take your eyes off the stone.'

Somehow the ceremony goes off without a hitch. – maybe it has something to do with Jake whispering instructions into an earpiece in Ernest's ear. Even more surprisingly, nobody seems to notice the almost tangible wall of ice between the best man and the bridesmaids and the robotic responses of the groom. Jake breathes a sigh of relief as Liz and Ernest welcome their last guest into the reception room. Taking to his feet, Jake taps his glass for attention, clears his throat and...

'Good afternoon, ladies and gentlemen - and the rest of you. First of all, I would like to say how beautiful the bride looks, I'm sure you'll all agree.'

Nods of approval and polite applause from some of the guests.

'And even the groom looks quite presentable.'

A couple of the guests laugh. He turns his attention to the bridesmaids, Sally, Candice, Randy and Rea.

'Have you ever seen such sheer loveliness in one place?'

He glances across at four stony, unamused faces - undeterred, he carries on.

'I can honestly say I don't think I have ever seen such bre... breath...'

Jake's super-senses suddenly go into overdrive. His gaze is drawn towards the far corner of the room, where a young woman is being shown to her seat. One by one, the guests all follow his gaze, until eventually everyone in the room is staring in the same direction.

'B...B...Breathtaking!'

Jake finally manages to stammer. Norma colors as she

realizes that it is her, gaining the attention of Jake and everyone else, including the bridesmaids. Jake is completely mesmerized, after that episode with the budgie-smuggling Olympian, he vowed never to even look at her again - but in that black micro-mini dress she is almost wearing, he cannot take his eyes off her... As Jake gazes longingly at her, almost devouring her with his eyes, the rest of the room seems to fade into a misty haze. Jake reaches into his pocket in search of the engagement ring he almost threw away, when...

# Chapter Twenty-eight

# The Island

*Five minutes later, the car park of the wedding venue*

'I've programmed in the coordinates you gave me, Jake – be careful with the controls. We followed your advice and made a few tweaks to the engines.'

'It sounds like you've also shaved a couple of millimeters off the axial-flow compressor blades.'

'How the heck do you...?'

'The engine idle is half an octave higher than the last time I flew this baby.'

'You son of a gun, Jake – you never fail to amaze me – just look after yourself!'

'You too, Snake.'

'Who vos that?'

'That was the General.'

'He must like you, letting you haf zis arrowplane.'

'I saved his life once. He'll never forget that – no matter how much they try to mess up his mind.'

'Svines! - You must be his hero.'

'Yes, there are some bad people out there, Arnie, but just remember - for every bad person there are thousands, possibly millions, of good people.'

'Are zere?'

'Well...'

'In a vay, you are my hero too, you sawed my life.'

'How so, Arnie?'

'You haf token me avay from zose boring cornfields, vithout you I vould haf not met Sally...'

'You're a bigger hero, Arnie – without you, Sally would have still have been stuck on that fire escape, the wind whistling round her...'

'Ya, zat vos a nice shirt.'

'It was my favorite shirt, it's not easy to get Ben Sherman shirts with that color combination nowadays.'

'I've had it invisibly mended for you.'

'Thanks, Sally – wait a minute! – What are you doing here?'

'That nice General said there was room for a little one.'

'Snake?'

'Yes – and he said the chopper would be better balanced if I was on this side.'

'Norma!'

'I thought you might need a translator.'

'Well, I might, but what happened to that Olym...'

'That was Norma's cousin, you knew that didn't you, Jake?'

'Of course I did, Sally, I'm trained to recognize family resemblances. I just didn't want to affect his aim – one wrong move with that sword and it would have been curtains.'

'He didn't have his sword with him, Jake.'

'How was I to know? I've heard you can get those retractable practice swords now - he could have had one down his Calvin's – he certainly had something down there. I was only thinking of you, Norma.'

'Zat's not vot you...'

'Look over there, Arnie – can you see it?'

'Vot?'

'A spaceship, look – over there!'

'Vere?'

'It's gone – they move pretty damn quick, those things. Keep an eye out for it, Arnie – we wouldn't want to crash into it.'

'No, vee vouldn't.'

'As I was saying – your safety is always my number one priority, Norma.'

'How sweet.'

Jakes glances in his rear-view mirror.

'Oh-oh, bandits at six o'clock. Buckle up - this could get hairy.'

'We have no belts back here!'

'Quick, you'll have to climb up here onto our knees and hold onto us.'

Two minutes later Norma and Sally are clinging desperately to Jake and Arnie.

'Norma, why are you naked?'

'The General said I would be too heavy with my clothes on.'

'Sally's still got her dress on.'

'She's a bit smaller than me.'

'Oh, I see – it's a shame though, because I loved that little black dress.'

'I've got it in my handbag, I'll try it on for you later.'

'You said it vould be hairy...'

A series of brilliant flashes light up the sky.

'Vot's that?'

'Heat seeking missiles.'

'Should I open the vindow to cool us down?'

'Best not to, Arnie, the cabin is pressurized, we'd all be sucked out. I'll take evasive action.'

Jake frantically presses a series of buttons and switches.

'Damn - the auto evade system has been disabled.'
He gently prizes Norma's legs apart.
'Excuse me, Honeybunch. There's a knob I need to get at.'
'Jake, I know you're only trying to take my mind off things, but is this really the right time?'

With superhuman effort and in excruciating pain, Jake nudges the quantum thruster forward just enough to reverse the polarity. The missiles shoot past, exploding yards in front of them.
'That vos close!'
'Too close for my liking – and we've still got those bandits on our tail.'
'Vot can vee do?'
'There is one thing we could try.'
'Vot?'
'I'm going to burn off some oil and put us into a tailspin, with any luck they'll think we've been hit.'
'Iz zere anyzing I can do?'
'Yeah, just push that cigarette lighter in, please, Arnie.'


*Three minutes later*


'It seems to have worked - they're heading back.'
'Yah, jettisoning Sally's dress vos a good idea.'
'I was surprised how much smoke was produced from such a small amount of material. I actually think it could have been a fire hazard.'
'How am I going to explain to Liz that we completely destroyed my bridesmaid's dress?'
'Never mind that, how am I going to explain to her that I

302

ruined her wedding?'

'That wasn't your fault, Jake – you weren't to know that all hell would break loose.'

'No, just because you programed your machines to go off ven you said "a toast to zee bride and groom." – Doesn't mean it vos your fault.'

'Jake – you didn't!'

'I had to, Norma, it was the only opportunity I had to get all the suspects together in the same place.'

'Well, I hope for your sake it worked.'

'Me too.'

'But, if they were all the suspects, why are we on this chopper?'

'That's a good question, Sally – there's one last piece of the puzzle I need to solve.'

Landing a prototype chopper on an uninhabited volcanic island with no runway is never easy, particularly when the landing gear has been damaged by debris from a couple of heat-seeking missiles, but somehow Jake manages to do it without waking the two naked stowaways. Jake gently moves Norma to one side then sprays the cockpit hatch with WD40 to avoid any squeaks. Using only his index fingers, he carefully opens the hatch, climbs through it and then indicates to Arnie to pass the two sleeping beauties to him. Arnie scoops both of them up and tries to pass them to Jake who shakes his head and mouths

*'One at a time.'*

Eventually the two women are placed side by side on the edge of the crater.

'The lava is nice and warm for them, we'll let them rest for a while.'

'Yah, gut idea.'

As Norma and Sally softly sink into the warm, steaming ash, Jake and Arnie wander off in search of water.

'If my instincts are correct, it will be in this direction.'

*One hour later*

'There's obviously no fresh water on the entire island.'

'Vait a minute, vere are zee vimmen? – Zey ver...'

'We're over here, men – under this waterfall, washing the ash off ourselves.'

'Zat woice came from ower zat ridge.'

Jake and Arnie hastily stride over the ten-meter-high ridge.

'Why don't you join us, the water is lovely and warm, I'm surprised you haven't been in already.'

'We would have, Sally, but we wanted to make sure the island was safe first, didn't we, Arnie?'

'You said vee needed to find vorter.'

'That's right, safe *drinking* water not safe *washing* water.'

'Oh, Jake – you think of everything, don't you?'

'I try, Norma – I try.'

Jake is grateful when Norma suddenly changes the subject.

'Where exactly are we, Jake and why have you brought us here?'

A deep, menacing voice booms out from over the next ridge.

'You're on Yokoate-jima island and you were brought here to serve me.'

'That's what you think, bud – did you really believe I would fall for that "you have won a fortnight's holiday for four on

304

an exclusive island retreat" routine?'

'Vell, zat email looked good to me, Jake.'

'It was a scam, Arnie.'

'Aww, iz zere no room serwice?'

'No and what's worse - no free towels!'

'That need not concern you, I can dry your lady friends off myself.'

'You keep your greasy hands off them.'

'Who said anything about using my hands?'

The fiendish voice behind the ridge cackles abominably.

'Who iz zat man, Jake?'

'If my instincts are correct, Arnie, that is a very large man with a hirsute torso, limbs like tree trunks and an extremely low forehead.'

A petite, slight, nymph-like brunette girl suddenly appears from behind the ridge, she shakes her little head.

'Close, but not quite right.'

The nymph is closely followed by something large and hairy.

'Herro and who might you be?'

'Vot iz zat, Jake? Eet looks like a dog, but eet eez talking.'

'It's a cross between an Australian Cattle Dog and Border Collie, sometimes abbreviated to an Australian Border Cattle Collie, both very intelligent breeds, but not normally noted for their vocabulary.'

'Eet's wery clewer.'

Jake notices that she is using one of Ernest's voice recorder machines to make it look like the dog is talking. He goes along with the illusion in an effort to find out more about this strange, beguiling woman.

'Queenie, be quiet! - I'm sorry, he tends to ramble on, he would speak the legs of a hind donkey if I let him.'

Jake is impressed  - he remembers his experience with one of those machines and admires her ability to curtail any unfortunate repercussions. Arnie is fascinated.

'Can zat dog do treeks?'

'Queenie – roll over!'

The dog jumps up and does a double somersault.

'She eez wery, wery clewer.'

'She is a he, actually.'

'And you called him Queenie?'

'He chose the name himself.'

Norma calls over to Jake.

'Jake, this water's starting to get cold.'

The nymph-like brunette pats her dog's head.

'Queenie, would you be a dear and put some wood on the fire?'

'Yesh, Bosh.'

The dog runs off to carry out its duties. Arnie joins the others under the waterfall, but, at present, Jake is more interested in the inhabitants of this mysterious island.

'Apart from you and Queenie, is there anyone else on this island?'

The nymph's voice suddenly takes on a robotic tone.

'There is no one here at present, sir.'

'Were you expecting us?'

'I cannot answer that, sir.'

'Please call me Jake.'

'Jake.'

Jake waits patiently for her to continue, but she is not forthcoming. Eventually, after looking blank for over five minutes, she continues.

'Can I help you with anything, sir?'

'You may call me Jake.'

'I may call you Jake.'

Another long pause.

'Where do you live?'

'I live on this island, sir.'

'Whereabouts on this island?'

'I cannot answer that, sir.'

Jake gives up on that line of questioning.

'We are hungry. My friends and I need food.'

Jake gestures towards Norma, Sally and then Arnie – the nymph's eyes nearly pop out.

'Is that what men look like when they are naked?'

Jake glances across at Arnie. 'Well, we don't all look *exactly* like that, but we have some similarities.'

'Do you wish to have a shower, sir.'

'Not at the minute, by the way, what is your name?'

'My name is Aurora, are you sure you wouldn't like a shower, Jake? It would freshen you up after your long journey.'

'I really must check out the rest of the island.'

'I'm going to have one.'

'Well, I suppose I could just have a quick one. Do you have any soap? I find shower gel a little harsh.'

Aurora picks a few berries off a nearby bush, squeezes them into a pulp and passes half of the mush to Jake - the smell is divine.

'This will cleanse your whole body and take away your hunger.' Jake takes a sniff.

'What hunger?'

*Three hours later*

'I really must explore this place, Aurora. What time does it get dark around here?'
'It will be daylight for another six hours.'
'That's handy, are there any more those berries around?'
Aurora disappears into a cave under the waterfall and returns moments later, with berries in each hand.
'While you were rinsing your hair, I gave some of these to your friends. The red ones make you feel sleepy and lethargic, the green ones fill you with energy and vitality.'
She throws the red berries away and passes Jake a large quantity of the green.
'Mmm, delicious – I feel wide awake – what color did you give the others?'
'They seemed to prefer the red ones.'

Jake suddenly notices they are alone.
'Where are the others?'
'They went back to the flying contraption that you arrived in. I think they are having a siesta.'
'Yeah, I suppose they'll need one after eating those red berries - by the way, where's that dog of yours?'
'The last I saw of him - he was singing them a lullaby.'
'I must just go and check on them.'
'Oh – they'll be alright.'
'You don't understand, Aurora – I am responsible for their safety.'
'I understand everything Jake Poisson, but you are all wet, let me dry you off with these leaves. I'll give you a good rub down.'

As the leaves touch his skin Jake stumbles to his knees.
'No, no... I...'
Jake is on the verge of passing out.
'Please!'
'Yes – I can please you – these leaves are an excellent exfoliant.'
On hearing that word, Jake comes to his senses a little.
'Ex - exfo - exfoliant! - Arnie, where are you - I need you.'

Jake starts feeling woozy. The last thing he smells is the intoxicating aroma of the leaves, Aurora holds them tightly over his nose and mouth. The last thing Jake sees is the naked nymph's blank, expressionless eyes. Then he loses consciousness.

*Six hours later*

Jake lies motionless on a cold concrete bench. He holds his breath as he listens intently to the heavy footsteps approaching from the blackness. Suddenly the room is bathed by an intense light, Jake blinks rapidly in an effort to see through the glare. A voice booms from the ceiling, echoing round the whole room.
'Captain Poisson, if you wish to save your crew, you must engage the Kraken in unarmed combat – do you accept the challenge?'
As Jake's vision clears, he notices a large, furry figure shuffling towards him.
'Is that the Kraken there – that thing with four arms?'
'It is.'
'It's hardly unarmed, is it? It's got an axe in one hand, a net

in another, a spear – and what's that?'

'An ice lolly - Krakens are very partial to Magnums.'

Jake is thinking on his feet, he looks round for a power supply to switch the refrigerator off.

'I know what you're thinking Captain Poisson, but all our equipment is solar powered.'

Jake glances up at the sky.

'And there are no solar eclipses forecast for another thirty-two years.'

The Kraken is now within feet of Jake's body. Jake lunges towards the foe, his every muscle taught, his every sinew constricted for maximum effect. As the figure of the Kraken disintegrates into thin air and Jake lands flat on his back, his perpetrator laughs contemptuously.

'Did you think you could come here and defeat my plans for complete global domination so easily, Poisson? That is just a small taste of what I can do to you!'

Jake winces and ruefully rubs his back.

'Jake, are you okay, Brudder?'

'Oh hi, Arnie – yeah, I'm just doing my early morning calisthenics.'

'I vos verried about you. I thought I heard you calling to me.'

'No need, I'm fine, how are Norma and Sally?'

'They are feeling wery gut, zey are vith zat old voman.'

'What old woman?'

'The old voman zat vos zere earlier.'

'Aurora? She's not old.'

'She told zee vimmen zat she vos sixty-four and zat the vorter kept her looking young.

'Where are they now?'

'Zey iz in zee vorterfall.'

*One hour later*

'Vot are vee looking for, Brudder?'

'Anything out of the ordinary, even if it seems ordinary. This island reminds me of a Star Trek episode. We need to find the computer which is controlling the inhabitants - but be careful, the fiend who created this contraption is capable of anything. Don't believe anything you see – it's probably a holographic illusion.'

'Vot eez a star twek?'

'It's a television series, Arnie.'

'Vot eez a telewision?'

'You've never seen a television set.'

'I haf newer had von.'

'Well, you've missed out on a lot of good shows.'

'Vot good shows?'

'Well, there's, ... er, ... umm, ... come to think about it ... - anyway, don't fall for any imaginary monsters with four arms – they're not real.'

'Who vud fall for a zing like zat?'

'Just keep looking for that computer, Arnie – let me worry about any krakens.'

'Zen, vot do vee do?'

'We ask the computer questions until it blows up.'

Arnie marvels at his brother's encyclopedic knowledge.

'Look - zere iz a tree ower zere!'

'Which one? We are in a forest, Arnie.'

'Zat one vith zee birdies on zee branches.'

'Ah, well spotted, brother – none of the others have birds on them, perhaps they are attracted to something.'

As Jake and Arnie approach the tree, they notice the temperature has dropped considerably.

'For a volcanic island, the temperature in this particular spot is very similar to that which I experienced when cycling twice round the Artic Circle.'

'Did you do zat for charity?'

'Only the first circuit, the second one I was looking for a way off.'

'Jake, vot iz zat buzzing noise?'

'It sounds like a solar-powered generator, probably used to power a refrigerator – keep an eye out for Krakens!'

As Jake investigates the trunk, Arnie trips over what appears to be a dead sapling.

'Vot's zis bloomin' bit of...'

He yanks at it and a hidden door creaks open.

'You've found it, Arnie.'

'Found vot?'

'The entrance to the underground laboratory which controls everything and everyone on this island.'

'Including us?'

'I'm afraid that's the intention of its creator.'

'Voo is zat?'

'That's what I aim to find out – you coming?'

Jake and Arnie slide down a metal ladder and head into a long, dark corridor. Jake pulls out his Ledlenser torch.

'By the sound of it, we're not that far away – look there's a hermetic door down there!'

Jake tries the door. 'It's locked.'

Arnie pulls the door completely off its hinges.

'Well, it's not hermetically sealed now.'

'I'm wery sorry, Jake.'

'Don't be, Arnie. I intend to destroy the whole of this laboratory before we leave the island.'

'Brudder, you haf not told me vy vee are on zis island.'

'That's right, Arnie, and since we don't know who or what is behind that door, I suppose now would be a good time to explain.'

'Ya.'

'Remember when I flew the plane from Rea's house to the airbase, and you followed us on your Harley?'

'Ya.'

'Well, I discovered from the onboard computer that someone had visited this island on a number of occasions during the previous four years.'

'Nein!'

'Close, Arnie – it was actually seven times.'

'Voo vos eet?'

'I have my suspicions – I think there's a very strong possibility we'll find the answer somewhere behind that door.'

'Zat's gut.'

'It's better than that, Arnie, it's the last part of the jigsaw. Once this piece is in place, we'll be able to save the world from mass mind destruction.'

Jake gives Arnie a brotherly hug.

'I know that since finding you, my brother, we have been in some dangerous situations, but this, by far, is the most dangerous of all – so I need to ask you. Are you willing to go through with it?'

'Ya.'

'Okay, let's go, but be very careful.'

Jake and Arnie creep slowly and silently along the long, dark, dirty corridor. As they approach the door Jake puts his finger to his lips and whispers.

'No sounds, Arnie.'

As Jake moves imperceptibly nearer to the door, he stops and mouths to Arnie.

*'There's a sign on the door.'*

'Vot does it say?

'It says:'

*"Gone for lunch – please leave any parcels behind the blue bin."*

Jake pulls at the handle.

'It's locked, do you think you can open it?'

Arnie grabs the handle and pulls with all his might.

'I'm sorry, Brudder, it's too heavy for me.'

'Well – if, you can't open it, Arnie, no one can. I suppose the best we can do is take this note for handwriting analysis.'

Jake carefully peels off the note.

'Aha – there's a notice underneath.'

'Vot does eet say?'

'It says *PUSH TO OPEN.*


Jake gingerly pushes the door open and peeks into the room.

'Eureka – the control center.'

Suddenly there's an almighty crashing sound behind them.

'My God – I think we might be too late!'

Jake's eyes frantically scour the room. He points at a large box.

'Arnie – grab that – and run like f…!'

Jake's message is drowned out by the crumbling walls of the corridor. Jake grabs Arnie - as he pushes him through the

disintegrating door frame, he screams at him.
'RUN!'

Arnie doesn't need any further warnings, he sprints up the corridor at breakneck speed, with Jake hot on his heels. The exit is almost in reach when an almighty explosion reverberates through the building. A huge ball of flame catapults them out of the exit and onto the forest floor. Arnie lands face down and Jake finds himself on top of his brother.

'Arnie, are you okay?'
'Yah.'
'If we'd only had a few minutes more we would have got that hard drive.'
'Vos zat zee box?'
'Yeah.'
'Eet vos attached to zee vorl.'
Jakes sighs with frustration.
'Yeah – just our luck!'

# Chapter Twenty-nine

# The Evacuation

Arnie rolls over showing Jake the box with half the wall attached to it. Jake laughs.

'Arnie, you are worth your weight in gold!'

'I am wery heawy.'

They both chuckle, as they brush the dust and debris off themselves.

'Wow, that was a lucky break!'

'Yah, and vee von't have to ask the computer any questions either!"

*Ten Minutes later*

In record time, a breathless Jake and Arnie reach Norma, Sally and Aurora at the waterfall, Norma sees them first.

'Honestly, you two – can't we have a few minutes to ourselves?'

'You've been in here for at least four hours!'

'Some of the dirt was ground in after that long flight.'

'We need to go *now!*'

'Can we not just have another hour, Jake?'

'The volcano is about to erupt, Norma, we may have days, but it could be only hours or even minutes – I can't be sure.'

'Is there any chance we could get a second opinion, Jake?'

'The only volcanologist I know happens to be five thousand miles away, Sally – and it's three a.m. there.'

'Have you seen Aurora's skin, Jake – and she's sixty-four – I mean, if there's any chance...'

'I see what you mean, Sally and I can understand why you...'

'So, you think Aurora's skin is much better than mine, do you?'

Jake realizes he's in a deep hole and his every word is digging him in deeper. He turns to Arnie for help.

'Arnie, tell them.'

'Ven I first saw Aurora I thought zat she vos much younger zan both...'

'Woah, hold it there, Arnie – I meant tell them about the underground laboratory.'

'Oh, yah! Zee vorls vere collapsing.'

'That's right, we were lucky to get out of that tunnel alive. We got here as quickly as we could to protect the women we love.'

'And who are they, Jake?'

'You know who – you and Sally.'

'I'm beginning to wonder!'

At that precise moment the earth beneath them starts shaking.

'Now do you believe me?'

'Well, I'm not entirely convinced, but I suppose we'll have to take your word for it.'

Jake breathes a sigh of relief.

'Head for the ship... er... chopper!'

'Vill vee be able to make it vith zee extra veight?'

Norma looks daggers at Arnie.

'I'm not jettisoning my black dress, if that's what you mean, I bought that specially to impress Jake, besides it doesn't weigh much – it certainly doesn't weigh as much as that wall you've got there.'

Arnie effortlessly tears the box off the wall and hands it to

Jake.

'This box contains vital information - besides, it's not half as heavy now that Arnie's removed the remnants of the wall from it.'

Then, in an effort to placate her, he hands it to Norma. 'I'm sure you'll look after it carefully.'

Norma beams with pride. As Jake turns to go, Aurora stands in his way.

'Jake, I need to apologize – I don't know what came over me, it was as if something or someone was controlling me, making me do things I didn't want to do.'

'I know that, but it's over now and it won't happen again, you're free. We must go now, Aurora, we haven't much time.'

As Jake follows the others on to the chopper, he turns back to help Aurora - only to see her waving from a distance.'

'Goodbye, Captain Jake Poisson – I love you!'

Jake pleads with her.

'Aurora... no!'

At that moment a massive fissure opens up, followed by a twenty-meter wall of flame, as she disappears from sight, Jake knows he has no alternative but to take off. The silence is deafening as the flame-engulfed island quickly becomes a speck in the chopper's rear-view mirror.

'Damn it!'

Jake loops the plane and guns the engines straight into the fierce inferno.

'Jake, you'll get us all killed.'

'If there's even the slightest chance that she's alive...'

'I know, Jake, but be careful!'

Suddenly Jake sees a small gap in the smoke, he delicately maneuvers the chopper through it.

'There – over there – do you see them?'

'Yes, well done, Sally – we need to alert them.'

'Can I use the loudhailer, Jake?'

'Of course, Norma.'

As Jake hovers over Aurora and Queenie, Norma clears her throat.

'Aurora, we are over you, over!'

Norma turns expectantly to Jake.

'Was that okay?'

'Brilliant, Norma – you were great!'

'She's seen us. Look, she's waving.'

'She's not waving, Norma, she's pointing!'

'Vot at?'

'That huge wave over there, the volcano must have triggered a tsunami.'

'Vot are vee going to do?'

'I'll do a one-eighty – Arnie, you lean out of the cockpit and see if you can grab them.'

*Two days later*

'GENERAL! – incoming at zero-two-zero – he's on a wing and a prayer. My God, clear the decks, no one's gonna survive this! Mayday! ---- **Mayday!**--- Red alert – Red alert – All emergency services STANDBY – immediate – REPEAT – **IMMEDIATE**!'

'Identification, soldier?'

'Negatory, General – no comms!'

'Dammit!'

'Wait – it can't be...! – It's not possible – it is **not poss...**– IT IS! - the eagle has landed!'

319

The general can hear a huge roar spreading throughout the base, he turns to his companion in bed.

'That'll be Drum, I'd better get dressed.'

As the general jumps out of bed, he can hear an even louder round of cheering emanating from the runway. The airman on the other end of the intercom coughs.

'Er, I don't think there's any need to, sir. They're disembarking and they're all naked, apart from one.'

'Apart from one?'

'Yes – wow, that's a beautiful, black micro-mini dress she's almost wearing.'

'I'll be right there, soldier!'

*Thirty minutes later*

'God dammit, Drum – you son of a gun! My staff tell me they've never seen anything like a landing like that, I told them.

"You don't know Major Tom like I know Major Tom!"'

Jake nods politely, but says nothing. The general senses Jake's indifference.

'We go back a long way, don't we, Major.'

Jake gives another non-committal nod. The general tries a different approach, he surveys the bodies seated around him. Most he recognizes, but there are one or two newcomers. He studies Aurora and Queenie, in particular.

'Are you going to introduce your new friends to me?'

'Later perhaps, I've got a few things I need to discuss with you, Snake, but...'

'I know, I know - you must be tired and hungry after your

long journey. Tuck in – there are plenty more quail's eggs where they came from. Tell me, what happened to your clothing?'
'We were low on fuel, we had to jettison it.'
'What's in the bag?'

The general nods towards a carrier bag containing the disk drive.
'Oh, you know, essential stuff, hairdryers, make-up – that sort of thing.'
'No matter, we'll see about getting some gear for you presently. There's bound to be some spare uniforms floating around somewhere in the barracks.'

As Arnie finishes off the base's month's supply of quail eggs and the women try on their newly supplied uniforms, Jake takes the general to one side.
'Snake, I'd like to thank you for the meal and the clothing.'
'It's nothing – I would do anything for the man who saved my life, you don't even need to ask.'
'That's good to know, it's getting hard to know who to trust these days.'
'You can always trust me, Major.'
'Well, I may need your help in the future, Snake - but, first of all, I'd like to know if you recognize this woman.'
'I sure do, that's Isla Ingblot, my new secretary, I've just left her in my bed. Is she in any trouble?'
'No, I was just wondering if she was okay.'
'Would you like me to go and get her?'
'No! We don't need to disturb her. Oh, and I'd be obliged if you didn't mention this to her. For her safety – and yours.'
Noticing the general's shaking hands, Jake takes a firm grip of his shoulder.

'Snake, just act naturally – I'll be in touch soon, okay?'

'Yes, Jake, certainly - anytime.'

'Oh, and one last thing – has anyone, apart from myself and Fox, ever had access to Prototype Two?'

'Not to my knowl... - wait a minute – there was an engineer a while back, who turned up from a top-secret agency – it was so secret even he didn't know what it was. I had to face the wall before he would even speak to me. He'd been gone an hour before I realized. He took all the CCTV tapes with him, as well – said if I ever tried to trace him, he'd use a rusty hacksaw to cut off my... '

'I get the picture - you've been very helpful, Snake.'

'Am I in trouble, Jake?'

'Just stay calm, Snake. Don't go anywhere – and triple the guard at the gate!'

As Jake gathers up the others and drives away from the base, he notices Snake hurrying off in the direction of the latrines.


*Ten a.m. next morning*


Jake is speaking to his old colleague, Harry Pusey, on his encrypted cell phone.

'That's right, HP, Keb Bleek, - Boy, Lincoln, Edward, Edward, King - a.k.a. Geek Bleek, last known whereabouts San Quentin jail.'

'Usual drop off point?'

Jake remembers the squirrel and, more importantly, the old lady and her dog.

'Negative, HP – drop off point zero, zero, two.'

'Copy that.'

Jake hangs up. One hour later Jake's encrypted phone rings.

'I hear you're going by the name of Jake Poisson now.'

'Geek, you son of a gun, how did you...?'

'You know better than to ask.'

'You've been watching my progress all along, haven't you, Geek?'

'Just checking on my old partner – life's been a bit boring for me since our experiment in Philadelphia – not that I can say the same thing for you.'

'Well, I've got something that should liven things up for you.'

'You've got the disk...?'

'Yeah.'

'How soon can you get it to me?'

'I've got a few loose ends to tie up first, then I'll deliver it personally. Do you still have the...?'

'I'm looking at it now, I've made a few minor tweaks to it – I hope you don't mind.'

'Not at all, Geek. I'm looking forward to seeing it - and seeing you – it's been far too long!'

'That's true – but, Jake, be careful, there are contracts out on...'

'I'm sorting those out as we speak, Geek – I should be able to get to you within the week.'

'You know the route to take, Jake – there's a lot at stake.'

Jake quickly cuts the call off before he runs out of rhyming words. He isn't looking forward to his next call.


'Hi, Sis.'

Jake's tone is sheepish, he still calls Liz his sister – even though she isn't really his sister.

'Oh, hi Jake, how are you?'

323

'I'm fine, Liz – I just phoned to apologize about the wedding. I hope I didn't spoil things for you and Ernest. I'll pay for any damages to the hotel.'

'The hotel staff were fine about it, in fact they offered us free accommodation for their swingers weekend next year – said we could bring along a friend, so we're taking Clarence.'

Jake doesn't want to let on.

'Who's Clarence?'

'You know Clarence, don't you? He's says he's an old friend of yours. I'll put him on for you.'

'Hi, Jake.'

'Clarence – I thought you were deaf!'

'I was, Jake, but that machine of yours cured me. It's marvelous – we've been using it all week.'

'That's good news because I need a favor.'

'Anything, my friend.'

'I'll be in touch - now put Liz on, so I can catch up on what's been happening.'

'Okay, Jake.'

'That's good news, Liz – so what have you been up to since I've been gone?'

'Riding.'

'That's nice - on Ernest's horses?'

'No, just on Ernest and Clarence.'

# Chapter Thirty

## Find Bleek

*The next day*

Jake is in the conference room (attic). He can hardly believe that a few short weeks ago he was sitting in his office across the road, bruised and battered, with a backside resembling the top of a latticed cherry pie. A lot had happened since then, he'd made new friends and cemented his friendships with old ones, he'd lost a mother, found a father, lost a sister, found a brother - he'd discovered skills he never knew he'd had, he'd...

'What are you thinking, Jake?'
'Nothing much.'
At least half a dozen voices bring his thoughts back to the present, he shuffles his papers and clears his throat.
'I'll answer all your questions in due course, but first I want to say thank you to all of you for the brilliant efforts you have made during these extremely difficult times.'
A chorus of approval echoes around the room.
'And for those of you who haven't already met our new recruits, I would like to introduce you to...'
'Can I introduce them, Jake?'
'Of course, Norma.'
'This is Aurora and Queenie and they're lovely.'
Jake pauses until the words of welcome die down, then resumes the debriefing.

'I believe that Aurora has provided us with the last piece of the jigsaw. The answer to the kingpins behind this fiendish plot to take control of the minds of everyone on this planet and I don't need to tell any of you the consequences of such a plan succeeding.'

'Certainly not, but could you just go over some of the main points?'

'Yes, Sven - there would be global chaos, governments would be at each other's throats, famine, war, pestilence, drought, viruses...'

'Good grief!'

'That's the best-case scenario, Sven.'

'Has eet already started, Brudder?'

'I think we're getting a taste of it, Arnie.'

Jake can feel the fear spreading through the room.

'But don't worry, if we all work together, I think we have just enough time to prevent the worst catastrophe the world has ever known.'

'What can we do?'

'We all have our roles to play, but unfortunately this puts us in great danger. I've arranged for protection for you all in a safe house.'

'Where's the safe house, Jake?'

'Any of you know Kokomo? - There's a nice little motel down there, I've managed to get us a good discount.'

Jake smiles at Norma.

'What about you, Jake?'

'There's someone I need to see - with any luck this should be sorted within the week.'

'Is there anything else we can do?'

'It might be a good idea to stock up, just in case. There's a special offer on baked beans at Walmart at the minute. We'll meet back here in a week - meanwhile, Norma's in charge. Arnie, Sven and Lars will provide round the clock security.'

Jake gathers up his papers, kisses Norma, shakes the hands of all the others and strides out of the room. Five minutes later he is on the highway, heading for his first rendezvous.

*One day later*

Jake is sitting in front of a bank of monitors, simultaneously typing onto a number of keyboards at lightning speed. Three men enter the room and point their revolvers at his head, Jake ignores them. Just as one of the men primes his Obregon, another man - larger, meaner and sweatier, but somehow more handsome and refined, than the others, barges in.
'PANCHO – STAND DOWN!'
As Pancho reluctantly lowers his weapon, the big, hairy man roughly shoves him out of the way and grabs, the now standing, Jake, in a massive bear hug.
'Ace, you son of a gun! I've spent the last two years making this place invisible and in you walk, cool as a cucumber and take over from where you left off.'

The three armed men immediately place their guns on the floor and hold up their hands.
'Forgive, my men - they are a little over enthusiastic, no?'
'Any friend of Geek Bleek is a friend of mine.'
The three men visibly relax, pick up their guns and quietly sidle out of the room.
'Thanks for not hurting them - Pancho, Ramone and

327

Ethelred have been with me since I relocated my headquarters from Quentin.'

'I see you're still using that as a holding address.'

'It keeps the IRS off my back, I pop in occasionally to say hello to the guards.'

'I can see how that could be useful.'

Geek is about to offer Jake the use of an empty cell next to his, when he notices one of the screens.

'I hope you like my improvements, Ace – sorry, Jake! – Old habits die hard.'

'That's okay, Geek – I haven't used the name Ace for the last couple of years, as I'm sure you know.'

'Yeah, I've been there with you wherever possible – virtually, of course.'

'I know that, Geek. You opened a few doors along the way - virtually, of course.'

'I'm afraid I couldn't keep up with you, Jake – no one could.'

'That's okay, Geek.'

Jake nods towards the bank of monitors.

'I like the improvements, by the way.'

'Thanks, Jake. I've been working on an algorithm for the last few months. If I can solve it, we should theoretically be able to create a fourth dimensional time shift in two paradigms, potentially creating a backshift delay of two parsecs.'

Geek points to one of the monitors.

'Where is it? -It was here – there was a stack overload – I can't seem to...'

'I noticed that anomaly, Geek - I've changed the codec, just let me run it.'

Geek stares in amazement as he watches the speed of the code accelerate exponentially, as each module of the

program is called, interpreted, parsed, and executed.
'You know what this means, Jake? This will give us the ability to accelerate photon momentum.'

Jake takes an object out of his breast pocket.
'Which will allow us to control the movement of light and sound - and if we find what I think we're going to find on this disk, we're going to need that power.'
'Remarkable! How do you do it, Jake?'
'I'm trained to think in binary – I can also meditate in hexadecimal.'

### Later that day

Jake and Geek are bent over a desk, soldering irons in hand, Pancho, Ramone, Ethelred are watching them with keen interest.
'That's it, Geek, I've connected the last circuit.'
'You were right, Jake – it's given us complete access to the whole of the disk – but how did you trace its whereabouts?'
'When my memory started to return, I was able to put the pieces of the jigsaw together. At first, I thought I was trying to uncover a local scam – routine stuff - but with Georgette's help...'
At the mention of Georgette's name all four men squirm in their seats. Jake looks up from his soldering.
'Do you know her?'
The other men shake their heads vigorously.
'Us? – No, no...'
'No way, seňor.'
'She's about five-two...'

'Oh, that Georgette – come to think about it, she did come here to ask about a machine she was developing, didn't she men?'

'Si.'

'Yeah – that was all – she never did anything else...'

'We helped her, but we've never seen her since, have we?'

'Was she not here, last week, Boss?'

'I'm sure Jake's not interested in how often we get our treatments, Ramone.'

Jake ignores the comments.

'I'm finished - all we need now is to test it.'

'How are we going to do that?'

'Well, Geek – I thought that part would be easy, but now Blowman has gone global I'm afraid we're going to have to extend our network.'

'How far?'

'The further the better.'

'I have friends in Mexico – I could visit them.'

'That's great, Pancho.'

'I haven't seen my Mama for ages...'

'Where does she live, Ramone?'

'Peru.'

'Perfect!'

'How about you, Ethelred?'

'I've been wanting to visit Denmark for a long time now.'

'What about me?'

'I need you here, Geek.'

'Okay, I suppose you're right, Jake.'

'Right, men – Geek will fill you in on the details. I have people I need to see – good luck!'

*Another day later*

Jake is sitting in Chief Pusey's office - the blinds are drawn and the two of them are talking in hushed tones.

'It's great to see you, Jake – your message sounded urgent. I'm afraid I couldn't find any info on Keb Bleek.'

'That's okay, I knew once you tried to trace him, he would contact me. We're in a race against time, HP - Blowman's gone global - and you know what that means.'

'From what you sent me in that top secret file, it could be the end of the world as we know it.'

'Too true – so, if you can suggest anyone with a detailed knowledge of the UK – anyone at all.'

'There is *one* person I can think of, but I don't...'

'Anyone, Harry – anyone at all – I'm really desperate – who is it?'

'Officer Crockett...'

'Crockett!'

'Yeah, he's from there – he knows the whole of the UK like the back of his hand, it's only a small place, you know. Crockett says you can walk from one end to the other in a couple of days, if you have a favorable wind behind you.'

Jake would love to query Crockett's logic, but he is desperate.

'Is there no one else – even someone who may have just visited or maybe had a connecting flight?'

'I understand your reservations, Jake, but after your sister's wedding, he's a changed man – we all are and I could send Lieutenant Columbo with him – he's found a way to temporarily deactivate Detective Crockett's internal...'

'No need to go into that at the minute, Harry. From what

I've been hearing, the wedding was a complete success, I must apologize again for having to rush away from it.'

'No need for apologies, we all know how busy Jake Poisson is – how did the trip go, anyway?'

'It was very productive and I'm working on a solution to the imminent global outbreak, but there's no time to lose. I'm afraid I've got another favor to ask.'

'You know me, Jake – I'll do anything for the man who saved my life.'

'There's a couple outside I'd like you to meet.'

'Bring them in!'

'Before I do, I'll come straight to the point – I want you to accompany them to the China Sea.'

'China? - Jake, you know I'm not a good traveler – not since that Bolivian Coffee Caper – surely you can find someone else...?'

'You're perfect for the job, Harry – you've got dog handling experience. Remember Shaft? That dog of yours won medals.'

'Ah, yes, Shaft – I loved that dog, but what's that got to do with anything. I'm sorry, but I definitely can't go.'

Jake pulls up the blind. 'There's the couple I want you to...'

Harry is out of the door before Jake has a chance to finish his sentence.

'So, we're taking a trip to China, I can't wait – what's your name, and what do you call this cute little doggie?'

'I'm Aurora – and this is Queenie.'

'What lovely names. I'll tell you all about my Shaft on the way.'

Aurora's eyes light up.

# Chapter Thirty-one

# The Final Countdown

On the seventy-sixth floor of a seventy-five-story skyscraper block, someone who considers himself to be the second most powerful man in the world, shakes his head in disbelief as he stares at a bank of monitors covering the whole wall. Blank faces stare back at him, pretending to listen to his every word.

'So, you're telling me that he is single-handedly preventing us from gaining control of the minds of the world's entire population. How can one man possibly...?'

Only one person is brave enough to speak up.

'He has a few friends helping him...'

'Thank you for clearing that up, Number Seven. We are allegedly the most powerful secret cabal in the whole world and you're telling me that Poisson and a few friends are outwitting us all? I understand it clearly now.'

'Thank you, sir.'

'I was being sarcastically ironic, you idiot – it's a good job you're not in a blimp, otherwise you'd be testing out Newton's laws of gravity by now! - So, who's going tell me - where is he now?'

A wall of silence and then, eventually, another face begins to stutter some kind of explanation.

'We've sent out all our best agents, sir – but no one...'

The screen flickers and then goes blank.

'Number Nineteen, we've lost connection – what's going...?'

One by one, the rest of the screens turn blank and then, after a short pause, they all miraculously spring back to life, this time displaying the same image.

'Hi, Charles.'

'Poisson! – What the...? – 'Where the...? – How the...?

'In one hour's time ALL global communication will cease.'

'You're bluffing, Jake – you wouldn't – you couldn't!'

Gradually the screens morph into one large clock, counting down the minutes and seconds. The self-proclaimed world's second most powerful man clicks his fingers at one of his minions.

'STOP HIM!'

*Twenty-seven minutes later*

The screens revert to their previous displays. Blowman and his minions punch the air. Their celebration is short-lived. The screens flicker as the countdown resumes again - Charles Blowman's smug, self-satisfied smile disappears from his bloated, dissipated face.

'That's impossible!'

'Obviously not – you idiot – someone stop him!'

As the clock continues its relentless countdown the atmosphere in the room becomes more and more tense, Blowman's fierce temper is ready to explode when, suddenly...

'We've got him, sir – target confirmed – hit authorized!'

Cheers echo around the room, then subside when the screens go blank again.

## Thirty minutes later

Jake sits alone in his attic cum office. As his eyes wander round the room, his thoughts turn to the events of the last few weeks.

*'I've been lucky up to now. If I can just keep the lid on this for the next couple of days, there's just a chance we can pull it off.'*

He takes a sip of his flat white.

*'Hmm, this is nowhere near as good as Sally's. I wonder what the gang are doing now.'*

His cell phone rings, disturbing his thoughts. He was expecting the call and knows who it is, but he plays dumb.

'Hello, who is it?'

'I've been watching the latest YouTube videos of the recent worldwide protests. It's amazing how susceptible people are to the slightest suggestions.'

'Who is this?'

'You must have known your plan wouldn't work, Jake – my men had us back online within the hour.'

'Oh no – is that you, Blowman. It sounds a bit like you...'

The man at the other end of the phone laughs gleefully.

'You are an idiot, Poisson - oh, and by the way, there's a reason why your coffee doesn't taste so good...'

Jake feels the room spinning, he sniffs the cup and realizes he only has seconds in which to act. Taking an old piece of pizza out of the waste bin, he licks the salt off it – then, crawling to the water dispenser, he just manages to aim three pints of water down his throat, thus creating a six-foot stream of greasy vomit towards the door. His vision too blurred to see, Jake crouches, listening carefully for footsteps.'

'*Good, there's only two of them.*'
He mutters to himself. He hears the door handle, then the bang and clatter as both intruders slide and fall on the vomit. Using their heads as stepping stones, Jake sprints out of the door and heads for the street, pausing only to throw an incendiary device into his pimpmobile. Five seconds later Jake is in the doorway of the bookshop, he detonates the device and crouches down to avoid most of the debris.
'Jake – in here!'
A secret hatch under the counter is swiftly opened, revealing a cellar which Jake effortlessly disappears into.

*Two hours later*

The hatch opens and the sudden, bright shaft of light causes Jake to shield his eyes.
'Are you all right down there, Jake?'
'Yeah, I've been reading Nineteen Eighty-Four to pass the time.'
'It's pitch-black dark.'
'Fortunately, I found a braille version.'
'I'm sorry it took so long, but I had to wait until the coast was clear and the Police and Fire Department had gone – they found a body in the car and they think it's yours.'
'I kept a cadaver with my DNA on it in my car, to convince them.'
'How did you do that?'
'Oh, you know, I added bits of my hair and nails to it every

now and then.'

'I see – what are you going to do now, Jake?'

'Well, Georgette, now that they think I'm dead I can put my exit plan into action.'

Georgette joins Jake in the cellar, switching on the light as she slithers across him.

'Why you didn't switch on the li...?'

'I was trying to save money, have you seen the cost of electricity these days?'

Jake quickly changes the subject.

'What about the shop assistant, Georgette – where's he?'

'He's a little tied up at the minute...'

'Can we trust him?'

'Oh yes – I took the liberty of having Feng Shui make me a miniaturized version of your machine, Jake. I keep it on me at all times – that's another reason why you had to wait so long.'

'Oh, it didn't seem so long, this is a good book.'

'It's back to front!'

'I wondered why it said the clock struck thirty-one...'

Georgette moves closer to Jake, as she does so, she readjusts her clothing, making herself even more provocative, she hugs Jake.

'That's the Jake that we all know and love – although now that you and Norma are an item, I suppose we'll have to ease off a bit.'


*Two days later*


Jake and Norma are in the honeymoon suite of the Yates motel.

'Jake, I can't believe you've done it.'

'It wasn't too difficult - I had a lot of help. Clarence told me what to expect and Geek operated the remote computer system. The boat's ready to take us to the island, we should be there in a couple of weeks. Arnie and Sally are already on the island – I showed him how to operate the chopper – he's a quick learner.

'He takes after his brother!'

Jake smiles proudly.

'He reckons the building work's almost finished, he's just waiting for the grout to dry in the swimming pool – he sent me an artist's impression of how it will look.'

'What if they find out you're not dead? - Aren't you worried they'll come after you, Jake?'

'Before Geek disconnects global communications permanently, Norma, he will broadcast something similar to MESH – they won't know that, of course, we are only wiping out the memories of their fiendish plan. I must admit though, I've added a little subroutine to turn them into kinder, more thoughtful people.'

'Do you think that will work?'

'Permanently? – Probably not, but I think it's worth a try – who knows, I still cling on to the hope that we may yet develop into peaceful, civilized people living in harmony on a beautiful planet.'

'That's a wonderful dream – can it happen, Jake?'

'Well, it is possible in the future, but not for a while, not while people are ruled by their carnal desires - which reminds me, I'd better inform your father.'

'Can I tell him, Jake?'

'Of course.'

Norma picks up her cell phone.

'No global communications, remember? – We don't want to be traced.'

'But - how?'

Jake passes Norma a sheet of paper and a pen.

'Write him a note.'

He heads for the garden and returns with a large wicker basket. Norma looks on in amazement as Jake reaches into the basket and pulls out a beautiful speckled pigeon.

'This one's called Speckled Jim – hand me your note, please – now, do you have anything belonging to your dad?'

'I've got this!'

Jake looks quizzically at the object, before gingerly accepting it.

'Pop's left it under his bed, I was going to wash it before I gave him it back.'

'That's perfect – Jake wafts the truss under Speckled Jim's beak for three minutes before launching the pigeon into the air. The pigeon lands heavily on his beak, before setting off haphazardly on his journey.

'Go get him, Jimbo!'

'Jake, you're so clever – how did you...?'

'I was trained in aerial comms.'

Norma pulls Jake to her.

'Can I ask you a question, Jake?'

'Of course, my angel.'

'How did you know who Mr. Big was?'

'The Head of Blowman? – It was easy, there was only one man smart enough, powerful enough, devious enough and greedy enough.'

'Who?'

'The senator – it's always politicians.'

'No!'

'Yes, all the others were just pawns – his aim was to use them to infiltrate, manipulate, orchestrate and facilitate his evils plans. He was doing it state by state, and your mom and pop could probably have coped with that situation eventually, but a chance meeting the senator had with a Professor Hando Kaxasaki at a seminar on Simulation versus Stimulation in an Everchanging Geopolitical Arena changed all that.'

'How so?'

'He realized that combining Kaxasaki's methods of stimulating the cerebral cortex of dogs with your father's cognitive simulation concoctions would enable him to produce bacteriological weapons capable of quickly spreading across the globe – maybe a bit further.'

'How did you find all this out, Jake?'

'I learnt the first part by being beaten, thrashed, tied, tortured and over-stimulated – I found out the rest on Kaxasaki's computer.'

'That explains Queenie.'

'Yes - God knows what that dog had to go through – fortunately the effects seem to have worn off. Now all he does is bark when he wants to go walkies.'

'But what has the Blowman Corporation got to do with the Dan Corleone Agency?'

'The senator used his pawns to infiltrate and manipulate our agency. Viggo was the first. For some reason, possibly the lure of easy money, he sold his own brother and the rest of us down the river – thank God Olga sussed him out.'

'Where's Olga now?

' 'She's in Patagonia with Wes and their children, Wes won't give up his search for a two-headed llama.'

'They've got children?'

'You didn't think that Hansel and Greta were mine, did you?'

'Well, Olga said...'

'I didn't even reach first base! I was saving myself.'

'For what?'

'I can't remember, now.

' 'Do you regret that?'

'No, of course not – well, a little, but I'll get over it ... I will ... I'm sure I will – in time.'

'But how did Wes?'

'There was a mix up about a big pizza order. Olga didn't get my note and thought I'd left her. Wes drove her to the airport and, well, one thing led to another...'

'Oh, poor Jake. Tell you what, why don't we have another go with your training – we can try for ten minutes this time.'

'Make it nine and it's a deal!'

*Six minutes later*

Jake is busily packing suitcases in readiness for their imminent journey. Norma is engrossed in her magazine *The Art of Bondage (Without Hurting Too Much)*. Jake stops packing and starts rummaging through his pockets.

'Have you lost something, Jake?'

'Er, no – nothing.'

Jake tries to rummage through his pockets more surreptitiously. 'These tsetse flies get everywhere.'

'Do we have tsetse flies in Indiana?'

'Oh yes, apparently there's new strain, they came across on the scirocco.'

'I thought the scirocco blew across the Mediterranean.'

'Apparently there's a new version which reaches here.'

Norma is watching Jake with interest.

'Look at that sunset!'

As Norma turns to look out of the window, Jake frantically pats another pocket.

'It's three in the afternoon, Jake.'

'Oh yes, I meant that plane.'

Jake is caught mid-pat.

'You've lost something haven't you, Jake?'

Jake's wide-eyed expression reminds her of a bush baby she once rescued from an acacia tree in the motel garden. How it got there, she never knew, but she remembered it cost a small fortune to have it air-freighted back to Central Southern Africa.

'I can't tell you, Norma.'

'After what we've been through, Jake – surely you can tell me anything.'

'I've lost your engagement ring.'

'I haven't got an engagement ring!'

'No – I mean the engagement ring I was going to give you.'

Norma drops her magazine and hugs Jake. 'Oh, Jake, you don't need a ring – just ask me!'

'Ask you what?'

'To marry me – sometimes you can be so...'

'But I wanted to do it properly – on bended knee and all that.'

'I wouldn't mind if you asked me while standing in the checkout queue in Walmart.'

'Is there something you need from the store?'

'No – just ask me, dammit!'

Jake bends down on one knee. 'Norma – will you'

'Stop, wait a minute...'

*'Just my luck'* Jake thinks *'she's changed her mind...'*

It's Norma's turn to start rummaging.

'It's here somewhere, I remember seeing it when I was packing for our trip.

'Here it is!'

'A trinket box?'

Norma carefully prizes open the lid of the box. Inside is an assortment of costume jewelry, broken necklaces and bracelets, old watches with flat batteries and other worthless items.

'These are my treasures - I've had some of them for years.'

'They're lovely.' Jake tries to match her enthusiasm.

Norma delves into the bottom of the box and retrieves a small octagonal, wooden box. It was originally painted red, most of the paint has flaked off, but the raffia tied around it is still keeping its contents secure - Jake's jaw drops – his throat is so dry, he can hardly speak.

'Wh...ere?'

Norma places the box on her palm and delicately loosens the bow.

'Norma – **wait**! – I've seen that box before - I have an image of it somewhere in the recesses of my mind. Where did you get it? – Can you remember?'

'To tell you the truth, I'd forgotten all about it until you proposed to me, but now I can recall it clearly.'

Norma's hand is shaking as she wrestles with the lid of the box.

'When I was little, a beautiful woman came to stay at the motel. I thought she was a princess and I would follow her around, - hiding, so she wouldn't see me, just staring at her. I wondered why someone so beautiful could look so sad.'

'She was sad?'

'Yes, but then one day, she caught me staring and her face lit up with a dazzling smile. She told me she was a...'

'A *fortune teller* in a circus!'

'How did you...?'

' 'Go on, Norma, did she say anything else – I need to know!'

'She told me that she had to leave the circus because of some...'

Norma hesitates, sensing Jake's sadness.

'Because of some kind of mishap – oh, Jake, I'm sorry, I'd forgotten about your acci...'

'Did she say what kind of mishap?'

'No, but she said she could never go back there – never!' She looked into my eyes and studied the palms of my hands. I can remember her nodding and smiling in a knowing way.'

'And the box, what has that got to do with it?'

Norma has freed the top off the box, she holds it over the base, unwilling to disclose the contents just yet.

'I only saw her once after that. It was the next day, just before she left. She made a point of coming to find me - that's when she gave me this box.'

'And you've never opened it?'

Norma pauses, unsure of what to say.

'This is going to sound strange - I'm not sure if I...'

'Please Norma – just say it – everything you can remember.'

'That's just it, as I said, I'd forgotten it completely, but now I can remember it as if it was yesterday.'

Jake nods his head excitedly, placing his hand over Norma's to steady it, his tone is soothing.

'I understand – take all the time you need.'

'She made me promise not to open it. She said I would know when the time was right and that the man who was with me would be able to explain.'

Tears stream down Norma's cheeks as she turns to Jake.

'I...I'm so confused, what's happening, Jake?'

Jake carefully takes the box from her and removes a locket. He opens the locket, revealing two small faded photographs.

'That's her, Jake – who is she?'

Jake is fighting back tears.

'And who are those boys?'

'That's me and Arnie.'

'Aww – how cute – but why would this woman have a photo of the two of you in her locket?'

'Because that woman is our *mother*!'

'She can't be, Jake. I know it's difficult for you – but you must accept it - she's de...'

'That's my mother and that's me and Arnie!'

'Jake it can't be – I wasn't born when you ki... when the spaceship chop... when your mother had that awful accident. I was a young girl when I met this woman.'
Jake is lost in his thoughts.
'I can see it clearly now. The woman in the accident was my aunt, Viggo's wife, she was looking after us while my mother was busy. My mother fled from my uncle. I see now why there was a rift between my father and my uncle – I never believed their half-baked story. – You know what this means, Norma?'
'What?'
'My mother is still alive – I need to find her!'
'Surely, the threat will be over by now – perhaps your father...'
'Blood vendettas last forever where I come from.'
'Where's that?'
'It's unpronounceable.'

*Thirty minutes later*


Jake has finished packing.
'That's it, Norma. I think we have everything we need.'
He hands her the wooden box.
'Put this in your trinket box to keep it safe.'
As he hands it to Norma a secret compartment springs open, revealing a small item. She hands it to Jake.
'Now you can do it properly!'
Bending down on one knee, Jake places the ring on the fourth finger of Norma's left hand – it fits perfectly.
'Norma, will you marry me?'
'Yes, yes, OH YES!'

*Ten minutes later*

Route Twenty-Six is quiet for the time of day and Jake is making good progress. He turns to Norma.
'Once I've got us to our safe place, I'm going to leave no stone unturned in my search for my mother – I won't rest until I find her.'
'I understand, Jake – I know how important it is for you – where is our safe place? You haven't told me yet.'
'It's top secret, I haven't told anyone yet - for security reasons, Arnie and Sally don't even know where they are, but now that you're almost my wife I think I can tell you now.'
'Oh, Jake – that's so sweet.'
'We're meeting Sven, Lars, Candice and Randy on the boat, we're going to somewhere where no one will find us.'
Norma's thoughts have returned to that day in the past, she can picture Jake's mother standing over her.

*'We **will** meet again – look to the west of the sky.'*

Jake tries to sound cheerful as he excitedly explains his plan to her, but he can't hide the anxiousness in his voice.
'Norma, I don't know how I thought of it, but I found an uninhabited island in the Inner Hebrides.'
'To the west of the Isle of Skye?'
'You know it, Norma?'
'I've heard if it.'
Norma settles into her seat, turning to Jake, she pats his hand and smiles reassuringly.
'Somehow, Jake, I think everything is going to work out fine.'

Printed in Great Britain
by Amazon

18088503R00200